STAR OF SAGE & SCREAM

OWL STAR WITCH MYSTERIES BOOK 1

LEANNE LEEDS

Star of Sage & Scream
ISBN: 978-1-950505-46-3
Published by Badchen Publishing
14125 W State Highway 29
Suite B-203 119
Liberty Hill, TX 78642 USA

CONTENTS

STAR OF SAGE & SCREAM

Of all the gods, she was most divine.
Her grey eyes glinted with her armor as
she broke into the sky.
Did the lonely cry of her owl surrender
a truth unknown?
Among soldiers and the wise, she was
relentless.
No endeavour could halt this girl woven
with bronze and ink.
Did her bright gaze gleam with tears, or
blood?
She was the rust coloured sky before a
storm.
She was their protector, the guardian of
their dreams.
They called her Athena.

— AUTHOR UNKNOWN

CHAPTER ONE

The ridiculous generates its own form of prejudice. I read that someplace.

The quote came back to me as I sat in an airless room being admonished by Imperatorial City's newest bureaucrat. Well, the city once known as Imperatorial City. Also previously known as the seat of all power in the paranormal world, a place the Witches' Council reigned over with an iron fist—until they were overthrown by some upstart clowns.

"Now, having pointed out all the complications with your department and how it contributed to the issues in our world, we do wish to acknowledge you for your service," Scout Trout, formerly the head of the werebear clan and now the elected Prime Minister of Paranormopolis—the new name of Imperatorial City—told us with a shrewd politician's smile.

As you might deduce by now, a lot of things have shifted around here.

"Are you firing us?" Glancing around the crowded hall, I observed a goblin I'd served with on a few missions standing tall, his face twisted up with indignation. The female goblin sitting next to him looked troubled. "If you are, just come right out and say it, you stupid bear." The crowd buzzed in agreement. "We're not some pansy group of pencil pushers, you know."

Scout Trout's face flushed with displeasure.

"You are ousting us, aren't you?" a muscled witch shouted from behind him. "You know, some of us are telepathic, you dolt! I can read it right there in your brain!"

"Now, we're not firing you, per se," Scout said, scrutinizing the anger-filled auditorium. The sober bureaucrats, just off the podium, nodded in agreement with a critical squint of their beady eyes. They clutched clipboards and pushed glasses up on their sharp noses while silently staring us down.

On any other day, they would have darted out of our way, fearful of attracting our attention.

Today, they practically reveled in the triumph of the paperwork nerds.

"Per Say?" The goblin frowned, peering down at his companion. "Who the heck is Say?"

Prime Minister Trout stared blankly at the goblin, drew a deep breath, and continued. "We no longer require Witches' Council guards since we no longer have a Witches' Council. It's that simple. The employment counselors up here"—he gestured toward the gleeful clipboard brigade —"would be delighted to talk to those of you that would still prefer to work for the ministry. We have several open positions—"

"Yo, Bob said I ain't no desk jockey, Fuzzy Wuzzy!" an imposing looking assassin snarled at the Prime Minister. The fellow next to him rose up and shook his fist, yelling his agreement. "This was a warriors' order, the Royal Guard was! A lifetime gig, they claimed!"

"Yes, well, situations evolve," Prime Minister Trout deadpanned.

"Look," Mercy Lawdottir, a former Witches' Council member, pushed up onto the dais and stepped slightly in front of Scout Trout. "We recognize the upheaval and changes impact you enormously, but I'm sure you recognize your functions are simply not required anymore. We are not going to hunt down rogue witches. We are not going to round up and imprison dissenters." She peered out over the crowd. "This is growth in our paranormal world. These are positive actions, ladies and gentlemen. It's good that we no longer have these roles in jeopardizing the autonomy of—"

"Not if that's all you know how to do!" the soldier yelled. The crowd rowdily agreed.

"And not when you were guaranteed a lifetime gig for signing up!" the goblin spat.

"What about our pensions?" a fat elvish woman shrieked in a strident voice. "I'm two years from retirement! What about that?"

"Well, Astra, you called it," Julia Rowland, a fellow witch, confided as she leaned in next to me. "You said they were going to fire us, and I thought you were crazy. I should have clued in when they took our crystal balls and gave them to those idiots in the Ministry of Trade." She tossed her hair and slid down in her seat. "I was actually looking forward to that pension yet."

The Ministry of Arcane Fugitives—our agency, or what was left of it, anyway—did not take the revelation of its dissolution well (even though anybody with half a brain could see it coming).

When your entire government goes from fascist dictatorship to allowing people civil rights and free homes and the ability to live however they want? Well, let's just say you lose use for your career soldier fugitive trackers. Especially when their principal job was to chase down misbehaving paranormals that mocked the dictates set out—admittedly, often on a whim—by the Witches' Council.

"Look, at this point, we're lucky they're not imprisoning us for war crimes," I murmured back as the rest of the group hooted, wailed, and objected. "At least we're only getting fired."

I stared around at the resentful faces.

It didn't seem like the rest of the room agreed.

* * *

I FINISHED GRABBING things to take to my mother's and marveled at how unemotional I was about this turn of events. It had been my home for the last ten years, and yet I only felt mild disappointment as I collected my meager possessions. We were lucky we were only getting fired, and maybe escaping a trial for war crimes was modulating my relief.

The Witches' Council had come up with a lot

of elitist, corrupt rules. In the last few years, the Ministry of Arcane Fugitives went after individuals that…well, that didn't seem like they deserved it.

But I did my job. Because that's what a good soldier does.

And I did my job well.

I didn't always believe in it, but it was hard to get up much steam to argue the right and wrong of a fugitive's capture when they got thrown in a magic cell provided with a maid, a swimming pool, and a chef. The prisoners we threw in the clink ate better and lived better than we did.

Were they free?

Okay, no.

And, yes, their magic was restrained.

But I knew a few fellow soldiers who would happily give up freedom and magic for a maid, a pool, and a chef. We'd heard of trackers who broke the law just so they could have a prolonged vacation.

"Where are you going to go?"

I looked up and found Julia leaning against the door frame, her duffel bag flung over her shoulder. She, like me, wore her MoAF Psychometer's garb. It was a sleek getup that made us look like Black Widow—if Natasha

Romanoff had a sleeveless summer outfit and psychometry powers she had to keep gloved. "Back to Forkbridge?"

"Yep. I have nowhere else to go." I shrugged, tossing in the last of my stuff and zipping up my own MoAF-issued bag. "Since they're cutting off our paychecks and still jerking us around about severance and a pension, I don't have much of a choice. You going in that?" I asked her, pointing to the official Ministry of Arcane Fugitives patch just above her left breast.

"I don't know where I'm going yet," she said, staring down at the patch that marked us elite henchmen (of a now overthrown regime). "I thought about going home, but my dad...well, you know." Her soft brown eyes looked up at me. "I'm in the same boat as you. No one in my family was happy I came here and did this. I never thought I'd have to go back and defend my choice after failing, much less ask them to air out my childhood bedroom so I'd have a place to sleep."

"First, we didn't fail. Second...yeah, okay, now we look like even bigger idiots since the sparkly revolution." I reached up and ripped my patch off with one hard jerk. "There. Now I look like slightly less of one. Not that my hippie mother's going to care either way."

"I don't know that I would call her that to her face if you're looking for free room and board," Julia quipped, tossing her chestnut hair again. Previously, we'd had to keep our hair in a tight bun. Both of us wore our hair loose, as if we needed to violate one rule to proclaim our newly enforced independence. "I could totally hear my father's judgment just leaking through the phone."

"You used a phone and not the cauldron?" I asked, my eyebrow lifted.

"What, I'm going to use the magical telephone, so I can get the full effect before I have to deal with it? It was enough I had to hear it. I didn't need to see the expression on his face, too. No, thank you. I'm putting that off until I absolutely have to deal with it." She sighed heavily. "Well, I've been putting off the conversation for years at this point. I guess I'll have to explain everything that happened here, too. I mean, I think they'll understand. Eventually." She frowned. "I don't know, do you think they'll understand?"

"Hell, Julia, I'm not sure I grasp what just happened here," I told her.

"Yeah, I hear you."

Heaving my bag onto my shoulder, I turned. "I just came here and did my job. I thought I was serving our people, you know? Keeping us from getting attacked, keeping people in line, keeping the humans from discovering our existence and killing us all. Protecting our community. We treated people we arrested well. I didn't know all that crap about the circuses and Gunther's mother being killed and...I mean, it's not like we were ever told anything. I followed orders," I added defiantly as if struggling to assure myself. "I did my job."

Julia blinked. "So, the following orders thing? Again, not an expression I would use with your family. Besides, you think anyone will care about that? Or believe it?" she asked me earnestly. "That we didn't know?" She gazed toward the hallway where more of our grumbling coworkers passed by with a brief nod as they left the dorm for the last time. "Are you taking a cauldron home?"

Cauldrons were the preferred communication and travel device in the paranormal world. A simple sustained thought, and you could connect with any paranormal in the world if they, too, had a cauldron. If the vats were big enough, you could even step into one and be teleported anywhere you made a connection. It was the quickest method of travel and one of the cooler perks of being supernatural.

If you wanted to get someplace fast.

Which, you know...I wasn't exactly in a hurry.

"I'm going to take the paratrain into Los Angeles, and then catch Amtrak to Florida."

"There's a train that goes all the way from Los Angeles to Florida?" she asked, astonished.

"No, but there's one that goes from LA to San Antonio. In San Antonio, I can pick up one that goes to Chicago. Then I can pick up a train in Chicago that goes to DC, and then down toward Florida."

Julia blinked again. "Isn't there a faster way?"

"I have no doubt there are many, many faster ways," I said with a straight face.

Eyebrow raise. "How long is that going to take?"

"A week or two?" I shrugged. "Maybe longer; the trains always run late."

Julia smiled. "Taking a long way around, are we?"

"I need some time in between here and there. If you know what I mean. Where are you headed to?"

"Baltimore, Maryland. Right outside DC."

"I'm getting one of those huge deluxe sleeper room things. Want to come?"

I made the invitation without thinking about it.

I'd been looking forward to the long train ride alone so I could have time to think about things. Prepare myself for moving from a rigid military life back into my mother's hippie-dippy instinct-driven flights-of-fancy life, determine precisely what boundaries I would need to walk in with—and cement them into place like immovable impact-deflection barriers before arrival.

Because let's face it—that's more or less what they would be.

But I realized in that farewell conversation I would really miss Julia, and it might be nice to have one more adventure together. Even if that adventure only involved staring out a picture window and drinking expensive train booze.

"You know what? I think I do want to come." She smiled, looking excited. "Let me give my dad a call and let them know I'll be delayed for a while, and I'll meet you at the front in about ten minutes. I wouldn't mind having someone to process this all with."

"I wasn't really planning on processing," I told her with a toss of my head. "I was planning on drinking and having the processing part just happen in the background. While I'm drunk."

"Well, then it's a good thing I'm coming with you. One, I can conjure up a mean margarita, so I'll save you a fortune on those little tiny booze bottles." She moved toward the doorway backward. "And second, I can keep you from crawling so far into a bottle that you never come out."

"Oh, I don't know about that." I followed her out. "I'm really good at crawling."

I closed the door without looking back.

* * *

ONE WEEK and forty margaritas later, I hugged Julia goodbye in our cabin and watched her family reunion through the window. She raced across the train platform into the waiting open arms of her father. Despite her surety the gruff man would be slow to thaw I spotted his tears across two train tracks. He hugged her so tightly it brought a lump to my throat.

"All aboard!" the conductor shouted. Julia pulled away from her father and looked back toward the train. She waved frantically and motioned for me to call her. I waved back, even though I wasn't sure she could see me.

With a lurch, the train pulled out of the Baltimore station and headed south.

Toward Forkbridge, Florida.

My hometown.

Forkbridge is a hundred-and-twenty-five-year-old small (like, tiny) town in Volusia County, Florida. We were about twenty minutes—and a hundred years—away from Orlando's theme park corridor. We also happened to be too close for comfort to Cassandra—a spiritualist community just across the river.

Their entire mission in life? To speak to as many dead people as possible.

By appointment only.

Cash and credit cards accepted.

Their constant calls to the undead meant that ghosts and spirits buzzed around the place like flies. Even more, though—when you have an entire community of spiritualists trying to talk to the great beyond? It attracts super-chatty dead people—and if they can't get in with one of the psychics, they'll yammer at anyone nearby that can hear them.

Thankfully, I could not see or hear the dead. On the other hand, my mother would carry on long-winded conversations with any ghosts that floated by. Because Mom felt an obligation to the dead, I would have to wait my turn.

Hence Cassandra's proximity was super annoying.

We lived in what my mother called "Arden House." The name came from our being the Ardens, and the house was our house. That's it. I never understood the reason for naming the roof over our heads. Still, Mom was insistent that the house needed a name so we would know what to call it during spellcasting.

People in town called it "the witch store," since my mother had converted the garage to a local new age shop, Athena's Garden. Other older residents called it the sugar house—it had been a plantation owner's home before my grandmother, rest her soul, bought it.

Whether you call it Arden House, the witch store, or the sugar house? Doesn't bother me. Choose one. Use the names interchangeably. Like I said, I think it's silly to name a building someone lives in. Pretentious. It's just the house I grew up in.

And my lack of attachment to the house and its name?

Just one more reason my mother and I don't get along.

Another is that I left home and joined the military.

Mother is a pacifist, you see. Even though her pacifism makes precisely zero sense.

She's the high priestess of the goddess Athena. Kind of like Athena's Pope? (Yeah, I know, it sounds kind of ridiculous to me, too. But some people believe this stuff.) The pagan gods are, thank goodness, not particularly popular anymore. Hence, we rarely get people showing up on our doorstep with offerings like Mimi did in the old days.

But it does happen.

And, yeah, pretty weird every time.

My entire family, by the way, is dedicated to Athena's service. We didn't have a choice in it. My mother, the moment we drew our first breaths, dedicated us to the goddess. So, we're dedicated. Or dedicants? I don't know. Something.

The Athena thing is why I am baffled that my mother is a pacifist, and was so against me joining the military. Yes, Athena is the goddess of wisdom. She's also the goddess of crafts and crafting, credited with inventing the ship, the chariot, the plow, and the rake. (Okay, granted, the rake doesn't seem all that impressive, but try picking up a whole bunch of leaves without a rake. I mean, a rake's a remarkable thing.)

Anyway, I digress.

Athena is also the goddess of war. Most of the time, she's depicted wearing a helmet and holding a spear. Despite this ancient truth, my mother was furious when I joined the military.

"No daughter of mine will serve the Witches' Council! The military? Are you out of your mind? Athena would curse you! Did you even bother to read what happened to Medusa? Do you want snakes coming out of your head?"

Anyway, I've never met the goddess and did not wake up green with snakes for hair.

And to be honest, I don't know that there's even one to meet.

I don't believe the old gods exist anymore, at least not in the way they were written about in the old stories. Sure, we are witches, and we are real. I'm not saying there aren't paranormal things in the world, because there are. I've spent my career chasing them.

Magic exists, too. I've seen magical items, magic done by magicians, witches, paranormal creatures. I can pick up vibes from almost any object.

But gods?

I believe in what I see. And I have never seen one. I would never tell my mother this, but from my perspective? There are no gods.

But, um, I'm probably not going to lead with that when I see my mother, the high priestess, for the first time in five years.

CHAPTER TWO

My rucksack felt heavy in my hand. Which wasn't really a literal problem, if I'm honest—I could curl a hundred pounds with one arm while sipping a martini with the other. The heaviness was, no doubt, an emotional thing. Like the bag held almost thirty-three years of broken dreams, relationship disappointments, and failed attempts to get away from the coven.

Well, the family.

No, I was right the first time.

I said coven. I meant coven.

My mother seemed to place more emphasis on the coven part, anyway.

Let's face it. Standing here on the sidewalk,

suitcase in hand, looking up at my childhood home? This wasn't where I was supposed to be, just days before my thirty-third birthday.

I'd been a Decanus. That's a rank (for those of you unfamiliar with the paranormal military's multitude of byzantine titles). I led a group of eight legionaries in the Ninth Cohort and was up for a promotion. I might have been second in command.

Might have been.

Somewhere at the bottom of my beat-up suitcase, a rolled-up piece of paper thanked me for my years of service to the Witches' Council. I fought the urge not to burn it on the spot. A piece of paper. That's all I got—a piece of paper.

In exchange for almost fifteen years of my life.

A Witches' Council, by the way, that was now blamed for just about every single problem the paranormal world's had for the past two hundred years. I spent half of my life training for, working for, and mastering my supernatural military career. A career now nothing more than something I had to defend.

Maybe even hide.

And because of a few bad actors—okay, maybe more than a few—the newly elected paranormal democratic government decided that our pensions, and the payment of those pensions, would be determined at a later time. After the investigations, they said. Which would be followed by the hearings. The committee meetings promptly after that—to discuss the outcome of the inquiry.

Last I heard, they formed a committee.

To discuss how to start the investigations.

So. Bureaucracy.

Yep.

Bye, pension. So long, future.

I looked up at the white house with black accents, squinting.

Hello, coven family.

My mother had told me my choice was a complete betrayal of my heritage when I left. See, since all the women in my family were witches living in the human world? She couldn't understand how I could take a job with the same military branch that hunted witches in the human world. She demanded an explanation from me multiple times over the years, and I kept trying to give her one—but it was never good enough. She never believed me. Or never respected my viewpoint.

Which, okay, was fair. I told Mom about my desire for service, my need for a more disciplined life, my discomfort with the soft side of magic she wrapped us all in like a pink, fuzzy blanket. But I never told her the main reason.

I wanted—no, needed—to get away from her, and it was the easiest way to do it.

I don't know. Maybe Mom sensed that. That swallowed truth I never admitted, but she felt floating around within me with her supposed goddess-granted insight, or whatever. Perhaps that's why she never approved of my choices.

I looked up at the pristine white colonial house with its whitewashed siding and well-manicured lawn. The windows were thrown open, my three younger sisters' laughter wafting out onto the street like music. I closed my eyes. Their joy just made the lump of failure in my throat even harder to swallow.

Mom told me I would regret leaving. Regret my choice.

And I did.

Just not in the way she hoped I would.

I could already hear the lecture I knew was coming. I arrived home jobless, career-less, prospect-less. Years of training I could no longer use, a piece of paper that was meaningless, and the possibility of a pension sometime later, maybe—but little more than that.

Oh, my mother would have a field day.

"Astra!" my twenty-year-old sister, Amethyst, screeched as she spotted me from the second-floor window. Leaning forward, her blonde hair a long, tangled mess, she smiled widely. "What are you doing out there? Come in! Come in! What are you waiting for?" While still waving, her dimpled face disappeared back into the house. "You guys, Astra's back! She's right downstairs!"

"Well, tell her to come inside the house," I heard my mother's sharp voice echo out. "We're not all going to run outside in our nightgowns, now, are we? What would the neighbors think?" Minerva Arden was always very concerned about what the neighbors would think. "Althea! Ayla! Stop arguing over that crystal ball! You'll break it!"

My three sisters—Ami, Althea, and Ayla— were over ten years younger than I was. I'd been the woops in Mom's youth, the mistake baby that wasn't supposed to happen. Proof that at one point, my mother's magic had been fallible.

Mom was just nineteen years old when she got pregnant with me, and if it hadn't been for Aunt Gwennie's help, I probably would have turned out to be even more of a misfit witch than I was.

It was too early in her life, Mom explained once, for her to be a good mother. She'd been too young to know what she needed to do to raise a witch well. Sometimes (after some coven ritual that required self-accountability), Mom would apologize for that whole "not knowing what she was doing as a mother" thing. Occasionally, she even blamed herself for my lack of proper direction in life.

Most other times she would blame me. She was a great high priestess, she would remind me, providing a charmed life of service for the greater good—and that should have been enough. It was enough for my sisters.

I closed my eyes and took a deep breath, inhaling the scent of my Aunt Gwennie's roses— red, luscious, perfumed roses that grew like weeds around the property—and remembered the last time I left for good.

* * *

"PERHAPS YOUR FATHER was some kind of rogue CIA agent," my mother said as she knitted, Aunt Gwennie beside her. "He seemed like a nice man, but maybe he had some deep, dark magic that infected you and blocked your natural goddess-given empathy. That could be it. Your father was a blocker."

"Blocker!" my five-year-old sister singsonged as she stuck out her tongue at me. With a quick surge of energy and a pastel sparkle, she made her tongue glow. "Your pa was a blocker, your pa was a blocker!"

"Minerva, don't tell her things like that. There's no such thing as an empathy blocker. You're just making that up," Aunt Gwennie admonished Mom. "Ami, that's very nice, dear."

"Well, then maybe she just needs more meditation," my mother told her sister as if I wasn't in the room. "She's a witch living in the human world. We help humans. Ami and Althea have connected with their desire to help already, and Ami's barely out of diapers. For goodness sake, Althea's still an infant and shows more compassion than Astra!"

"Hey!" Ami shouted, her tongue shooting pink sparks. "I'm almost six!"

"Yes, dear," my mother said without even looking at her. "So clearly, the problem isn't with me. I produce empathetic witches just fine. I don't produce murderous witches who want to spend their lives arresting others of their kind just for being a little different from everyone else! Goddess forbid."

"Mom, I'm eighteen, and I don't lack compassion," I told her sullenly from my seat on the couch. "I know what I want to do in life, and I know what I don't want to do. I don't want to sit and read tarot cards for humans looking for a boyfriend. Or spend my days mixing up anti-anxiety lavender lip protector to sell in the shop. And I don't need more meditation. I hate meditating. It's boring." I crossed my arms. "I want to join the paranormal military. I want to catch bad guys."

"Nonsense. I still think you're just not trying hard enough," my mother said dismissively and refocused on her knitting. "If you just try, dear, I'm sure you'd find some empathy somewhere. Maybe a vision, hmm? Your psychometry powers would be wasted in service to the Witches' Council, not to mention a betrayal of the goddess herself. They have plenty of people who can do that. The town of Forkbridge only has you." She looked up. "I absolutely forbid it, so there's no point in talking about this further."

* * *

SHE WAS RIGHT. There was no point in talking about it further. So, a week later, I ran off to Imperatorial City, the seat of power for all the paranormal world, and joined the magical military.

I pulled myself out of my memories and spotted my Aunt Gwennie, her muumuu flowing behind her, skipping down the steps of the house. Her eyes were alight with love and affection.

"Hi, Aunt Gwennie," I told her, forcing a smile.

"Astra, darling, you look wonderful," Aunt Gwennie told me warmly. She wrapped her arms around me tightly and squeezed, her rose-scented skin imparting an instant healing effect. I suddenly felt happier than I had in days. "You look like a female Indiana Jones. Or that Lara Croft person. What a svelte figure, and those arm muscles! My goodness." Aunt Gwennie tapped my hips with her finger. "Have you lost weight since I last saw you?" Her twinkling eyes sparkled in the morning sunlight, and my mood lifted even higher.

Her magic, not mine.

"Thanks." I glanced down at her. Though I had no telepathic or empathetic abilities, I still caught a hint of worry in the lines of her face. "Let me guess. Mom's not happy I'm home?"

"Oh, Astra," she sighed, tilting her head. "I don't know what it is with you and your mother. She hasn't said a single word to you yet, and already you're looking for friction. Of course, she's happy that you're home! You're her first-born daughter. She never wanted you to leave in the first place, if you recall." She placed her hands on my forearms and squeezed. "We're not used to the Arden women running off into the world to make their own way, you know that." She let go of one arm and tugged on the other. "Something is missing, always missing, when you're not with us, dear. Come inside, see your sisters. They're very excited you're back."

"They're just excited it's my birthday, and they'll get to have cake," I teased, hitching my duffel back over my shoulder and grabbing my rolling suitcase. "Not many Taurus girls in this family." My mother and sisters were all Libras—which was a shame. As fair as Libras tried to be, they were not great at sharing birthdays.

Or cake.

"Oh, don't be such a curmudgeon," Aunt Gwennie chastised me, opening the creaky door to the house. "They look up to you, you know. They were very proud of their famous sister, chasing down bad guys and keeping the world safe for witches."

"I would have thought Mom would have magicked that point of view right out of them," I said. The two teens flew at me. Now twenty, Ami held back, waiting for a more dignified greeting. "Whoa, whoa, whoa!" I said as soft limbs embraced me from multiple directions. "Let me put my stuff down. You're going to knock me over!"

"Do we have to call you Decanus Arden and salute you, or is that over with?" Ayla, a pixie-like thirteen, giggled as she pulled away. I rolled my eyes at the reference to my now meaningless military rank. "You don't look any smarter, you know."

"You do look taller, though. That outfit is wild, just wild," Althea, a buxom fifteen now, said as she stretched to tap me on the head. "When did you start wearing heels?"

I looked down and smiled at my sisters' bare feet, amused that the grass stains on them looked very similar to the ones they had as children. My mother taught us as youngsters to ground ourselves as much as we could. Grounding, or direct skin contact with the earth, was essential for our health and connection to the goddess, she claimed.

I lost count of how many days I showed up to public school barefoot by accident.

"I've been wearing my uniform for more than ten years," I told Althea, recalling my collection of t-shirts and ratty old jeans stored in the attic with a shudder. "I'd feel weird in regular clothes at this point."

"So you have work clothes, but no work?" a harsh voice called across the foyer. "Ironic, isn't it?"

My mother's voice was tinged with judgment as she loosed it toward me like an arrow. Its sharp point popped the bubble of sisterly excitement and sailed through the protective cloud of rose-scented happiness my Aunt Gwennie previously wrapped around me.

Some things never changed. Mom's sharp voice could still slice through joy and happiness like a hot knife sliding through cold butter.

"Hello, Mom," I said as my sisters dropped their arms, their smiles, and moved a few steps back from me to clear the way for the queen of the house. Aunt Gwennie moved closer. "The house looks good."

"Of course it does," she answered haughtily

from the archway between the foyer and the kitchen. "Every Friday, still, Astra, you know we make sure to do any repairs we can. The same as we always did." She tossed her hair to one side and smoothed down the flowing silk gown she wore. It was purple as always, woven through with golden flowers embroidered by hand. "Well, dear, aren't you going to give your mother a kiss hello?" Her voice hardened. "Or do I have to request one?"

She opened her arms wide and waited for me to cross to her.

A subtle power play I recognized from my psyops lessons.

It immediately annoyed me.

It wasn't enough that Mom was the oldest witch in this house, the high priestess of the coven, the unchallenged matriarch. It wasn't enough the house was in her name, that she owned the new age business in the garage, or that she technically employed and supported everyone in the place. It wasn't enough she decided for everyone.

Nope.

Mom had to remind everyone—in big and small ways—she was the queen.

The most important witch.

The most important woman in the lair.

The chosen of the goddess Athena.

I knew what she was doing—Mom wasn't nearly as slick as she thought she was. I knew the small act was meant to instantly make me lesser and her more. To make me come to her was her not-so-subtle way of forcing me to dance to her tune. Of making me subject to her demand—simple as that demand might be.

And for a split-second, I thought about refusing.

The stubborn rebel in me balked at even this little show of allegiance, this small admission of Mom's superiority. I had my own contubernium, for goodness sake. (A contubernium? A Decanus leads a contubernium...oh, fine, it's a squad. I had a squad.) I commanded people—and more people than she ever did. And people I didn't give birth to. Adults. Warriors. Not children.

Or...

...I used to.

The reality of my situation required me to ask myself if this was really a hill I wanted to die on. I had precisely zero job prospects and zero money, unless I wanted to become an assassin for hire. Or a barista. Didn't everyone in the human world

STAR OF SAGE & SCREAM | 33

become a barista at some point when they couldn't find another job?

On the other hand, I could make coffee. Beans, hot water, stick it in a cup. How hard could it be? I didn't need to put up with these games.

I took a deep breath and tried to calm myself.

Aunt Gwennie was right—it's not like I didn't know this was how Mom was. Starting a confrontation with her over this (not even five minutes after I hit the door) was probably stupid. Maybe even a little childish.

And the bottom line that calmed me down?

She did ask. Whether she realized it or not, she did ask.

This means whether or not she realized it, I sort of won this one.

"Of course, Mother," I answered formally and crossed the five feet from my independent outside world straight back into my mother's attempt at control. "Thank you for welcoming me home," I told her as I hugged her lightly. She thrust her cheek toward my face and waited. I kissed her cheek formally.

As we pulled away from one another, I caught her expression.

It was one of triumph.

"Why don't you go get settled in and wash up?" She waved. Glancing at Ami, she ordered her to assist me with my luggage. "Unfortunately, we turned your room into herb storage, so you'll be in the alcove off the attic. Your sister Ayla translocated your furniture up there for you, so the room should be all set up."

"Why can't Ayla just translocate the luggage?" Ami asked with exasperation as she grabbed the heavy suitcase. "I don't see why I have to carry it when she can just put it there."

"What did I say?" my mother asked Ami without answering her question.

Ami grabbed the suitcase and lugged it up the stairs step by step without complaint.

I hadn't been home for ten full minutes, and my mind had already wandered. Exactly how hard is a venti, half-whole milk, one-quarter 1%, one-quarter non-fat, extra hot, split quad shots (1 1/2 shots decaf, 2 1/2 shots regular), no foam latte, with whip, two packets of Splenda, one Sugar in the Raw, a touch of vanilla syrup and three short sprinkles of cinnamon to make, anyway? (Julia and I once looked up the most complicated coffee to make. This, apparently, was it.)

"If you need proper clothing, I'm sure one of your sisters will be happy to lend you some."

I looked down at my slick, form-fitting bodysuit.

Well, she got her hug. And a kiss on the cheek.

Her Highness wasn't taking my bodysuit.

CHAPTER THREE

"It takes thirty-three years for the cycle of lunar years get back in sync with the solar year. When the cycles align again, the sun returns to the same house as the day you were born and the ascendant returns to its original sign," my mother told us, her voice breathy, over flickering candlelight. "We as witches know the celestial cycles guide all that is and all that will be, yes?" She gazed meaningfully at each one of us. "Astra's thirty-third birthday is a meaningful one, yes?"

I struggled not to sigh in frustration. This wasn't a birthday party. It was a coven ritual. It just happened to take place around the dining table, and the ritual sacrifice was a Black Forest cake.

It was hard not to be frustrated. I'd arrived home to the same situation I'd left fifteen years before. Oh, sure, my mother was older—but she still ruled over the household with an iron fist wrapped in a velvet glove. My Aunt Gwennie chased after her, smoothing over hurt feelings and consoling frustrated nieces. My sisters maintained a cheerful facade as they performed whatever magical tasks were demanded of them despite their hidden misery.

Well, I assumed it was a facade.

And I assumed they were miserable.

No one could be that happy living with my mother. They had no hope of moving out, no prospect of an independent career. They lived with the likely possibility any love partner wouldn't stick around longer than it would take to create the next generation of Arden women. Because they never did.

Then again, maybe I was the black sheep of the family, and everyone was cool with the situation other than me.

"Astra, tell the girls why the thirty-third birthday is so special," my mother encouraged me, her eyes shining.

Great. I glared at Mom. My birthday celebration and there was a test.

"I think you just did, Mother." I glanced briefly at Aunt Gwennie, then over at my younger sisters. "Look, it's getting late, and I have to be up at six o'clock to work out. Do you think we could wrap this up and get to the cake? I don't want to eat that much sugar too late."

The pause in her response was almost undetectable.

Almost.

"Of course, Astra, we wouldn't want to inconvenience any of your plans." The softness in Mom's face hardened as she waved an imperious hand toward Aunt Gwennie. The latter immediately grabbed a cake cutter from the table. "It's not like your leaving to join the military inconvenienced any of our plans."

"I'm glad to hear it," I responded dryly.

Mom looked at me sharply. "Well, of course, they did slightly."

Of course they did.

"Your Aunt Gwennie and I had to work twice as hard for the goddess and the shop. We had no one to help us with the younger girls. Of course, we were worried about you for weeks since you didn't bother to tell us where you'd gone and what you'd done."

"So, a little inconvenience, then." I nodded.

"We managed." Mom glared at me, her eyes cold. "I suppose you're just not quite as flexible as we are. We can make sure your birthday doesn't interrupt your workout—"

"Minerva, it's her birthday, and you promised me," Aunt Gwennie said to my mother through clenched teeth as she handed her the first slice of cake. "If you want to talk to her about leaving, there are better times for that. For now, I need to remind you we are here to celebrate her life."

"Humph," my mother mumbled.

Predictable.

Now, maybe you're wondering why this is all coming up fifteen years after I walked out of the house. Surely, you're thinking, this Astra chick and her mother talked about the military thing in the last fifteen years. Didn't she come home on holiday? Family visits? Didn't she call her mother?

She did, actually. Until about five years ago when she stopped.

Um, when I stopped.

I stopped because every visit home went the same way, contained the same lecture, and the same recriminations. My mother was like an ex-boyfriend that just couldn't accept the relationship was over. You ever had one of those? One of those people you told repeatedly why you'd done something, why you'd made a choice, and because it wasn't what they would've done or what they wanted, they simply dismissed your reasons?

My mother believed Athena's Garden was the responsibility of every female sitting around this table. A small magic shop in Forkbridge, Florida. It seems ridiculous when you think about it. But for some reason, she passionately believed it was our responsibility as priestesses to serve the human public—and anyone that walked away from it abdicated their commitment to serve.

I didn't understand her view of service. She certainly didn't understand mine.

"Do you at least know what this alignment is called, or have you forgot everything I taught you?" my mother asked, her voice slightly less sharp.

"I'm still a witch, Ma. This year is my solar-ascendant house return."

"That's so exciting," Althea said, her eyes shining. "And you really do have a whole new life!"

"Yep." I accepted the slice of cake Aunt Gwennie held out. "Lucky me."

Had I known what the next moment would bring, perhaps I would've infused that statement with even more ironic sarcasm.

The distinct doorbell chime saved me from having to field any more magic pop quiz questions. Aunt Gwennie and my mother looked at each other, their faces mirroring one another's shock. "Could it be?"

I looked at the two suspiciously. Glancing down at my phone, I marked the time. Who randomly dropped by at nine in the evening? "Could what be what?"

My sister Althea pushed her chair from the table so quickly she wound up running toward the door, still holding her fork. We all listened as the door opened. "Holy moley, you guys are not gonna believe what's on the front porch!"

"They will if you bring me in," a sarcastic male voice answered.

"And it can talk!" she squealed. My other two sisters jerked their chairs away from the table and took off toward the front of the house. "You guys have to see this!"

"Instead of gawking, could you bring me inside, please?" the male voice said, sounding more annoyed and more insistent. "If that's too much to ask, just open the door, and I'll take myself in. I told her this stupid golden cage would be a bit much."

"Told who?" Ami asked.

"Oh, wow, he's adorable!" Ayla squealed. "Can we keep him?"

"Look, there's a note," Ami said.

"Don't touch that!" he snapped, and the sound of metal rattling followed. "And get me inside!"

My mother and aunt hadn't moved, so I hadn't either. Their expressions were vaguely startled.

"You don't think..." Aunt Gwennie's whisper trailed off.

"She never told me that she would be..." Now it was my mother having trouble finishing her statement. "Surely, she would've told me! Why would she not have told me? Me! Her high priestess! This seems like something you would tell a person!"

"Look what was on our front porch!" Althea shouted.

We all turned to look at my exuberant sister, her arms wrapped around a tall, golden cage. She struggled with its weight, but Althea rebuffed any attempts Ami and Ayla made to assist her. With a clunk, she placed the gigantic cage on the floor.

"Watch it, sister!" the cage's inhabitant snapped. "You're about as gentle as a drunk giant dancing on an ice sheet!"

My mother rose from her chair and glided elegantly toward the cage. "May I have your name, sir?" Her voice had the priestess echo threaded through it, and her shoulders were thrown back like a queen. "May I have your name and the reason we have been blessed to have you visit our household this evening?"

"Are you Astra Arden?" the owl asked gruffly.

My mother stopped and stared. "No, I am—"

"Then no, you can't have my name. I'm not here for you." The owl swiveled its head to look at Ami. "What about you? Are you Astra?"

"I'm Astra Arden," I answered without sitting up or getting to my feet. I wrapped my hand around a knife just in case the bird represented a mortal threat.

My mother might be acting like this was some kind of blessing on our house or something, but I just left the military after an insurrection.

I wasn't taking any chances.

The owl swiveled its head so fast it was difficult to mark the actual turning. Its intense eyes blinked once and then once again. "You, the one in the military uniform. You're Astra Arden?" he asked, incredulous.

My mother bowed. "We've been trying to convince her to take it—"

"Was I talking to you?" the owl snapped at my mother without looking at her. Its dark eyes watched me through the bars of its golden cage. "Are you sure you're Astra Arden?"

"I am completely sure I am Astra Arden. What is it you want from me, bird?"

"I want you to put the knife down. That's the first thing I want," the bird responded congenially. Despite his sudden friendliness, a deliberate lean made it clear he knew about my defense preparations and wasn't in the mood to trifle with them. "I'm not here to hurt you. Well, not intentionally. My talons are pretty sharp. Some idiots stick out their arms like they want me to hang out on them. Hopefully, you're smarter than that."

I stood up and tossed the knife onto the table. It landed with a clatter.

"What kind of damage did you think you were going to do to me with a butter knife?"

"You want to find out?" I leaned forward toward the table and slowly reached out my hand. "I can if you don't tell me what you're doing here within the next ten seconds. I'm sure there is a recipe for roasted owl somewhere in this house."

"Oh, you're a feisty one, aren't you? I can see why Athena sent me for you." The owl shook his feathers out with a quick movement. "When I heard you were a girl, I figured the goddess made a mistake. I usually get the tough guys. You know, the bikers and the ex-cons and the martial artists. But then I realized the goddess doesn't make mistakes. I mean, that's why she's the goddess, right?" The owl's head tilted until his head was at a ninety-degree angle. "Oh, that's right. I forgot."

"You forgot what?"

"You don't believe in gods, do you?"

I could feel the shock in the room, hear the gasps. I wanted to rush across the room and throw the owl out the nearest window for opening up a can of worms.

But I still didn't know what this thing was, what its powers were, or what it was doing here.

"Are you here to have a theological conversation with me? If that was all you wanted, you could have used a cauldron," I responded. "I'd rather finish my birthday, have my cake, and go to bed. I'm not interested in discussing my beliefs with a bird."

"We could do that if you want." The owl

paused and preened its feathers. "I'm actually here to give you a birthday present. Well, I am the birthday present. Or at least one part of it." His head swiveled. "It's kind of a two-part thing that goes together."

"I don't need a bird, thanks. What's the other part?" I asked him.

He struggled to spread his wings and rattled the cage. "Open the door, and I'll show you."

"Tell me, and then maybe I'll open the door," I countered.

"Oh, for heaven's sake," my mother said as she moved toward the cage.

"No!" the owl shouted. He glared at my mother menacingly, his voice echoing with power. "Nothing about this is about you, Minerva. I know that's probably hard for you to understand, much less accept. As to your self-centered question, you weren't told anything because this doesn't have anything to do with you." The owl glanced at me. "Astra must choose to open the door."

"I thought you just asked my sister to open the door? Now, suddenly, I have to do it?"

"Well, now I'm inside," the owl responded. As if that explained everything.

All heads in the room turned and stared.

I didn't like it. Some strange talking animal shows up on the porch unaccompanied? And on my birthday, no less.

The soldiers and I had talked on the train as we headed away from Paranormopolis. Many of us wondered if we would be targeted in our civilian lives because of what the Witches' Council had done. If we had cause to be concerned for our safety. We exhibited the usual bravado and prayers for any who would tangle with us. Still, none of us wanted to spend the rest of our lives fighting in defense of a past ripped away from us. Those conversations were ringing in my head as I stared at the caged raptor.

This could be some kind of Trojan...owl.

I knew one thing for sure. I didn't believe in the goddess Athena as anything other than a myth. No goddess sent me a snarky bird as a birthday present.

"You don't have to believe in her," the owl told me quietly as if it had heard my thoughts. "She believes in you. If she didn't, she wouldn't have sent me with the gift I'm about to give you." He lifted his feet and swayed his body back and forth —though his head didn't move an inch. "You spent the past four days sulking that you don't have a purpose anymore."

"And that's your gift?" I asked with a laugh. "You're bringing me a purpose?"

"Open the cage and find out, tough girl."

The thing that always got me in basic training?

I was way too curious for my own good. And I'm confident.

Those two things can get a girl in trouble.

I should've thought about it longer. Probably should have talked to my mother, even though that would have been a blow to my ego. I could have called Julia or other folks in my old squad to see if they, too, had a wisecracking magical animal show up on their doorstep.

But I did none of that.

I walked across the room, and I opened the cage door.

The moment my fingers gripped the cage door, I was blinded by a white light. Heat raced over my skin like a current of electricity, snapping and sizzling. I heard my mother praying to the goddess Athena as I stumbled backward, but her words sounded far away.

"She'll be fine!" the owl shouted. "Don't touch her. Athena knows what she's doing! Leave her be!"

Of course those jerks listened to the bird.

No hands touched me as I fell to the floor, reeling and in pain. Images shot through my mind at such a speed I felt them all like hammer strikes to my forehead, but I couldn't describe a single one. It could have been hours, days for all I know. When I finally stopped writhing like an idiot, every muscle in my body ached as if I'd run a marathon.

"What the hell did you just do to me, bird?" I crawled to my knees. The owl stood on the floor next to me, his eyes glued to my face. "What was that?"

"That was the essence of the goddess Astraea, the last of the immortals to live with humans. She abandoned the earth and ascended to heaven," he intoned. Then the owl made a noise that sounded like a cough. "Because humans were starting to really tick her off."

"Astra, honey, are you all right?" Aunt Gwennie asked, worried.

I nodded—even though I wasn't entirely confident that I was.

"'There's an end to all hope of justice more. Astraea's gone indeed, let hope go too!'" my mother whispered behind me, quoting a Robert Browning poem. "She became the constellation

Virgo, her love of Dike and justice symbolized by their nearness to one another."

"Mom, is Astra a goddess now?" Ayla asked, awestruck.

"No, of course not," my mother responded quickly.

"Minerva, I think we need to ask that owl a few more questions before we make any final pronouncements about what Astra is or is not at this point," Aunt Gwennie declared. My aunt looked at the owl and gestured toward me. When he didn't respond, she hurried over to help me up off the floor. "Mr. owl, sir, what is it that just took place here?"

"Athena wanted to give Astra a purpose for her birthday," the owl told my aunt. He then silently flapped his wings and flew up onto the table. "The goddess knows she did her job as well as she could and was honorable in her service— even if those she served chose not to be." The owl paused and leaned down to grab a piece of steak off my mother's plate. The bird then tossed it in the air with one talon and swooped up to grab it. With a loud and satisfying gulp, he flew back onto the table silently. "Athena's got a new job for her."

"Oh, yeah? Does it come with the pension?" I

asked with a small stab of uneasiness. "And if you're going to keep shocking me with electricity, I'd like medical insurance, too."

"Athena's getting kind of annoyed at people, too. Instead of booking off to the cosmos like Astraea, though, she decided to do something about it. Well, more to the point," he said with a flap of his wings, "she decided that you're going to do something about it."

I frowned. "What does 'the goddess' think I can do?"

"You got half of Astraea's energy," the owl explained. "The other half has been set loose into the world to look for wrongs that can be righted before they're wrong-ed." The owl pronounced wrong as if it had two syllables.

"That's not a word. Well, it is, but that's not how you say it."

"I'm a goddess's owl. If I said it, not only is it a word, but it's gonna wind up in some epic poem at some point." He tilted his head again at that unnerving ninety-degree angle and wiggled his tail feathers. "Your sister, the seer,"—the raptor pointed his wide wing toward Ami—"will do readings for people, and if a card with a star comes up—"

Ami frowned. "There's already a star card, and it comes up a lot—"

"I didn't say the star card will come up; I said a card with a star will come up in the reading. You'll know it, little lady, because it will glow with golden starlight." The bird flapped its wings again and teetered awkwardly on the edge of the table. "Trust me. You'll know it. It's unmistakable."

"And then what?" I asked.

"And then, Astra Arden, you make like a metaphysical paramedic, figure out what's about to kill the human, and you stop it. People are killed in this world all the time, and some aren't supposed to be. They were destined for better things, or they were going to do something fantastic and then blammo!" The bird dove off of the table and rolled on the floor. It came to a stop on its back, feet up, wings wide, tongue hanging out. After a few seconds, its head popped up. "You get what I'm saying?"

"So, you don't want me to go after murderers —which is, by the way, what I'm actually trained to do. Go after people that committed a crime—"

"Is that really what you did, though?" the owl asked, his tone unconvinced, rolling himself up back onto his feet. "I know that's what you were trained to do, and that's what you thought you would be doing, but I don't think that's really what you wound up doing." He paused as we stared at one another. "I mean, I'm just saying."

"How am I supposed to prevent a murder?" I asked. "These people will be strangers."

"Archimedes at your service." The owl swept his wing in front of him and bowed. "I have fantastic powers. Amazing powers. I mean, I'm the goddess's own owl, right? Well, one of them, anyway. I am here to help you with the task Athena has laid upon you. You and me, kid, we'll get it done."

"And if I say no?"

The owl looked at me, its expressionless face managing to look a little surprised. "So, I wouldn't do that. Athena is really benevolent. Like, a lot. But when she makes offers..." The owl paced in front of me, slowly. "Let's just say when she makes offers? You really can't refuse. I mean, you can try...But from my perspective, you don't want to do that." The owl stopped pacing and looked up at me. "Do you?"

The owl apparently wanted a reply to assure him we were in agreement.

I didn't believe there was a goddess, even now.

As much as I wanted to reject being told what

to do by anyone (after so many years of being told what to do by everyone?) I had to admit— running around preventing people from being killed (which would inevitably involve digging up and dealing with bad guys) was the best job offer I'd had since I came home.

I glanced over at my mother. She nodded excitedly.

Maybe this was my mother's way of helping me find a purpose. Maybe she did understand me, at least a little bit, and this magical farce was the only way she could show support for me.

Without, you know, actually showing support for me.

And I'd have to work closely with Amethyst since she would find my targets.

It would give me a chance to get to know my sister after being gone for so long. It also gave me a reason to stick close to the shop—which would make my mother ecstatic. Not to mention the fact that my mother would think I was doing this for the goddess she worshiped.

Even though I was sure there was no goddess, and I suspected my mother magicked the whole thing because it was easier than having a conversation with me.

"Okay. I'll do it. But I'm not calling you Archimedes."

"My friends call me Archie. We're not really friends yet, but for the goddess energy you've been entrusted with? I'll let it slide." Archie swept his wing in front of him and bowed regally again.

Well, sort of.

Owls don't have waists.

CHAPTER FOUR

*W*ithin a recessed alcove, Archie sat with his talons wrapped around a wooden rod. It was initially intended to hold clothing but now would apparently be the perch for a snarky owl. He watched me with those intense eyes of his as I removed my makeup. "So, riddle me this, owl man. Why would an ancient goddess decide that Forkbridge, Florida needed your attention? Why not New York or Los Angeles or Washington DC?" I asked him. "Or Myanmar? Have you heard what's going on in Myanmar lately? Surely those people could benefit from your wisdom and some dead goddesses' energy more than some dinky town in the swamps of Florida."

"First, it's not 'dead goddess energy,' you disrespectful nitwit. And second, beyond the disrespect, I'm detecting a certain amount of sarcastic sass in your question," the owl replied, tilting his head. He blinked his wide eyes rapidly just once as if to punctuate his statement. "Normally, this would annoy me. In fact, I think it's supposed to annoy me—I am a divine creature, after all, and not used to putting up with lip from anyone. People don't normally sass divine creatures, you know." The owl shrugged his wings. "But I actually like a certain amount of sass in my disciples, so I'll let it pass."

"Disciples? I don't think so. And you didn't answer the question."

"And I'm not going to, not in the way you expect." The owl spread his wings without releasing his grip on the rod, then ruffled his feathers with a self-satisfied click from his beak. "Your question assumes a goddess like Athena is ignoring the rest of the world in favor of blessing Forkbridge and Forkbridge alone. I can assure you that is not the case. Secondly, this isn't about Forkbridge, Astra. This is about you."

It was later, much later after the party. The owl had enjoyed copious amounts of attention (and strips of a raw filet mignon I'd been planning to barbecue tomorrow) from my three younger sisters for most of the evening, giving me little time to ask him questions. Despite the typical stereotype of a witch never being far from an animal, my mother had a strict no pets policy in the house. Thanks to that, all three—even Ami —were enthralled by the mysterious raptor.

My mother accepted—heck, insisted—Archie would now live in our home with no argument. He was now happily ensconced in a small area off of my unfinished attic room.

And staring at me with unsettling intensity.

I finished brushing my hair and turned toward him. "So there are hundreds of owls all over the world in towns big and small racing to stop catastrophes using a bunch of paranormal military veterans that couldn't find a job?"

"Now you're assuming there's a parliament of divine owls."

"A parliament? Like a governmental body?"

Archie ruffled his feathers and blinked again. "A group of owls is called a parliament."

"Why on earth would it be called a parliament? That's the dumbest name for a group of owls I've ever heard of. Who came up with that?"

"Because we're known to be intelligent and

wise, you numpty." The owl leaned forward and narrowed his eyes fiercely. "Why don't you ask me what you really want to know instead of dancing around with small talk? You know you want to." The owl chuffed. "Or don't you have the guts?"

I didn't like how the owl seemed able to read my mind. The truth is I wasn't sure what I wanted to know from the owl, and even if Archie answered my questions? I wasn't sure if I could trust him. "You're not going to goad me into doing what you want."

The owl continued staring at me with a blank look. As the silence dragged on, his expression looked sour—though I couldn't have told you what features on his face changed to make me think that.

"You know I'm nocturnal, correct?" said the owl placidly. "I have all night. Your sisters made sure I was well fed."

"With my steak, yes. I know. Okay, what do I really want to know?" I tried to make my tone reasonable to not agitate the prickly bird, but he simply shook his feathers again and stared back. "What? If you have something to say, why don't you just say it, Archie? Isn't that the whole point of you being here? To whip me into shape for mother while pretending to be some kind of divine messenger from the gods or something?"

"First of all, I am a divine messenger from the gods, but I'm not going to waste my breath on someone not ready to hear those messages. There's no point, right? Second—you really don't believe in the gods?" It seemed far more like an accusation than a question.

"I really don't." I got up and stepped behind the brick wall dividing the two sides of the attic. Grabbing a t-shirt and sweats to sleep in from my duffel bag, I hung them over a chair and peeled off my skintight uniform. "Look, I think all of the god-bound families are essentially engaging in the paranormal equivalent of LARP-ing."

"Harping?"

"LARP-ing. Live action role playing. Just being a run-of-the-mill normal paranormal isn't enough for them, so they create something complicated that makes their family seem special. Everyone needs to feel special, I guess. More special than everyone else." My mother more than most, hence the elaborate enchanted barn owl.

"Your mother didn't send me. First, Minerva

doesn't have the magical prowess to conjure me. Second, I'm not some enchanted barn owl designed to help you find a life that's compatible with what you want to do and what your mother wants you to be." As I slipped the t-shirt over my head, I heard wings flapping. "To be honest, it doesn't matter to me whether you believe me or not, whether you believe in Athena or not. She's not some wilting flower goddess that needs people to fall at her feet."

"Then why are we having this conversation?" As my head popped out, I came face-to-face with the smirking owl balancing on the back of my chair. Though, again, I couldn't tell you why I thought he was smirking. But he was. "You're the one that asked the question about the gods out of nowhere."

"It wasn't out of nowhere. You're thinking about it. And you were the one that started asking the questions about the gods and why She chose Forkbridge, Florida."

Darn it. He was right. "I'm thinking about everything that happened tonight, Archie."

"That's fair," the owl answered with a flap of his wings. "But I think you would get further if you just asked me what you want to know. I know a lot, you know. I'm Athena's owl. I'm very wise." With a sudden lurch, the owl dove toward a box. Seconds later, he muttered curses. "Stupid lizard. I'll get him next time." He looked back up at me. "Sorry. Not hungry, but he was right there. Taunting me."

"Not a very good hunter, are you?" I asked.

The owl looked stricken. "Wiggle your finger, sweetie, let's test that theory."

"Maybe you should pray to the goddess for slower prey."

"Okay, now you're just dialing up the sass to be difficult. Besides, you don't believe in gods, anyway, right?" Archie flew back up and perched again on the chair. "So why would you suggest that?"

In a mirror of humanity, there were both religious people and secular people in the paranormal world. Once, the spiritual far outnumbered those that had little or no belief, but now? There were far more secular people than religious people. I always wondered how and why it switched, but not enough to ever look into it. I just didn't need a goddess in my life. Most of my friends didn't need gods.

If Archie was sent by the goddess Athena? It

seemed maybe they needed us—since I didn't seek her out.

"You're really gonna be a handful, aren't you?" the bird quipped. His talons scratched the wood on an antique chair I'd found stored in the dusty attic. "You know, I could have picked a really nice village girl in Africa with a tiger problem."

"I guess that depends on what extent you're planning to try and control me," I told him. Turning away from the pouting owl, I hung up my uniform and smoothed it out. "Look, I don't mean to come off like I'm ungrateful or anything. Honestly, this sounds like it's going to be a lot of fun."

The owl opened his eyes wide. "Stopping a murder sounds like fun to you?"

"Trying to kill a lizard is fun to you."

"That's different."

I crossed my arms and leaned against the brick wall. "I didn't join the military to get a desk job. I wanted to be out, scouring for clues, tracking enemies down. I'm trained to fight. I'm trained to sneak around. I'm trained to jump out of bushes and catch people. I learned how to track and stalk and catch my prey without anyone ever seeing me coming or going.

Remember, I'm not living here in Forkbridge because I want to," I said, shifting uncomfortably. "I'm here because I don't have anywhere else to go."

The owl blinked once, and for the first time that night, I found his slight lean and placid expression somewhat charming.

"I'm positively adorable," he cooed, his head tilting coquettishly.

"Stay out of my head, owl," I warned him.

"Yeah, so, I'm sure you already figured this out, but that's not going to happen."

* * *

Now, maybe you're wondering why my reaction wasn't very...reactionary?

I might give the impression that enchanted owls showing up out of the blue on the doorstep of witches happens every day in my world, but it doesn't. The supposed 'gods' sending magical gifts with a card and a message? Doesn't happen often, either.

However the owl showed up, whoever enchanted him so I had my own predatory Jiminy Cricket? I just rolled with the star magic. That's what military folks do, you know? Whatever shows up, whatever problem walks in front of you, whatever weapon your target might be holding and whatever their intention might be toward you? You have a job to do, and you just have to do it.

You can't stop in a gunfight, call a timeout, and discuss the situation.

In an attack? You don't think about how you feel.

You process all of that later.

Well, if you process it all...which, I'll admit, some of us don't.

Okay, sometimes I don't.

Not that this was a gunfight or anything.

I'd been in the military for a long time. I knew how to adjust to new situations, and things didn't surprise me.

Even if they surprised me.

And it was better than sitting behind the counter at Athena's Garden selling rose-scented body lotion designed to make that perfect man fall in love with you.

Which was where I was when she walked in.

"I am so excited about this!" Her shrill voice made me look up from the customer I was ringing out. The voice belonged to a thirty-something woman with hair dyed a deep blue-black—which was an odd choice considering her rosy pink complexion. She entered the magic store alone. "My friend Rosie told me that this was the best reading she'd ever had!" She took no notice of the customer in front of me and barreled in like she was the only one in the room. The woman smiled, her rosy red lipstick smeared on her teeth. "Are you Amethyst?" she asked me excitedly.

I handed the previous customer her rose-scented lotion, and she hurried out the door, her face down. "Ami!" I called toward the back. "I think there's a woman here who wants a reading from you!"

"Oh, my gosh, is that an owl?" the woman asked, her eyes wide. "That's an actual owl, isn't it? A real live owl. In a store! Oh, I just love Florida. You never know what to expect."

"Well, she's a bright one, now, isn't she?" Archie asked sarcastically from his perch next to the cash register. "I guess we can cross veterinarian, wildlife rehabilitator, or Harry Potter reader off the list of things we suspect she does."

"Oh, I think he's talking to me!" the woman squeaked excitedly, hearing a series of whistles and coos instead of Archie's snarky observation. "I didn't realize owls were so chatty!" She reached forward toward Archie's face.

"Yeah, me neither," I muttered as I jerked forward to grab the woman's hand. "Please don't place your hand anywhere near the owl. Owls do bite, and their talons can be very dangerous."

"You're ruining all of my fun," Archie muttered darkly.

"Oh, that adorable little cuddle bug wouldn't hurt me. Would you, sweetheart? Would you, baby?" Now she was talking in baby talk, cooing and wiggling her fingers at the bird. "You're just a little love, such a little sweetheart. Yes, you are. Yes, you are!"

"Ami!" I shouted even louder. "You have a customer!"

"Coming!" Ami raced down the three steps and landed with a clunk, her peasant skirt flowing behind her. "Sorry, I was just finishing up with the 'Love Yourself' soap, and it has to be wrapped in silk before it can be stored." She flashed me a look of apology and then turned to the dark-haired woman. "Ma'am, did you want a reading?"

"I did, I did!" She tore her eyes away from Archie and looked Ami up and down. "My goodness, my friend Rosie was right. You look like you walked right out of a fairytale with your long flowing clothes and your bare little feet! It's like I went to a Renaissance Faire! Only this is a real store, and you are just adorable!"

I cringed. The woman was talking about my sister the same way she had just talked about Archie. Her infantilizing first the owl and now a twenty-year-old woman grated on me like fingernails being dragged across a chalkboard. Archie and I shared a glance.

"Yes, well, just more comfortable without shoes. If you'll step back here, we have a reading corner set up in a semiprivate area." Ami didn't miss a beat, steering the woman toward a table for two with a crystal ball in the center. The ball was actually just for decoration, but people like the stereotypical experience, so Mom insisted. "Were you looking for a card reading or some other type of reading, Miss...?"

Raven-head sat down on the red velvet chair and placed her elbows on the table. "Marianna Black. I want whenever my friend Rosie got—and then whatever is slightly more expensive, so I can rub it in her face that I got a better reading than she did," Marianna told my sister without the slightest hint of irony.

"Um, you don't really get a better reading just because you pay more," Ami responded as she pulled out her cards. "A card reading is the easiest and the cheapest, but it's only the most inexpensive because it takes the least amount of time and effort. An aura reading is slightly more expensive because it takes a bit more effort on my part. I can't do any more for a few hours," Ami explained (without mentioning it was slightly more expensive because she had a good chance of swimming around in someone's aura while it contained all manner of nasties, and she didn't like it much). "My sister Ayla can contact anyone on the other side for you, but that's easier to do at night, so you'd have to wait a few hours. And my other sister Astra,"—Ami gestured toward me —"can read objects if you need that done."

"Objects? Why would I want to pay you people to do a reading on my watch or lipstick or something?" Marianna Black frowned. "That seems a little silly."

"Okay, so you don't need psychometry, then," Ami nodded kindly without missing a beat or expressing any reaction. "Why don't you tell me what your question is, and maybe we can figure out the best reading to give you?"

"I want to know why Bartholomew Chandler has not asked me to marry him yet," Marianna told Ami with an evil little smirk. "The two of us have been dating for two years, and it's well past time that he put a ring on it. If you know what I mean." She frowned. "I want to know what the holdup is."

I could tell her what the holdup was. At least, if the man had any brains in his head.

And I didn't need any oracle cards to do it, either.

"Okay, I do need to let you know, though, that the best readings are about you and not someone else," Ami said as she shuffled the cards to clear them. "Asking the universe to tell you about somebody else's motivations? It doesn't really give you any actionable information to improve yourself, and these—"

"I don't need to improve myself," she answered haughtily.

"You should've let me bite her finger," Archie told me flatly.

I tried to stifle a laugh.

"Yes, well, okay. If you could just shuffle the deck, please. Then cut it into three piles toward me," Ami told Marianna, handing her the deck of cards. "Clear your mind of any other distractions while you're shuffling, and think only of your question."

I was impressed with my sister, Ami. She was cool as a cucumber and incredibly charming to the unpleasant woman. Mom always told us that anyone who walked in our door needed to be here. It was drilled into us that even if the customers were rude, unpleasant, uncooperative? We still needed to show them the goddess's mercy and the goddess's love because the goddess Athena had sent them to us for help.

I didn't believe that bunch of malarkey, either.

I didn't know if Ami did, but watching my sister handle that woman made me wonder if I had more in common with my family than I thought I did.

Ami was unflappable, like a soldier.

* * *

"YOU STILL HAVEN'T GIVEN me my answer!" Marianna's voice raised several octaves, and I stood up from my chair, muscles tense. "I came in here asking one question. Just one question. I don't want to know all this other stuff about how I need to show more kindness and stop being so greedy."

"Marianna, I—" Ami's face looked frustrated as the woman cut her off.

"I want to know one question. What is the date my fiancé will propose to me, and if he hasn't decided to propose to me yet, why hasn't he proposed to me? That's all I want to know. Can I get him to do it tonight?"

He hadn't proposed, but she was already calling him her fiancé.

Poor Bartholomew Chandler, wherever he was.

I had been (of course) listening to the last twenty minutes of the card reading while feeling sorry for my sister. Marianna Black was a narcissistic woman used to getting whatever she demanded. Her frustration right now was that she'd ordered her boyfriend to propose to her.

For reasons I could guess, he had chosen not to acquiesce to her demand.

Ami had tried to gently guide her toward some of the reasons that could be the case. Like Marianna's unkindness toward his cocker spaniel and her repeated statements to Bartholomew that he would have to find another home for the dog when they got married. Like Marianna's rudeness toward the elderly Mrs. Chandler, Bart's beloved mother.

By the time I was done listening to the reading, not only wouldn't I have married this woman, I would've moved out of town at the first opportunity.

"Oh, no," Ami said. Her tone was demoralized as she stared down at the table. A strange glow illuminated the lower half of her face.

"What is it?" Marianna demanded. "Is that glowing card going to tell me the answer that I want?"

Wait. What now?

"Did she just say glowing card?" Archie asked, perking up on his perch and straining toward the back of the store. "I could swear I just heard that woman say glowing card."

"Astra, there's a card here with just a star on it. Um, in gold, and"—she swallowed and rubbed her eyes—"I swear it's glowing. Like, sparkly glowing." Ami looked up at me. She picked something up off the table with her left hand and held it up in my direction. "Is this it? I mean, that's almost a stupid question, isn't it? This has to be it. It has to be."

"It has to be what?" Marianna snapped. "What does that card mean? Is it like a scratch-off where, if you remove the sparkly bits, it will tell me the date?"

"Are you sure that the starlight card points toward someone we're supposed to save, owl?" I asked, my tone clearly expressing my suspicion that the starlight card was a little broken, maybe. "You said we were going to save people that need saving." I looked at Archie and pointed toward Marianna. "This is how we're starting? Seriously?"

"What are you people talking about?" the woman asked, agitated, as she looked back and forth between Ami, me, and Archie. She looked down at the incandescent star card and appeared to register for the first time that something about it didn't seem...normal. "Why is it doing that?" Marianna asked Ami. When she didn't respond, the woman then whirled to face me. "And are you actually asking that owl?"

"Ms. Black, please calm down," I told her.

"That card is glowing!" she said hysterically. "That's not normal!"

Archie turned to glare at her with undisguised dislike.

She jumped under his scrutiny.

I looked at Archie. "I'm sure there's an explanation—"

"You people are crazy," she whispered, cutting me off. Then she nodded vigorously. "This is some kind of crazy gypsy con artist thing, isn't it? You're about to tell me I'm cursed, and I need to pay you thousands of dollars for an egg or something, aren't you?" Marianna threw a twenty-dollar bill down on the table, hugged her purse close to her, and made her way toward the front door—walking sideways like a crab. Hence, she never turned her back on us.

"That's very antiziganist. Please don't say that," Ami admonished Marianna while standing up to go after the hysterical woman. "Gypsies aren't—

"What is a ziga-noised? What is that!" Marianna demanded angrily. "You have your money for your reading. I'm done. Even though I shouldn't even have to pay you. You didn't tell me what I wanted to know. I'll tell everyone I know not to come here! Rosie must hate me to recommend this cursed, ziga-noised place!"

Finally making it to the door, Marianna Black forcefully pushed it open and raced out. Bells jingled as the door closed.

"Astra, are you sure that we're supposed to save people who get the star card?" Ami asked quietly, glancing back toward the table. "Because I have to tell you, that's not someone I would assume should be saved. She's a horrible woman."

"The bird's supposed to be our guide through this." I turned and crossed my arms. "Well, Archie? It seems it was definitely the card, but my sister's right. She certainly didn't seem to deserve divine intervention. Isn't there some seven-year-old you could send me out to help?"

"I don't get to pick, and the goddess must have her reasons," the owl said, but his expression spoke volumes. Whatever goddess or magic or witch had a reason to mark Marianna Black for help? Archimedes, divine creature of the goddess Athena, certainly didn't seem to comprehend what that reason could be.

"So what do we do now?" Ami asked, looking nervous.

"We go on the computer and find out who Marianna Black is," I told her. "Tell Aunt Gwennie or Mom they need to come to watch the shop. Then you go and write down everything you remember from that reading. Anything she told you, any names she mentioned, companies she works for or owns, where she's from. We'll organize that information and see if we can find out who she is."

"Right." Ami stood, not moving. Then she sighed. "I might need to run to the store and get more paper," Ami said finally.

I raised my eyebrow.

"When we get to making a list of who might want to kill her?"

"Yes?"

"That list might be really, really long."

CHAPTER FIVE

*T*here have only been a handful of times researching a target made my jaw drop, but the search results on Marianna Black got added to that list. "Ami, you will not believe this," I told her as I scrolled through the images. Marianna Black dressed in a leather bodysuit on a red carpet. Marianna Black posing in front of a cheering crowd. Marianna Black, dirt-caked and bloodied, carrying an automatic weapon. "She's a Hollywood starlet. Like, a well-established Hollywood actress."

"No way." Ami scurried up behind me and peered over my shoulder at the screen. "I need to see more films because I'm obviously out of the loop." Leaning down, she examined the web encyclopedia entry. "She was a child actress? Really? What on earth is she doing in Forkbridge, Florida?"

"She mentioned nothing to you during the reading about her career? Nothing about performing at all?" I found it hard to believe someone's celebrity wouldn't come up, either from their statements or the reading itself.

"I really felt she was just independently wealthy or something. She didn't bring up any kind of career or anything like that." Ami stood up and put her hand on her hip. "It was all about getting married, and Bart Bart Bart. 'Why hasn't Bartholomew asked me to marry him? Doesn't Bartholomew realize we are meant to be together? Is Bartholomew upset with me, and that's why he hasn't asked me to marry him?' Listening to her, you would think there was nothing else in this woman's life other than that man."

"She's filming around here." I pointed. "At the Parrot Paradise. Wow, is that place still around?"

"Are you kidding?" Ami said with a snicker. "There is no way Randall Ford would ever leave those birds. He's still out there day after day with his parrot shows, whether one tourist shows up or twenty tourists show up. Hey," she said, peering down at me. "Didn't you go to school with Ricky Ford?"

"Yep," I said and continued scrolling through all the intelligence on Ms. Black. Ricky Ford had been the most popular guy at Forkbridge High—not altogether the circles I ran in, if you know what I mean. We did have a couple of classes together over the years. Once, we were assigned to be partners on a six-week project. If it hadn't been for that project, I probably never would've spoken to him. "We had a few classes together in high school. You know, back when mother would allow us to go to public school."

"Mother never allowed us to go to public school. Mother allowed you to go to public school, and she was so upset with how you turned out that none of the rest of us were allowed. Thanks for that, by the way," Ami said, scowling with annoyance. "All the rest of us really owe you for the homeschool thing."

"It's not my fault Mom thinks public school made me decide to run off and join the paranormal military. If she really stopped to think about it, she would have realized her theory made exactly no sense whatsoever. I didn't run off into the human world." I shrugged. "Don't blame me. I did great in school."

"I don't know, Astra. She might have been less disapproving if you had run off into the human world." The tenor of her voice was light, but her eyes were veiled by something I couldn't quite name. Ami blinked again, and it was gone. "Anyway, Ricky Ford now goes by Rick Ford, and he works with his dad at the Parrot Paradise."

"Ricky Ford, the quarterback of Forkbridge High's football team?" I looked up at her with an eyebrow raised. "Homecoming king three years running? That Ricky Ford? Works at Parrot Paradise doing parrot shows? Are you sure?" Rick and I had talked about family expectations a few times and the fact that both of us had goals my mom and his dad couldn't understand. I realized my dream. I don't recall his involving parrots.

"I go over there sometimes just to spend time with the birds, and he's definitely there. In a really adorable little safari uniform." Ami swooned a little and shivered. "Oh my gosh, Astra, you should see the guy's thighs. They're so tight you could bounce a quarter off of them."

I stared at my sister in astonishment. "Have you gone out on a date yet?" I asked.

She looked offended. "With Ricky? Of course not. He's way too old for me."

I cringed at my sister's unintentional slight.

Ricky and I were the same age. "No, not him—though, honestly, you could do worse. He's a really nice guy. I mean with anyone."

"No, why, is it that obvious?" She looked at me for a moment, her cheeks pink with embarrassment. "You know Mom's rule about not dating customers that come in the store. I don't meet anybody else, so where would I find someone to date, much less have a relationship with?" Ami sighed and sat down next to me at the table. "Between the store and the coven, I don't have any time." She glanced at me, her expression jealous. "I bet you went out with tons of people when you were in the military."

I set the laptop aside and looked back at my sister. "No, not tons. Active military service doesn't give you a lot of time for establishing relationships. My life wasn't much different from yours, at least as far as having free time. I was in the MoAF—"

"I know. Believe me, Mom never stopped griping about it."

"Anyway," I said, ignoring her observation about my mother. "We chased after fugitives, and it was a pretty solitary job. They assigned everyone to go after someone, so you never knew when you'd be back at the base or on the other side of the world. Almost impossible to have a stable relationship."

Just then, Archie flew in through the window and skidded across the kitchen table, his talons gouging the wood as he slid. He'd appeared so stealthily (well, until he tumbled into the tabletop) his arrival made Ami jump five feet.

"You have a lot of bunnies in the backyard," the owl told Ami. Archie leaned down and rubbed his beak on the edge of the table.

Ami took one horrified look, and her eyes widened. "You did not eat a bunny in the backyard, did you?" Ami asked.

"I did not eat a bunny in the backyard," the owl told Ami as he hoisted his head and locked his black eyes on her. "I took it to the roof so no one would see me. I'm kind of a sloppy eater."

Ami took a heavy, steadying breath and rubbed her cheeks with her hands. "You must be joking. You have to be joking." She lifted her hand to her throat, and tears appeared in her eyes. "I named some of those bunnies!"

The owl blinked once, then twice. "I'm just teasing you, kid," Archie told her, opening his wings wide and stepping back and forth. "I wouldn't attack one of your garden bunnies. That would be scandalous." Lifting his wing higher to shield his face from Ami, he clicked at me and shook his head yes. Then he rolled his eyes.

"I'm going to go wash my face," Ami said, her face still looking stricken. "I presume after what we discovered, you'll want to go over to Parrot Paradise?"

I nodded. Once my sister was out of earshot, I turned to the owl, my voice low.

"Okay, apex predator, which bunny did you eat?"

"The slow one," he whispered back.

* * *

WE PULLED up to a stone marker off Killian Drive. It was a tremendous boulder that marked the entrance to the wildlife park. Just behind it, taped over the brightly painted sign indicating Parrot Paradise's hours, was a notice that the eco-park would be closed to visitors for the next two weeks. However, there was no guard at the front gate—just a chain across the drive that led to an information building and the parking area.

"Now what?" Ami asked.

"It's a chain, not a militarized border crossing," I told her as I hopped out of the Jeep.

"We unlock it, drive in, lock it behind us, and pull up there where there are people."

"But it's locked," she called out the window.

"You're really not good at breaking the rules, are you?" I called back. I unclipped the chain and walked it across. "I'm back in town after being abroad. My high school friend Ricky Ford works here, and someone just gifted me an owl that I know nothing about." I dropped back into the Jeep and put it in gear. "We're not here to visit the park." I hitched my head toward the backseat. "We are here to receive information on how to take care of this stupid bird."

"Hey!" Archie snapped and thrashed his wings. "No need to be disparaging, you twit!"

"Speaking of, maybe you don't want to act like a bird that can hear and understand all the conversations around you for the next hour or so," I told Archie, glaring at him through the rearview mirror. "You were the one that picked this woman to help, so you need to do your part, too. This is a group effort, remember?"

"Will anyone else be able to understand you if you talk?" Ami asked Archie.

"Only the Arden women. Well, and anyone god-touched," he responded. "Other humans will just hear clicks or hoots or whatever they expect a normal owl to sound like. Don't worry about it. You two just need to make sure that you don't react to anything I say, and you especially shouldn't talk back to me. People will think you're crazy."

"People already think we're crazy, Archie," Ami told him pleasantly. "We are the homeschooled witch girls of Forkbridge. Even the spiritualist kids think we're nuts."

"I wasn't homeschooled."

"Yeah, but you're done up like a spy in a Russian movie, Astra. Or Black Widow from the Marvel movies. Or Lara Croft!"

Exhaling loudly, I frowned at my sister. "We live in Florida; this could be a surfing outfit. Or a diving outfit. Or maybe I'm on my way home from work in Orlando at one of the tourist shows. Or Disney World. This is Central Florida, Ami. No one's normal here."

"That does not look like a surfing outfit. Surfing outfits don't come with black leather boots, sis. Believe me, you don't look any more normal than the rest of us, and there are plenty of normal people in this neck of the woods." She peeked back behind us. "Why don't you just wear regular clothes, anyway? Are you really wearing that just because Mom told you to take it off?"

"Because this is comfortable—and bulletproof, and slash-resistant," I told Ami as I pulled into a parking spot. "It's also got some magical defense built-in. You find me a t-shirt and jeans that do all that? I'll retire my work uniform. Until then, it stays on."

I didn't mention it to my sister, but it was also moisture-wicking. Like, magically moisture wicking. In this sticky hot humidity that was the entire state of Florida? There was no way I was giving up my bodysuit. Just not going to happen.

"What if someone shoots you in the shoulder?" Ami pointed at the bare skin between the top of my arm-length gloves and shoulder.

"Then it's going to hurt. Which, Archie, you should keep in mind. Keep off my shoulder. " I held out my arm in front of me and motioned for the bird to jump on, which he did. He wasn't as heavy as I expected him to be, but the owl had some heft to him. "Remember, act like an owl."

"I am an owl," he retorted.

"And don't eat anything," I warned.

"I'm full, thanks to the"—he glanced at Ami with a quick swivel of his head—"crackers you gave me earlier. Wheat crackers. No rabbit in them at all. Nope."

"I wonder if we can trade him in for a parrot," Ami muttered darkly.

"You know, there's a bunch of parrots called kea in New Zealand that look like hawks and eat like hawks. You think I'm bad? They attack sheep," he told her as he shifted on my forearm. "Parakeets in the Antipodes eat albatross eggs. We all gotta eat, babe."

"Don't call me babe," Ami told Archie absently.

"Yes, everything has to eat, but don't eat here," I warned him as we climbed the steps to the information building. Just as we reached the top of the stairway, a door opened, and a stunning man in blue jeans and a Parrot Paradise t-shirt (with a large macaw on his shoulder) stepped out. He stopped short and stared at the owl on my arm.

"Astra?" the man asked, surprised. "Astra Arden? Is that you?"

"Are you asking the owl or me?" I joked, noticing he couldn't take his eyes off of the owl perched on my forearm. I squinted, and somewhere within the ruggedly handsome thirty-odd-year-old man's face, I could see the hint of a boy I once knew. "Ricky, is that you?" He smiled warmly and nodded as he glanced at me.

Almost immediately, his eyes were pulled back toward the owl as if by some force.

"Guy's got two pretty women on his front step, and he can't take his eyes off the owl," Archie quipped and shook his feathers. "Not surprised I don't see a wedding ring on this dude's finger, I'll tell you what."

"Dude's finger, dude's finger," the parrot squawked. "Pretty women, pretty women."

"They are pretty women, Thor," Richard 'Ricky' Ford told his gigantic macaw. He stepped forward and looked Archie over with an expert's eye. "Is the bird injured at all? Is he able to fly?"

"Injured? No, he's not injured. Why do you ask?" I turned and looked at Archie, concerned. "Do you see something wrong with him?"

"Since you showed up here when the park's closed with an owl, I assumed you had found him and were bringing him here. I'm a registered wildlife rehabilitator." He gestured toward Archie. "You're not dropping him off?" My old English class partner sounded somewhat disappointed.

"Astra got him as a birthday present," Ami volunteered, stepping forward. "We just don't know much about taking care of owls, and I remembered you had a lot of birds here, so we were hoping you could tell us a little bit about him. Maybe give us some advice about taking care of him?"

"Don't you even think about leaving me here," Archie warned me, his talons digging into my arm through my glove. "I have no interest in spending one minute more than I have to in a place infested with rainbow-colored bird-brain divas."

"Bird brain, bird brain," Thor cackled, casting a dark eye at the owl. "Rick, I'm a pretty bird. I'm a pretty bird. Right, Rick? Right, Rick?" As Rick assured Thor he was a beautiful bird, I realized two things standing on the porch in the Florida heat.

One? That parrot could understand what the owl was saying. At least, it could hear the words and repeat them. What the bird understood and what it didn't? I had no idea.

Two, my owl appeared to be a racist.

If animals have races.

Wait. Do animals have races?

Anyway, the owl clearly didn't like parrots.

If the parrot knew what Archie was saying, it was possible the feeling was mutual.

* * *

"YOU NEED an outdoor aviary at the very least," Rick said as he walked in front of a vast library and scanned the titles. His attitude had changed slightly, and he seemed somewhat uncomfortable. "There are no books that tell you how to keep an owl as a pet because you're not supposed to. I mean, if you'd asked me whether you should keep an owl as a pet? My answer would be no. A hundred, thousand times no." He grabbed a book and turned back to where Ami and I were sitting. "Owls are one of the most precisely adapted wild raptors on earth. They are, without a doubt, wild creatures that should not be kept in captivity."

"You do realize you own a tourist trap that lets people come in and play with parrots, right?" I asked him as he handed me the book. "Not an attitude I would've expected from you. I mean, what's the difference?"

"What's the difference? That's a solitary creature." Rick pointed at Archie. "Parrots have flock instincts, and that makes them good pets. An owl has no such instincts. That owl has evolved to hunt and kill," Rick said, stepping back. "If you don't know how to handle a raptor, you can hurt yourself. His talons? Razor-sharp."

"You know it, baby," Archie told Rick proudly, his beak in the air.

Rick's head jerked back slightly. "Did he just click at me?"

I glared at the owl. "Archie isn't your average owl. I appreciate what you're saying, but for reasons I cannot explain right now? The owl has to stay with us for a while."

"What can he eat that doesn't involve…killing things?" Ami asked Rick. "Can we feed him vegetables and rice? I have fresh vegetables from my garden." Her eyes widened as if she just had a great idea. "How about kibble? Is there owl kibble? Birdseed?"

"If I eat your sister in her sleep, I want you to know it will be entirely her fault," Archie huffed.

Rick looked horrified. "The owl is a meat-eater. Like, strictly a meat-eater. It's a wild carnivore, and it doesn't eat anything other than meat," he told Ami, causing her face to fall into a frown. "Again, it's evolved into one of the most lethal predators on the planet. It needs meat; it needs space." Rick frowned and looked back and forth between us. "Didn't you learn any of this before you got your license?"

"What license?" I asked him.

"You can't keep an owl without a license. I mean, lots of people keep them illegally, but you shouldn't do that. There's a reason it's illegal to keep an owl as a domestic pet. You're only supposed to have them to rehabilitate them. Once they can survive in the wild, even as a rehabilitator, I'm required by law to let them go." He shrugged sadly. "I know in this day and age, no one follows the rules."

"I follow the rules," Ami piped up. "I am a rules follower. All the way."

"Well, I guarantee you, that owl doesn't want to be kept locked up."

"Oh, look who psychic, now," Archie said sarcastically.

"We don't keep him locked up," I said somewhat defensively. "He can come and go as he pleases, and if he chooses to leave, that's really his business. If he chooses to stay, I want to take care of him as best I can. But if this is about the owl's freedom to choose, I'm not gonna tell the owl he can't stay if he wants to."

Rick didn't respond, but he looked troubled.

"Okay, you got in. You did all the owl talk. Dudley Do-right over there is about two seconds away from calling US Fish and Wildlife, so maybe we should shift the conversation to Marianna Black?" Archie snapped with a flap of his wings. "I prefer not to bite the face off a game warden, but I'll do it if I have to."

Suddenly, the door on the other side of the room burst open, and a man I didn't recognize ran into the building. He had on muddy boots and clutched a CB radio. Through the speaker, we could hear frantic shouting. "Where's your phone?" he panted.

Rick pointed to an old-fashioned rotary phone hanging on the wall.

The man raced over, dialed three numbers (while cursing loudly at how long it was taking), and shouted into the receiver. "Send the police right now! Marianna Black has just been kidnapped!"

CHAPTER SIX

arrots squawked, and men raced within the enclosed aviary. Any security that could've stopped us from following Rick into the zoological park had obviously left their post as soon as the alert was raised. I grimaced as I observed everyone stomping through the potential crime scene. "Fools. If they were working to try and secure the scene, they should have done that before people started running around like chickens with their heads cut off," I told Ami as I waved her to the side. We squeezed ourselves against a fence and watched the chaos unfold.

"What are we doing in here?" she murmured.

A frantic security guard rushed in front of us. He blew by us with scarcely more than a glance.

"Blending in and determining what we can find out." I reached into the pouch on my tactical belt and plucked out sunglasses. It was bright inside the place—the protective netting covering the acres of the fake jungle did nothing to shelter us from the hot Florida sun, but the glasses had a secondary purpose. Slipping them on, I tapped the border of the frame to assure they were recording all I looked at. "Over there."

We moved back onto the trail and headed in the same direction Rick had gone just minutes before. A rich canopy of glistening leaves and damp palm fronds hid a cacophony of screeching birds. Snatches of radiant sun periodically highlighted bright crimson and blue parrots in the trees. "This place usually sounds so tranquil, but now it sounds...nervous. Like, agitated," Ami observed as we ventured further into the park. "It's like the birds realize that something is awry."

"It wouldn't surprise me if they do," Archie said as he traveled on my arm. Off to the right, something grunted from within a stand of bamboo. "Most of the birds are hanging out above us. If Marianna was snatched from here, inside the aviary? They likely saw it take place."

I peered up. The vividly hued birds shifted and moved, clawing along the vines and branches as if they were pacing. I noted most cast their gaze in one distinct direction, and it wasn't the direction we were moving.

"Stop," I announced, grabbing Ami's arm. "None of the birds are looking that way. They're looking over there." I pointed east toward a chained-off dirt pathway. It was unmaintained, with twisting tree roots crawling over the faint route. "Let's go that way."

Ami balked. "It's dark. I don't think we're supposed to."

"We're not supposed to be in here at all, so I don't see how taking that path will change the situation. Come on, just follow me, and look confident we're supposed to be here. Right now, you look like a rabbit on the edge of a clearing. Don't act like you're afraid to get caught."

"I am afraid to get caught. Is this what your job was like?" Ami whispered as we moved further into the dense jungle planted to mimic the Amazon wilds. "Creeping around and hoping you don't get caught?"

"That was probably what it was like for the people I chased," I told her. "I never worried about getting caught. Confidence is half the battle. Of course, that was probably because I was the one with the badge."

"You don't have a badge anymore, though."

"Yeah, the curious thing about the badge? It's not so easy to put down. Especially not after fifteen or so years." The air was growing even thicker with moisture, and decaying vegetation mingled with an overly sweet floral perfume. Tropical flowers bordered the path and hung low, large, and lush in this sheltered area.

I sneezed.

"Bless you," Archie mumbled, his eyes searching ahead.

The unmistakable rumble of rushing water or a waterfall grew louder as we made our way even further. No one passed us, and the sound of people rushing this way and that grew further and further away. A few more steps, and we wouldn't be able to hear it.

"Look over there on the ground," Ami said with a start. "Is that a piece of cloth?"

Archie dove off my arm and seized the fabric. Turning, he launched up with a single flap of his mighty wings and released it into my outstretched hand. "Does that look like anything she was wearing?"

I raised my eyebrow. "Aren't you presumed to

be the shepherd on this adventure, Mr. Know-it-all?"

Archie stared. "I'm colorblind. My eyes are a hundred times more sensitive to light than yours, but colors? Not so much. My sense of smell is pretty much garbage, too." The owl suddenly reared its head and froze. "Hearing and vision are pretty spot-on, though—and it sounds like there's something in the water up ahead." Archie turned and stared at me. "It's way bigger than a fish, and it's in trouble."

I thrust the material in my pocket and darted toward the water.

Thirty seconds later, the dense path opened into a man-made grotto with a large circular pool surrounded by gently sloped uniform banks. A rocky outcropping directly across from us rose high in the air, so tall it cut off the sun and made the small pool seem mysterious and gloomy. A frothy cascade of water tumbled from it, swirling and churning around…

…a slight woman, sprawled face down over the bank, her legs bobbing in the waterfall's churn.

"Ami, go get help!" I called out as I vaulted into the water. The pool must've been designed for the animals because it wasn't deep, and I ran across the smooth bottom toward the woman. As I drew closer, I could see her hair was soaking wet, and her lips were blue. "How on earth did you almost drown in this dinky little pool, lady? The water's only up to my knees," I murmured, pulling her from the water. Once I had her out, I shook her. No response.

I checked for breathing.

Damn it.

Then her pulse.

Nothing.

Laying her on her back, I tipped her head to clear her airway and stuck my cheek near her mouth to see if I could feel any breaths. Her chest didn't move up or go down, and I could pick up no hint of air stirring.

Nothing.

Pinching her nose, I breathed into her mouth. Once, then again, then again, and again. After the final breath, I leaned back and looked, scouring for any sign of life.

The young woman was lifeless, so I started CPR.

About thirty seconds in, she coughed. I quickly jumped off to roll her over on her side, and relief washed over me as she continued coughing up the water in her lungs. Her eyes flickered open weakly, and her eyes found mine. The poor girl looked horrified.

"You're going to be okay. I sent my sister to get help. Just stay here, don't try to get up. Concentrate on breathing slowly. In and out, in and out. That's it." I wrapped my hands around her arms to warm her. "Someone will be here soon, and hopefully, they'll have blankets. If not, we can just use my sister's skirt. That thing is huge," I told her with a smile.

"They took Marianna," she mumbled hoarsely. "I tried to stop him, but the man saw me following them here. And then the other guy, he held me under the water."

"The kidnappers took Marianna through here?" I asked, looking up. The area around the grotto had such dense vegetation I couldn't see which way they'd gone. "Is this how they got her out of the park?"

"Through the waterfall," she confided, her finger pointing toward the fake gray outcropping of rocks. "They reached the waterfall and escaped."

I twisted and looked at Archie, jerking my head toward the waterfall.

"Are you out of your mind? What do you take me for, a pelican?" he bellowed from a tree branch on the side of the pond. "Owls don't get wet. We're not waterproof. If I get doused, I won't be able to fly for hours. Forget it. You want to know what's behind that water? You go look." He shuddered as if in revulsion.

I looked back down. The color was coming back to the woman's face. "Who are you?" she croaked.

"My name is Astra. I just stopped by to visit an old friend that works here. Who are you?"

"I'm Marianna's personal assistant, Christine Chandler," she responded and suddenly coughed again. "I tried to stop them from taking her, Astra. I really did. I yelled for help, but I guess nobody could hear me."

"Your last name is Chandler?" I asked, my eyes narrowing. "Any relationship to Bartholomew Chandler?"

"Marianna's boyfriend?" She gave a frail nod. "He's my older brother."

* * *

AMI and I watched the emergency medical crew roll Christine Chandler's stretcher out of the waterfall area and back up the passage toward the center of the place. Two guys with CB radios stayed back. As soon as Christine and the paramedics were out of earshot, they advanced to block the route, turned toward Ami and me, and demanded (rudely) who we were and how we had found Christine.

"I'm a friend of Rick Ford's. I thought I saw someone come down the path, so I followed." I crossed my arms and lifted my eyebrow. I consciously did not give them my name. "And who the inferno are the two of you?"

"My name is Hayward Beals. I'm the producer of *The Fabulous McCaws*." I didn't burst out laughing—though I was surprised Hayward said the film's title with a straight face. "This is the director, Joel Clemens." Joel nodded but didn't speak. "And this is a closed set, so I'm sure you're not supposed to be here. And if you're not supposed to be here on a day when the star of our film got stolen?" Hayward smiled widely in a way that seemed anything but amiable. "I'd say that makes me concerned you could be a suspect."

"Since I was standing in the information building with Rick when someone rushed in to let us know Marianna had been kidnapped, I'd say that makes you wrong. There are three cameras in the building, at least; you can go look if you're interested."

I'd been apprehensive, on alert, since the paramedics left with Christine, and the two men remained behind in this out-of-the-way private section of the park. That apprehension was added to when they prevented our exit. On the one hand, what Hayward Beals said made sense—he didn't know who I was, and he just found me with someone who claimed to have been forcefully drowned by kidnappers. A sensible reason to be dubious, if you ask me.

The thing is, though—the fellow brought paramedics back here, but no police.

And they didn't go with Christine. Which seemed an odd decision.

And they didn't bring in any of the ten or so security guards I saw flying around just up the path, there. Which also seemed like an odd choice.

I shifted my head and went on. "It's strange, though—despite what you said, you don't really seem concerned. Like, nothing in your manner leads me to believe you're concerned."

"You don't know anything about me, lady," Hayward responded defensively.

"I know you're blocking my way out of this grotto."

"Yeah, like, again—you seem like a suspect. Or

like you might know something." Hayward said the last part hurriedly as if he didn't want me to focus on it too closely. People did that sometimes. They said something fast or tried to be super casual about the exact thing they wanted to know.

"I know a lot of things." I paused, but he didn't say anything. "What, specifically, do you think I know?"

It was almost imperceptible, but the silent director's eyes darted toward the waterfall. Now, the waterfall was the main feature in this small area, and someone glancing at it? It didn't necessarily mean that someone knew it was the means of escape for kidnapping.

It didn't necessarily mean that someone didn't know, though.

Ami stood slightly behind me and said absolutely nothing. I turned and glanced to make sure she was all right. Her eyes were unfocused, her face soft as she watched the two men. I knew that look. She was reading their auras, taking stock of their souls, reading what type of man they were, and trying to determine how frightened she needed to be of them.

"Look, I'm sorry, I'm just a little on edge with the kidnapping and what happened to Christine."

Beals switched tactics, almost like a car slamming from drive directly into reverse with a clunky lurch. His tense, confrontational stance relaxed, and his hand moved casually to rest on his hip. "I'm a little freaked out over what's happened here today. I'm sure you can understand. And you do look a little"—he looked me up and down —"odd, if you know what I mean."

"Can't imagine what you're talking about."

"Right, right, Florida." He smiled. "Anyway, did Christine tell you anything before the paramedics showed up? Anything that might be useful?"

Look at him.

Not sure how to approach me, not sure how to get the information he wants without making me suspicious of him. Sure that he's in no danger. Not even comprehending how his lack of concern for Christine's health makes him look suspicious.

He was clearly more concerned about what she said to me than what happened to her. He didn't ask me what I saw. Didn't ask me if I saw anyone else here. He asked me what she said when she woke up.

And that made him suspicious as hell.

"Hey, I get your curiosity. I'd be curious, too," I

told him as I waved Archie over. The owl swooped over, settled on my forearm, and turned to stare at the two men. Slowly, carefully, I made my way around the grotto toward the path. Ami followed closely, still saying nothing. "I think, though, I'm going to wait and talk directly to the police." I smiled. "You understand."

A flash of anger. Then a politician's smile. "Of course, of course."

I was prepared for the two men to stop us from leaving. I could feel Archie's tense grip and knew instinctively that he, too, would have acted if either man had become actively threatening. They watched as I grew closer, Hayward and Joel's eyes searching my face for my next move.

My only next move was to leave.

But I could see they weren't sure of that.

We all arrived at the head of the path. Silence. Tension.

I stared at them, waiting for them to step aside.

It took several seconds, but they finally did move.

* * *

"OH MY GOSH, that was the scariest thing I've ever been through," Ami said as we raced to the Jeep and jumped in. "Wait, aren't you going to talk to the police?"

"Are you out of your mind?" I lifted my arm up, and Archie jumped into the backseat. "That guy was right. The police in this little podunk town? At some point, they're going to realize that Marianna was kidnapped through that waterfall and the fact that we were there at all? Suspicion will fall right on us. I don't have time for it, and besides, if I had to guess? Frick and Freak back there had something to do with it."

"The director and the producer?" Ami asked, surprised. "You think they had something to do with Marianna's kidnapping?"

"You know, for a seer, your instincts are kind of crappy." I threw the Jeep in reverse and pulled out just as local law enforcement was driving up. "It certainly took them long enough to show up here," I said with frustration as we passed the two patrol cars. "I thought the police have to show up when the paramedics do? How did the ambulance get here before the police?"

"Astra, they're looking at us," Ami whispered, her eyes wide.

"If they show up at Arden House, we'll talk to

them, but we need to look into this a little further before that happens. I want to know more about this film set, the film company, everything." I frowned as the Jeep picked up speed on Killian Road. "Something weird is going on here. I can sense it."

"But how are we gonna find out? I doubt we can just search for it on the internet."

"You'd be surprised. Besides"—I reached down and pulled out the cloth we'd found on the path —"I'm a psychometrist, remember? Let's get back to the house and see what story this piece of fabric has to tell."

CHAPTER SEVEN

*A*rchie flew off toward a thicket of woods before we even hit the front door. I said a silent prayer for any bunnies hopping around the woodland. I presume the owl wasn't into research, which was first on the schedule. I wondered what the owl actually was into. Other than the death stare and wild rabbit population management, it didn't seem like he had much in the way of powers to help us.

Anyway, the research wasn't demanding. I hadn't been at the computer for more than two seconds when thousands of links came up detailing Hayward Beals' checkered Hollywood history. I became so immersed in the drama of

Hayward's life I totally forgot to look into the director.

Later, you'll remember I said this.

You'll also realize this was a huge mistake.

But I digress.

Beals appeared to be around forty, maybe forty-five—no one seemed to have an exact birth date. A gossip site snagged pictures of the guy racing out of a plastic surgeon's office, too, so I wasn't sure I could discern his age solely by the way he looked. The guy shot to stardom when his first independent film, *Bird on the Line* unexpectedly snagged critical acclaim and several Academy Awards.

Huh, I thought, tilting my head. Apparently, the guy has a thing for birds.

Just as quickly as his career's success exploded, that's how quickly his career—followed by his life—imploded. Box office flops made him unemployable in Hollywood. Loans and financing for unmade movies remained unpaid, and eventually, Hayward was driven into insolvency.

Bankruptcy took his two sports cars, his beach house in Malibu, and his wife, Trista. Trista headed for the exit with Hayward's beloved bulldog Spike in tow.

Ouch.

As far as the film he was shooting now? The buzz about *The Fabulous McCaws* was less than stellar—and that's when I could find information about it at all.

I know, shocker, right?

"What on earth was Marianna doing in a film like this and working for a guy like that?" I muttered, scanning the dozens of articles on her career. "Beals seems like he's one bad film away from producing discount dinner theater down in Miami."

"Are you asking me?" Ami called from the other room.

"No, just thinking out loud, really," I called back.

Marianna Black's information was just as plentiful and far less unseemly. Though we'd initially thought she was a Hollywood diva? A deeper dive into her story made clear she was a recognizable working actress with some success, a bit of fame, but no breakout roles to catapult her to the top. Conversely, there was no publicized fall from grace I was able to find.

In fact, all the articles I pulled up wrote about her in mostly favorable terms. One indicated that she was absolutely professional and reasonably successful in the B-movie action genre. Another said she was well-liked with a reputation for kindness among crews. While not an A-list celebrity by any stretch, she still appeared to stand a good chance of being recognized on the street—at least, if Instagram was any evidence.

"What are you musing out loud about?" Ami asked as she returned to place oiled candles on the table.

"Marianna Black donated her entire salary for the film *Blood Feud in Africa* to a Nigerian orphanage just three miles from where the film was shot," I told Ami. Scanning, I read part of the article out loud. "'The philanthropic Miss Black spent much of her downtime visiting the orphanage, and members of the crew report she became quite attached to a young girl named Daraja.'" I looked up. "This doesn't sound anything like the woman we met. Would you think the self-absorbed woman in the shop this afternoon was the same woman that donated her entire paycheck to an African orphanage?" I shrugged. "She must have a great publicist."

Ami looked at me as if I'd whacked her across the face. "We only met her for half an hour, Astra. Maybe she was just having a bad day."

"Who's having a bad day?" Althea asked as she and Ayla shuffled into the dining area from the great room. "Should I go and get some of Aunt Gwennie's flowers? One snoot from those babies, and you'll be in a good frame of mind for twenty-four hours." She dragged out the chair opposite me and sat down with a clunk. "What are we doing?"

"We are investigating a producer and a director we met," I told Althea.

Ayla's eyes grew wide. "You saw someone that worked in movies? Which movies? *Star Wars? Harry Potter?*" She wiggled her shoulders with childlike excitement. "*Twilight?* I love *Twilight.* Have you seen *Twilight?*" She looked around the table. "Where's Archie?"

"He went out to stretch his wings, and I see someone in this house actually pays attention to popular culture, so that's good. You'll be useful in this investigation." I winked at Ayla, and she blushed. "Unfortunately, this producer and director were not on the level of anything like those movies. I doubt you've seen anything he's done. At least I hope you haven't. Sounds like several hours you wouldn't be able to get back."

Ayla finally sat down next to Althea. "Does this have to do with the star card thing? Mom said you and Ami took off to go investigate something because the goddess gave you a job."

I came close to popping off a sarcastic response, but Ayla was only thirteen years old. I didn't know what her religious beliefs were or whether she'd begun questioning the things our mother taught us, but I was sure it wasn't my place to rattle her cage just yet. "We had a woman in the shop today, and Ami flipped over the sparkly star card. Now, we are trying to figure out what's going on."

"What's happened so far?" Althea asked.

"Well, I did a reading for this woman who was really narcissistic. She just kept asking over and over and over again why her boyfriend Bart hadn't proposed to her," Ami told Althea as she placed the last of the candles on the table. Her words came out in a rush. "Then she got freaked out when the sparkle card showed up because she thought we were going to claim she had a curse or something, and she ran out." Ami rubbed her neck as if it was sore and bit her lip. "Honestly, if she'd pulled out a cross and started throwing holy water at us, I wouldn't have been surprised. Not at all. But her aura wasn't that black, you know? It was just strange." She sighed. "Anyway, we found out that she's actually a Hollywood actress, and she's filming a movie over at Parrot Paradise."

I stared at my previously quiet sister in surprise. Ami hardly spoke up when we were at Parrot Paradise, and now the words poured from her like competing ideas were fighting to break free. She turned and nodded as if to open the floor to me.

Interesting.

"Unfortunately, when we went over there to check her out, she got kidnapped," I told my younger sisters. "So, now Ami and I are trying to figure out what happened to her."

Althea blinked. "So. I mean. That doesn't seem like you're good luck for her at all. I mean, she got kidnapped when you went over to see her. That's not good luck. I would think if the goddess pointed you toward her, you'd be good luck. But…I mean…" Althea shifted in her chair. "Bad juju, man."

"She didn't get kidnapped because of us, Althea. And if we find her before anything happens to her, we will be very good luck. If anything, that's probably why the card showed up."

"But the card showed up before you left. You were probably supposed to stop her from being kidnapped. I mean, obviously." Althea's fingers absently toyed with the oiled candle in front of her.

"Then perhaps the goddess should have been more specific with her instructions or just sent a text," I popped back sarcastically.

Althea stiffened, her eyes wide.

Oh, lord, I thought to myself. They're really on guard around me. I tried to remind myself they were young, sheltered women, and I'd been gone for fifteen years. I needed to be a little careful not to be...well, me.

I smiled at her, and she relaxed again, but her expression remained guarded. I continued my warm, friendly, affectionate smile. Finally, Althea returned it. "In any case, we are where we are now, so we'll work with what we've got," I assured her.

"Well, Astra, the police might think we did it since we found that drowned woman in the pool," Ami pointed out. "I still think they're going to show up on our doorstep any minute now." She let that hang in the air a moment and then turned. "Should I keep a toothbrush in my pocket or something?"

"You found a woman drowned in a pool?" Ayla asked slowly. Ami nodded. "Was she dead?"

The thirteen-year-old looked around the room. "If she is, she didn't come back with you. Though, I mean, if I thought it was your fault that I died, I don't know that I'd come back with you, either."

My sisters had a brake on their mouths that made them swallow their words or say none at all, and that thing was off, apparently. "No, ghost whisperer, she didn't die," I told Ayla.

"She didn't. Astra actually saved her life. It was amazing. Talk about something out of a movie," Ami told Ayla and Althea with a severe look on her face, her words coming quickly again. "She jumped in the water and dragged Christine out with, like, no seconds to spare. I was so shocked it took me like five seconds just to run after she told me to." Ami shuddered at the memory. "When I left to go get help, I could swear she wasn't breathing. When I came back, she was talking." There was a slight pause, and then Ami jumped slightly. "Oh, and get this. The woman that almost drowned?" She looked out over the table. "Marianna Black's boyfriend's sister. Isn't that crazy?"

"Who's Marianna Black?" Ayla asked, confused.

"The woman that's been kidnapped," Ami answered.

"And who's Christine again?" Althea asked.

"That's the woman that almost drowned. After all that happened, that's when we met the producer and the director." I closed my laptop and slipped it underneath my chair. "They were pretty sketchy, and that's why we were checking into them. But right now, we're going to see what this little baby has to say." I pulled out a piece of torn fabric roughly six inches long and about four inches wide. "We found it on the ground near where Christine was attacked. If you guys want to help, you're more than welcome."

"Can we?" Ayla asked, excited. "This is so cool. This is just like being in a movie!"

"Except it's not, Ayla," Ami told the thirteen-year-old gently, pouring water on her fiery excitement. "This isn't a movie. A woman's life is in danger, and the goddess thinks we can help her. This isn't a game, and we don't know what we'll see. Are you ready for something like this?"

"You know, I'm not a little girl anymore, and none of you are deathspeakers!" Ayla glared at us, frowning, then folded her arms across her chest. "I've talked to a ghost that got stabbed by another ghost, you know. He was all totally freaked out! I didn't go running to Mom because I got scared."

She lifted her chin defiantly. "I'm a witch, too, just like you guys. Stop treating me like a baby."

I half-smiled at my feisty sister. "I think she'll do fine."

Ayla's angry face melted into a smile, and she beamed back at me.

* * *

WE EACH SAT AT A QUARTER. If you don't know what that is, the four of us basically formed a plus sign—I sat opposite Ayla, and Althea sat opposite Ami. Between each of us, Ami lit candles and whispered a prayer of protection. Effectively, this formed a circle.

Witches like circles. It's a thing.

The prayer thing may be confusing, too. Religious witches? They pray. Nonreligious witches cast spells. In some ways, these distinctions were meaningless since, of course, there were no gods.

But my sisters' didn't cast spells seeking to force their will on something or someone. They asked the gods to grant them the results of whatever magic they cast—yeah, I said cast. Ironically, they have to cast to make it clear to the "gods" what they want.

Follow me? (And can you spot the irony?)

Anyway, Ami asked Athena to protect us. So the goddess wouldn't have to put herself out too much, Ami went ahead and cast the protection spell for Athena to allow or not allow, as is her (the goddess's) will. The prayer that accompanied the spell was just a request for her to let it go through and an acknowledgment that if Athena chose not to protect us, we were super cool with that. We were supplicants, after all, existing solely by the will of Athena.

If she let us die? Cool.

Of course, the spell always worked.

Fancy that.

Like I said, to me?

The distinction between prayer and spell was meaningless.

I didn't know whether the distinction was meaningless to Ami, so I murmured the words "If you will it, so mote it be" at the end, along with everyone else. I didn't want to be rude—when in Rome and all that. But I didn't believe it made a bit of difference one way or another, so it didn't cost me anything to say it.

And if it was true and Athena was real and decided to just leave us dangling?

I could protect myself and everyone else at

this table if need be, and I didn't need magic to do it.

"The circle is cast," Ami said, smiling. "Astra?"

"Okay, let's see what this has to tell us." I reached forward and snatched up the fabric.

"Aren't you going to say a prayer first?" Ayla asked, her eyebrows arched.

"Nope." I stripped off my gloves, unzipped my jumpsuit, and pressed the cloth flat against my throat chakra with the palm of my hand.

Images flooded through my mind almost immediately.

"I see two men dragging Marianna down the path we were on. She's fighting them, but she's weak, almost drugged. She can't stand. She hits one of them. Good girl," I murmur as I observe the memory of her in my mind's eye. She desperately thrashed against the bigger, stronger men. One of them shouts, and they're all tangled up with one another. Her blouse rips and the piece pressed against me flutters to the ground. "She tried to get away, but she just couldn't. They were too strong."

"That's just horrifying," Althea whispers. "Can you tell who the men were?"

"I wasn't trying to get details that time," I responded, my eyes still closed. "I'm going to go back and watch the whole thing again, slow it down. Are you guys ready with your pencils and paper?"

I heard murmurs of agreement.

"Okay, here we go. I'm going to start at the clearest part, which is on the path."

Psychometry, or the reading of an object, tends to show a particular moment in time. Decisive moments make imprints that sit and float right on top, just waiting to be examined by someone like me. The more emotional that moment was, the more substantial the impression and the more that can be read of that moment. The problem with intense moments like that? The further away you get from that moment in either direction, the fuzzier the images become— as if the heightened moment overwhelmed anything else imprinted.

"One man is tall, about 6′2″. I put the other one at six feet. They're both wearing ski masks, and the masks match. They are khaki or tan. No, wait…These aren't ski masks. Well, it is, but it's a military ski mask, like a balaclava. The shape of the eyes and the mouth are different on those. I'm sure of it; it's a tactical ski mask. The eyes and mouth aren't right for a regular one. Neither is the color."

"Are their shoes military? What about their outfits?" Ami asked.

"Black leather, but just on the bottom. The soles are thick. They look tactical to me, too—leather and nylon, I think. Like a leather strip all around near the sole and then nylon up on the top?" I tried to look closer but couldn't shift the image enough to read a brand. "There's a tag with the name on it; it's yellow with red writing. But I can't make it out. The words, I mean."

"Got it." I heard pencils scratching.

"I think they are wearing raincoats," I said, a little surprised. "They have one for her, too, and they keep trying to wrap her in it, but she's fighting them."

"Are they saying anything?" Althea asked.

I shook my head no. "They're breathing heavily like they're out of breath, but they're not saying anything. It doesn't look like either one of them has facial hair, at least from what I can see through the hole in the mask." Something shined in my eyes. "The tall one. He's got a gold ring with a big red stone in it."

I started to get dizzy.

"Astra, are you okay?"

"I think I'm too far in, I'm too close," I said as the ground lurched away from me. Ripping the fabric from my chest, I opened my eyes and breathed deeply to steady myself. "Marianna was completely messed up. I don't know what they gave her, but she couldn't tell up from down or left from right. That dizziness was horrible."

I felt like I had only been in the memory for a few minutes, but the candles had burned down halfway to the holders. Ami handed me a tall glass of water filled to the rim with ice, and I accepted it gratefully.

"I guess we start looking for boots on the internet?" Ayla asked.

I shook my head and held up the fabric. "First, we watch what I taped while we were at Parrot Paradise and see if anything stands out and looks familiar. After that, I track the shirt this belongs to."

"You can do that?" Althea asked, surprised. "I don't mean to be rude or anything, but why didn't we start with that? This woman was kidnapped."

"Because you never go into a situation that could turn violent without knowing as much as you can about what you're walking into. I don't even know if I'm going to go over there and rescue Marianna—assuming I can track her with this." I paused and gulped down the rest of the water. "I needed to know how many people took her and what I could be facing at the other end before I'm comfortable trying to track her down."

"Are you comfortable now?" Ayla asked, her eyes wide. She looked frightened.

I met my thirteen-year-old sister's eyes and realized I would have to be much more careful with my words from now on. "Maybe comfortable wasn't the right word—I'm comfortable I can prepare myself. Going into a situation where there could be violence? That's never comfortable, Ayla. It's something you should never do unless you're trained to do it."

"I understand," she lied.

"I'm not coming with you?" Ami asked, looking disappointed.

"Not this time."

CHAPTER EIGHT

I'm a psychometrist. I can touch an object or a person and get impressions. Sometimes it's memories, other times a tug in a specific direction. It could be as little as a feeling or as big as an explosion of truth in my mind. I never know, really, what I will get.

But I always get something.

You may have heard of psychometry. Maybe you haven't. A physician named Joseph Buchanan coined the word in the 1800s. He claims to be the first person to have developed the idea that all things—people, trees, items, rocks—give off an emanation.

I know what you're thinking.

Some doctor in Kentucky less than two hundred years ago "discovered" concepts that religions worldwide had been talking about for eons? To be honest, I had the same reaction when I learned the history. But, yep, he thought he was the first and that his ideas would revolutionize science and bring about the dawn of a new civilization.

Needless to say, it didn't. Well, science was revolutionized—but it had nothing to do with Doctor Buchanan and his "revelation" that psychic energy was a thing.

I'm digressing. What was I saying? Oh, right. Psychometry.

It takes many forms. The one most people are familiar with is how it's portrayed in movies. Someone grabs an object—and they stiffen with a start (as if the power sneaks up and surprises them every single time). Maybe their eyes roll back in their head. I don't know, something dramatic, right? Then they immediately zero in on the information they need to know, and it's totally compelling and usually just-in-time to save someone or find someone.

How it's portrayed in the movies?

That's not how it happens in real life. Not at all.

Reading an object isn't easy. It's wholly inanimate, and it has no consciousness. It doesn't have a desire to help, and it doesn't have a desire to hinder. It just is what it is, and what has been imprinted on it is just what has been imprinted on it. The strongest memory or moment may be the least useful to me as a tracker. Often, it's so useless that taking my gloves off appears, in retrospect, like a waste of time.

Objects that "belong" somewhere, though?

Totally different situation.

A watch has imprinted on itself that it belongs on a particular person's wrist. A particular pillow belongs on one specific person's bed. A painting hung in a particular room belongs on one specific wall looking out on a specific view. The longer an item is affixed and imprinted in or on a particular place in space and time, the easier it is for me to use it.

In this case, this particular piece of fabric knows it's part of a shirt. And even though it has no consciousness, even though it has no desire? Even a piece of cloth has an identity, and it pulls toward where it thinks it belongs. Even things that are inanimate prefer to be whole.

As I drove to Parrot Paradise, I muttered a prayer that the ragged fabric would lead me to

Marianna's shirt—which was hopefully still on Marianna.

* * *

It was dark when I pulled up to the back of Parrot Paradise. The wildlife park backed up to dense overgrowth, tall grasses that undoubtedly hid hundreds of slithering Florida snakes. Archie perched on my Jeep's back bar within seconds of the vehicle's stop and scanned the darkness. "We're not here for you to eat," I told him. I threw the Jeep into park and pulled up the parking brake lever in the center console. "This has to be where they took her out, so I want to poke around."

"If a snake tries to bite you, can I eat him at least?" Archie asked.

"Well, clearly, that would be defense of a fellow soldier. You'd practically be obligated." I glanced over toward the tall slatted fence as my eyes adjusted to the dark and listened. The wind rustled the trees, and birds flapped their wings, but I heard no human sounds. "I don't hear anything. Do you?"

Archie took a few steps along the front seat

harness bar and stared toward the fence line. "I hear a lot of parrot yammering and squawking, but if you're asking about humans? I don't hear any talking or feet shuffling."

"They couldn't have finished collecting evidence that quickly, could they?" I moved toward a tall iron gate in the fence line. The gray stone outcropping peeked out above it. We must be directly behind the waterfall grotto. "That gate, look." I pointed. "There is no lock on it." I walked toward it slowly, searching the ground carefully for any clues (and snakes, because…um, snakes). If there had been any evidence dropped, either the police had found it or the kidnappers were careful.

"Are you really going to go in there?" Archie called from the Jeep.

"Are you really going to sit in the car and do nothing?" I called back. "What if I'm attacked by a snake? Wouldn't you feel just terrible if I died and you didn't get to have a snack?"

I removed my glove and placed my palm against the metal. Taking a deep breath, I closed my eyes. So many people had been in and out of the place it was just a blurry and flurry of images —workmen coming in with wooden boxes, janitorial staff removing bags of garbage. In and out, day after day. "Come on, fence, show me something useful," I muttered.

"Does that help?" Archie asked. "Asking the gate what you want to know?"

"No. It just makes me feel better." A flash of an image whizzed by, and I mentally chased after it. "I think I have something. Joel Clemens was back here talking to someone at the fence line."

I watched the nervous director lean through a small break in the fence. Looking right and left, he handed something in a paper bag to a large man. The man nodded, shoved the bag into the pocket of his heavy jacket, turned on his heel, and left. Just as the image ended, I glanced up at the sky. The sun had been just over the set of trees to my right, and once I checked my compass, I could pinpoint the time.

"It was this morning," I told Archie as I opened my eyes. "If I had to guess, maybe nine? In almost all of the other images I saw, there was a large silver lock hanging off here." I pulled back the spring-loaded latch and yanked on the gate. "Everything else I saw, there was always a lock hanging from right there. Sometimes open, sometimes closed, but always there." I pointed to a metal loop next to the latch. "Today? It wasn't there. Not even this morning."

"That doesn't sound like it was an accident," Archie observed. Then he sneezed.

"Bless you," I called. "I didn't know owls could sneeze."

"We can, but that wasn't me." He carefully preened his feathers with his beak. "That was your sister Ayla. She's hiding under the canvas in the back of the Jeep." Archie swiveled his head and perched sedately as if he hadn't a care in the world. "Sorry, didn't you know?"

* * *

"I just wanted to see what you were going to do," Ayla protested after I ripped the canvas off her. "I wasn't going to let anyone see me! I was just curious!" She sneezed again. "It's just so dirty back here."

"It's a Jeep; it's supposed to be dirty," I snapped. "Haven't you heard the thing about curiosity and the cat, Ayla? What on earth were you thinking?"

"I thought you wouldn't find me!"

"I'm a tracker!"

"Well, maybe not a very good one," Ayla muttered sullenly with a stare of rebellion.

I glared back. "Do you have any idea how dangerous this is? Just for a start, there are no seat belts back there." My fingers closed roughly around her arm, and I lifted the thirteen-year-old up. "We're at a crime scene. A crime scene is no place for a thirteen-year-old. Ayla Arden, you should know better than this!" I let her go and she grudgingly climbed out of the back and slipped into the backseat. "Did you even tell anyone you were going?"

"Well, no, it's not like anyone would've let me!" she told me with a huff.

I turned toward Archie. "And you, you knew that she was back there the whole time?"

"Well, of course, I'm not an idiot." Archie tilted his head to the side and blinked. "I thought you were some super soldier that could sense danger around every corner. Are you telling me that you didn't know a thirteen-year-old hid in the back of the Jeep?" Another blink of deliberate nonchalance.

I realized at that moment the adage about not working with children and animals? There was probably some truth behind that advice.

"Get in the front seat. I'm taking you home," I told Ayla as I marched back to the front of the Jeep and hopped in. "You've added an hour to my work tonight, thanks very much. Probably two once mother realizes you snuck into the Jeep and I didn't realize you were there. I am never going to hear the end of this."

"Mom would be fine with me going. We're doing work for the goddess. That's never wrong, you know." Ayla crawled over the bar and slammed down into the passenger seat sullenly. With a jerk, she yanked the seatbelt across her torso. "I just wanted to see what you did. I wanted to spend time with you." After clicking the belt, she dropped her hands into her lap and stared at them.

"That's fine, but—"

"I barely know you, you know," Ayla whispered, her voice thick. "You left to join the military before I was even born, and then you never bothered to come back and visit." Her chin lowered to her chest. "It's like I only have two sisters, not three," she muttered under her breath.

Her words hit me like punches. I didn't even have to stop and contemplate why she felt that way or look back to see what I could have done to make her feel the way she did. Ayla was right. And I knew it. And what's worse, I always knew it.

I knew what she looked like because everyone sent me pictures from back home, and I'd seen her several times throughout her life...

But not recently.

I had not seen any of my sisters in the last five years, and before that, my visits were...infrequent.

I nodded without responding and started the Jeep.

"Are you strapped in?" I asked quietly.

"I have my seatbelt on," Ayla responded hotly.

"Good. Is Griselda's still open?"

Griselda's Ice Cream Shop had been a staple in Forkbridge for almost seventy-five years. I'd be surprised if anyone's first date ever ended anywhere else. It had the biggest, baddest, goopiest ice cream sundaes around, served in soda fountain glass dishes by carhops that never skimped on napkins, for a reason. The Jeep would no doubt need a visit to the car wash.

"Yeah, why?" Ayla asked sullenly. Then she popped up, her eyes wide. "Yeah, they are open until ten. Why?" Her face shined with hope.

"You and I are going to stop for ice cream on the way home, and we're going to talk for a few minutes," I said as I started up the Jeep and pulled out. "I don't have a whole lot of time—there's a woman whose life is in danger, and I can't stop what I'm doing to…deal with this the way I should." As soon as I groped for the words and found the wrong ones, Ayla's face fell. "I did not mean you were something to deal with. Ayla?"

"Okay," she whispered and faced forward.

I sighed. This was definitely not within my realm of expertise.

* * *

"Okay, you are absolutely right. Death by chocolate is fantastic." I spooned another shockingly sugary mouthful and swallowed. Ayla had ordered the most giant chocolate concoction on the menu. It was so insanely large, I was convinced at least a pint of heavy cream had gone into the whipped cream topping alone.

"I told you." Ayla beamed, chocolate smeared on her chin. "Ami says that chocolate is magic, and I totally believe her."

"I think Ami might be right." I tried to keep

my voice light, but it was a wasted effort. Ayla's face was blissfully happy, the joy that only a child seemed able to fully express. "I do want to talk about what happened back there."

"Back where?" she asked, her mouth full.

I raised my eyebrow. "I'm not mad that you want to spend time with me, Ayla, and I am sorry if your feelings are hurt that I didn't come back to visit as often as I should have. I promise that had nothing to do with you."

"Oh, I know, it had to do with Mom. Aunt Gwennie told me you and Mom don't like each other very much, even though you love each other. I used to not get it, but now I'm thirteen, and I totally get it." She nodded like she was a wise old woman that understood all the secrets of the universe. "I love Mom a lot, but sometimes? She's really all up in my business, and I just want to turn her into a frog for a little while."

I blinked and suppressed a laugh. "Well, I'm glad you can understand." I put the spoon down and let my sister finish the chocolate ice cream (with chocolate sauce, chocolate-covered nuts, and chocolate whipped cream layers). "I wish I could've gotten back to see all of you more often, but it was just really complicated for me."

Ayla looked at me with a stare of burning

intensity. "Just because I understand now doesn't mean it didn't hurt, you know. And that was really complicated for me. Especially when I didn't understand. Because I didn't before."

Ouch. Gut punch. "I can't really do anything other than apologize and try to make it up to you."

She held up the half-melted chocolate mess. "This is a good start. I think I just hit the brownie. You want some?"

"There's a brownie under all that?" I asked, surprised.

Ayla nodded. "The brownie is the best part. So, do you? Want some?"

"I think if I eat any more of that, I might be sick."

"I've built up a tolerance. I'm good," my baby sister told me cheerfully as she dug out the brownie.

I waited to give her time to devour it.

She needed little.

Ayla spoke two minutes and half a brownie again later, but her mouth was full, and I could barely understand her. "I just want to get to know you, Astra. And, well…Ami is a seer, and Althea is an herbalist. They don't deal with really dark stuff, you know? It's all positivity and rainbows and unicorns and stuff." Ayla's eyes shifted around the parking lot as if to make sure no one would overhear her. "I sometimes do. Deal with the really dark stuff. The ghosts that come visit me? Sometimes they've had nasty stuff happen to them, or they're terrified. I don't tell them—Ami and Althea—about it because I don't think they would understand."

"Have you talked to Mom or Aunt Gwennie about it?" She shook her head. "Why not?"

Ayla flushed with self-consciousness. "They'd just tell me not to talk to the ghosts or to banish them."

Her statement surprised me, but also…didn't. It was just like my mother to be a hypocrite, one set of rules for her and one set of rules for Ayla. Sure, Minerva needed several hours a day just to speak to the dead, but Ayla should banish ghosts that annoy her, or ignore them. Instead of pointing out my mother's hypocrisy, I bit my tongue and continued listening.

"That's just so rude, though, you know? I mean, they come to talk to me because they need something. It's my power. I can't just turn my back on them. But I can't not do what Mom and Aunt Gwennie tell me, either."

It was an ironic statement coming from the

girl that hid in the back of my Jeep, and for a second, I thought about pointing that out. A second later, I realized my sister might be going through something very similar to what I'd gone through when I ran away to enlist. If that were the case, the first thing she needed was someone that would listen.

So I did.

Ayla's muscles tightened, and her jaw set as she looked off into the distance. "I don't want to just run from things. I want to learn how to be better." She glanced back at me and smiled. "Sorry. I know you have to go soon."

I nodded. "I do, but...Ayla, I promise I will help you figure out how to handle some of the darker stuff you have to deal with. And I appreciate your trusting me enough to talk to me about this." She smiled with noticeable relief. "But in return, you have to promise me that you will not do what you did tonight. If I tell you that you can't come with me? There's a reason for that." I leaned toward her and grabbed her hand. "I love you, and I don't want anything to happen to you."

Nodding with thirteen-year-old exuberance, she smiled even wider. "I appreciate that, but I can be useful, you know. Like, really useful." Ayla's eyes twinkled with impish amusement.

"I have no doubt that you can be."

"Like right now? There's a ghost standing outside the Jeep, and he says he knows where Marianna Black is. She's being held at the old Thompson place. And since you can't talk to him? I guess you're going to have to take me with you."

CHAPTER NINE

Griselda's Ice Cream Shop's parking lot was not ideal for discussing ghosts, the kidnapping, or the old Thompson place. The whole town (and neighboring townsfolk and tourists) seemed to mill about the parking lot every evening eating far more empty calories than should ever be in a single dessert. I wasn't familiar with anyone after being away for so many years.

I did remember Stephen Thompson, the former owner of the old Thompson place. The quiet, disciplined man disappeared twenty years ago under mysterious circumstances. Theories abounded about the thrifty man's vanishing, from kidnapping to being abducted by aliens. He had lived a solitary, childless life on his farm. With no heirs to inherit—once he was declared dead—the property sat abandoned. It was already in disrepair by the time I left for Imperatorial City.

Aunt Gwennie told me people had tussled over custody of it periodically. The historic farmhouse dated to 1895, and developer after developer eyed the place for vacation homes or condos due to our convenient location between the coast and Disney World. In the end, possession always seemed to fall through, and deals never seemed to get made. Aunt Gwennie mused it was almost like the property was cursed.

Thompson's disappearance wasn't the first weird thing that happened there, either. In the 1930s, during the Great Depression, the builder Russ Joseph committed suicide on the property. After that, a succession of farmworkers employed by the Thompsons (Stephen's parents) over the years smelled mysterious perfumes they couldn't explain or would find farm equipment belching smoke and burning through fuel when they arrived in the morning—even though no one had been at the farm overnight.

"This isn't a good place to discuss—"

"You can't take me home. You need to know what he said, and he can sneak in there while we're on a stakeout and tell us what he sees," Ayla said. She stopped speaking and turned as the charmingly adorable carhop bounced up. "Hi, Lisa! This sundae was great. As always, right?" My sister handed the gigantic glass bowl to the server. "Whoever made the brownies tonight? They were just awesome. I mean, just awesome!"

I gave her a sidelong glance.

"So glad you liked it, Ayla." The older teen steadied the tray on her shoulder and gave my sister a wink. "Can I get the two of you anything else?" Before I could answer, the young woman turned toward me and then blinked in surprise. "Oh my gosh. Are you Astra Arden? You are, aren't you?"

I nodded. Before I could speak, my cell phone rang. Glancing down, I could see it was the store phone. I snatched it up with a speed that would've made a poltergeist blink, sure my mother was on the other end. "Hello?"

"Is Ayla with you? I can't find her anywhere!" My mother's tone was accusatory.

"She is. We went out for ice cream. We're at Griselda's."

"Why didn't you ask me if you could take her? I've been worried sick!"

"Because I didn't think I needed to ask you

whether I could go out for ice cream with my sister, Mom," I lied. (Well, it wasn't really a lie—if I had just intended to take Ayla to Griselda's, I wouldn't have asked.) I could almost see her frown at my non-groveling tone. "I'm thirty-three years old."

"And she's thirteen years old! Considering how you wound up—"

I clenched my jaw and breathed air through my nose to steady myself, biting back a response I'd regret. "Mom," I began in a courteous tone, "I'm sitting in the parking lot at Griselda's with our waitress standing outside the Jeep. Now, if you'd like Lisa the carhop to know all of our family business, I'd be happy to have this conversation with you right now. If that's really what you want." Both Ayla and Lisa were watching me intently. "Otherwise, we can talk about this when I get home."

Mom paused. "You're coming straight home?"

"When we leave," I assured her. "Why would we delay? You're making coming home sound so appealing," I added with a touch of sarcasm. I could hear Aunt Gwennie in the background urging my mother to watch her tone, assuring her that Ayla would be fine. "I took care of an entire squad, Mom. I can take care of one thirteen-year-old girl." I paused and listened, but Mom didn't respond. "She's safe with me. I promise."

"Let her go, Minnie. Let them spend some time together," Aunt Gwennie's told Mom loud enough I could overhear clearly. "This is what you wanted, wasn't it? So why spoil it by getting upset?"

A few more seconds of silence, and then Mom snapped, "You and I are going to have a talk when you get home." Then the call disconnected.

"Wow, that sounded like a conversation with my mom," Lisa smiled as I pulled the phone from my ear. "That's crazy. You're so old, and you still get into fights with your mom!" Her hair wisped around her youthful, grinning face. "I still can't believe that you're *the* Astra Arden!"

I slipped my phone back into my tactical belt. "Why would that be so hard to believe?"

"Well, there have been rumors that you're dead. For, like, years," Ayla said. Lisa nodded. "The town was sure you wound up in the bottom of a swamp somewhere."

"Nope, not dead," I told Lisa. "Though if I don't get Ayla home, death is a distinct possibility before sunrise."

"Oh, everyone knows your mom, Astra," Lisa

laughed with a cute little shrug. "She's a whole lot of bark when she's agitated, but she's hardly any bite. Hardly any. Maybe a little. But just, like, band-aid level."

I stared at the girl—who couldn't have been over seventeen years old—as she told me about my own mother. I should have been offended, but I realized she potentially did know my mother better than I did. Especially if she was a customer at the magic shop. "Yes, well, I think my mother saves all of her best for biting for me. If you know what I mean." I raised my eyebrow. "It was nice to meet you, Lisa, but Ayla and I have to get out of here." I passed over a stack of bills that covered the ice cream and a generous cash tip. "Keep the change."

The teen's eyes lit up. "Wow. Thanks! It was good to see you tonight, Ayla! Glad you liked the sundae! And nice to meet you, Astra!" Lisa flounced back toward Griselda's with her tray.

* * *

"WAIT A MINUTE. You're not heading toward home." Ayla leaned out of the Jeep and looked back at the turn I didn't take. "You're heading toward the old Thompson place." With the top off the Jeep and our speed about forty, my sister had to yell over the wind noise. "Can I ask you a question?"

"Yep, you can ask me anything."

"Would you be taking me with you to the old Thompson place if Mom hadn't called you and told you to take me home?"

In the distance, ominous thunder clouds gathered, and they were issuing loud warnings to take cover. A sharp bolt of lightning zigzagged, lighting up the road ahead. "Ugh, Florida, and its stupid thunderstorms," I muttered. My sister didn't press me for an answer to her question.

"I think you just can't stand to do anything that Mom tells you to do, and so you're taking me with you. Even though you weren't going to."

"I hadn't decided whether I was going to take you with me or not, especially after you made the announcement about the ghost." I pulled over as the raindrops pelted us and scrambled to put the top and the doors back on the Jeep. Without being asked, Ayla unclipped her seatbelt and helped.

Archie hid under the canvas, clicking his beak in agitation.

"There, that'll keep us from getting wet," I said as we jumped back into the Jeep. Yanking out two of Aunt Gwennie's beach towels, I handed one to Ayla and used the other to dry my hair. "So, did a ghost really come up to you in the middle of an ice cream parlor parking lot, or was that just you trying to manipulate me into taking you?"

Ayla's jaw dropped, and she looked hurt. "I wouldn't lie to you just to get you to take me. That's completely insulting."

I chuckled. "You wouldn't lie, but you would sneak into the back of my Jeep? I do not see the honesty distinction between the two."

Ayla gestured toward the dashboard of the dusty Jeep Wrangler. "This isn't your Jeep, you know. It's Aunt Gwennie's. I can't even believe she let you drive it. She won't even let Mom touch it."

I tried not to get an intense thrill out of borrowing the Rubicon. And Ayla was right—Aunt Gwennie was an empath. When empaths have emotional attachments to vehicles, they can get darn possessive over them. It didn't surprise me she wouldn't let my mother drive it—though since it was a manual, I doubted my mother could have driven it even if Aunt Gwennie would've allowed it.

Anyway, Aunt Gwennie liked going out to get away from everyone so she could get distance herself from other people's emotions. Years ago, she realized the easiest and fastest way for her to do that was to learn how to off-road. When I returned with no money and no job, she handed me the keys and made me promise that when she needed to get out of Dodge for a while to decompress, I would give it back, but other than that condition?

This was my Jeep now.

"Astra, look," Ayla whispered, pointing toward the front gate of the old Thompson place. "I didn't realize we were so close to it."

"I don't think you need to whisper. No one's going to hear us out here. Especially not with this storm."

"What do we do now?"

"What did your ghost say back at the ice cream shop?"

"Just that Marianna Black was at the old Thompson place. Then we—you and me and Lisa —started talking, and he just kind of faded away." Ayla frowned. "The ghosts do that a lot. Fade away, sometimes in the middle of talking to me, which can be annoying. That doesn't necessarily mean that they disappeared or anything. He might still be here. He may just not want me to see him," Ayla told me, still half-whispering.

I knew little about talking to ghosts. To tell you the truth, I was grateful deathspeaking wasn't one of my skills. It seemed aggravating, just having some random dead person come up to you in the shower or while you were sleeping and start a conversation as if you had nothing better to do.

Having ghosts work for you, though? I knew a few deathspeakers back at the ministry with dead partners, and they could rock cases faster than anyone else. Ghosts were super-effective spies.

At least, if you developed a working relationship with a ghost and didn't just trust some random dude that walked up to you in an ice cream shop parking lot.

"Okay, so this is what we're going to do," I said, and I pulled out my pendulum.

Oh, right.

So, a pendulum.

Pendulums are symmetrical objects that hang from a chain or cord. It can be anything, really, but it can't be magnetic, or you can get wrong readings. Sometimes people use crystals, or a ball, or even just a key.

Personally, I use a specifically manufactured metal pendulum from the ministry. So…Yeah, I use an essential military-issued pendulum.

Anyway, lots of people use pendulums for dowsing all kinds of things. I could use it to find water, or answers, or even people. Still, since I am a psychometrist, I use it combined with psychometry for tracking.

"If I wrap the cloth around my hand and then steady the pendulum," I told Ayla as I held my arm up with the chain hanging down, "we can see if the rest of the shirt is in the direction of the old Thompson place."

Ayla stared as the pendulum came to a stop, held its position for five seconds, and then swung diagonally. I looked up to make sure, but the pendulum was definitely swinging toward the old Thompson farm.

"The ghost was right?" Ayla asked.

"Well, it looks like Marianna's shirt is over there," I said as I wrapped the chain around my hand, pulled both off, and put them in my waist pouch. "He might've been. You sure you don't know anything about who he was?"

She shook her head no.

"Can you call him back?"

"It doesn't really work like that. I mean, it can, but I can't do it sitting in a car in the middle of a storm, you know? And I need quarter candles and crystals and some incense and maybe a chalice or two," Ayla sing-songed as she ticked the items off on her fingers.

If trackers needed to do all that to call their ghost partners, they'd never find anyone. I shook my head at my mother's requirement that magic be both pomped and circumstanced—even though it was far more valuable when used simply, strategically, and quickly.

"You probably don't need any of that garbage, but that's a conversation for another time." I leaned forward and tried to see through the wind-driven rain. What had been gentle had progressed into an unremitting downpour in just a few minutes. Which, for Florida, wasn't that out of the ordinary. "Okay, I need you to stay here. I'm going to run over there and take a look, see if I see anything."

"In this storm?" Ayla asked, looking up nervously.

"My uniform will protect me from any lightning, and I've been in harsher storms than this. It's not a big deal." I reached back into my duffel bag and pulled out a large rock. "Archie, are you still hiding under the canvas? The roof's on the Jeep now, you know."

"It could leak. I hate water," a muffled voice

called from the back. "I'll stay right here, thank you very much."

"Fine, stay here, then." I handed the rock to Ayla. "This is a military issue ensorcelled protection rock, or MIEPr." Ayla's eyes grew wide as she stared at the crystal. "Some witch back in Imperatorial City cast a spell on it that enables it to hide anything smaller than thirty feet by thirty feet. Give or take," I explained as she turned the white rock over in her hand. "Once I leave the truck, I need you to place both hands on the rock and say 'Corium.' That's all you have to do to make sure that no one sees the Jeep or you two. Can you do that?"

Ayla nodded vigorously.

"Okay, now, when you see me come back out, I need you to un-hide the Jeep. To do that, you say 'videtur.' You got that?"

She nodded again.

"Okay, show me." I sat back and pointed.

Ayla placed both hands with ceremonial reverence on either side of the rock. She lifted it up as if it was the Holy Grail itself. "Corium!" she shouted. The Jeep sparkled with a pink hue.

"While there was a little more stylish flair than needed, and you don't need to shout, that's fine. It worked. Now, make us visible again?"

"Videtur," she said with an annoyed shrug as if she was telling me she wanted chocolate cereal for breakfast. The sparkle faded away.

"You don't have to act like it's nothing, either. Just say it naturally," I said with a half-smile. "Look, Ayla, I know you and the family do things with a lot more pageantry because everything is ritualistic and religious to you. But I was in the military. I don't care about ceremony or style. It was just not something we were taught to value— well, in the field, anyway." I rolled my eyes at the memory of my six-hour graduation ceremony. "Our job is to get things done as quickly as possible and in the most efficient way possible. You know what I mean?"

"Yeah, I guess." She glanced out the front window. "Hey, the rain's letting up a little bit. Maybe you should go check the Thompson place out now before it starts up again?"

I nodded and slipped out of the car. "I'll be back in twenty minutes," I told her through the open door. "Whatever happens, though, you need to stay in this vehicle. You understand?"

She nodded, picked up the Corium rock, and disappeared from view within seconds of the Jeep door closing.

* * *

THE OLD THOMPSON place was dark as I came down a narrow trail toward the back of the decrepit farmhouse. The last of the light had faded hours ago, there was no electricity at the place as far as I could tell, and no streetlights to cast so much as a shadow. I could sense no movement, no sound—but I knew from experience silence could hide many threats.

There was no fence around the property, but as I crept closer, I could see there was nothing left to steal. Anything of value to be scavenged had walked away long ago.

The farmhouse itself had caved in. Well, half of it folded in a wooden accordion arc, while the other half remained standing. The ground was uneven, the wood rotted, and the rain-soaked muddy ground was difficult to trudge through as silently as I would have preferred.

I froze. The sound of boots scuffing on rocks reached me from about ten feet away. In response, I threw myself to the ground. Scanning to the right and left, I tried to pinpoint the noise's origin, but the driving rain confused everything.

"Who's there?" A stern woman's voice called out sharply, followed by the click of a flashlight.

Before I could turn my head to spot the origin of the light beam, the light beam found me. "You there! Marianna? Is that you?"

"Nope!" I called and pushed up, but the distinctive click of a gun being cocked stopped me cold.

"This is Detective Emma Sullivan of the Forkbridge Police Department! Do not move! Without getting up, identify yourself!"

I dropped my head and cursed quietly.

Now the police were on the ball? Come on.

I could probably explain what I was doing here kneeling in the mud at the old Thompson place. I had no doubt I could come up with something if asked about the grotto at Parrot Paradise (and why I found Christine Chandler half-drowned on the same day Marianna Black was kidnapped). I could even dance around why I illegally have an owl.

Probably.

For the life of me, though, I was not sure how I would explain the magical Jeep Rubicon reappearing out of thin air in front of the old Thompson place if the detective got a gander at that.

"Identify yourself now!"

I sighed. Nope, nothing coming to me.

CHAPTER TEN

Sullivan's gun stayed trained on my center of mass. I rose up from the grass slowly, my eyes blinded by her flashlight. "No need to get twitchy, Detective," I told her slowly. Standing up straight, I raised my hands, palms out, and tossed my head to get a strand of damp hair out of my eyes. "I'm unarmed."

"You're trespassing is what you are," Sullivan responded in a monotone. I practically felt her staring at me, examining me as a threat, for a good five seconds. "You also still haven't identified yourself."

"Astra Arden, Detective Sullivan."

"Astra Arden?" A hint of surprise crept into

her voice. "I thought you were missing. Or dead." Sullivan lowered the flashlight, and as the circles of after-light faded from my eyes, I spotted her looking at me with a quizzical expression. "You're the oldest girl of that witch that owns the magic shop? The one in the building on the side of Arden House on Chanway Road?"

Detective Emma Sullivan looked to be about my height and close to my age. She had rich chestnut-colored hair, striking cheekbones, and a curvy figure. In a state full of blonds (both natural and bottled), the detective was stunningly different. Her vibrant eyes glittered in the darkness as we took stock of each other.

"Not missing, not dead, yes, yes, and yes," I responded, my hands still up. "But I do have one quibble with what you said."

"Oh?"

I raised my eyebrow. "I'm not a girl. I'm a thirty-three-year-old woman. If you were a man, I'd probably get more defensive about the 'girl' thing. But since you're not a man—and you have a gun trained on me—I'll just politely point out I would prefer not to be classified as a girl. I left childhood a long time ago."

Detective Sullivan relaxed her stance slightly,

the gun lowering toward the ground, and gave me a slight nod of acknowledgment. "You're right, Ms. Arden. I apologize for any disrespect." Sullivan holstered her weapon and stepped toward me. "None was intended." She watched me intently. "I'm just curious—you don't have any problem with me calling your mother a witch?"

"No, my mother is a witch," I responded with confidence. "And I mean that in more ways than one."

The detective gave me another peculiar look. Then she took a deep breath, tilted her head, and the distance returned to her tone. "What are you doing here, Ms. Arden?" Her eyes swept over me from head to toe. "And dressed like you just left Comic-Con?"

Why was everybody feeling a constant need to comment on my outfit? There used to be a woman in West Palm Beach that sold hot dogs from a cart dressed in a bikini. A pair of men tried to burn down a house dressed in a bull costume a few counties over. A guy stole a car and got caught—his poor pet monkey clinging to him as he was handcuffed. A woman in Seminole Heights went jogging in a puffy unicorn costume.

Daily.

I was hardly the weirdest thing Florida offered these days.

"This outfit makes it easier for me to do parkour," I told the detective with a straight face. I mean, technically, I could do parkour. I've even done parkour. I was just usually doing it while chasing after a fugitive racing through some city trying to get away from me.

"Uh-huh." Her answer dripped with disbelief. "You have a habit of not answering questions unless I ask them several times. Again, Ms. Arden, what are you doing in the grass at the old Thompson property?" I could see her growing impatient with my obfuscation.

"You've known me for all of two minutes, and you think you know my habits already?" My tone was more defiant than it needed to be, but my detour to the ice cream shop meant the clock was ticking faster than it should have been. Things not following my well-planned...um, plan? It always made me crabby and impatient. "Fine, you know what? I don't really have time for this, and I doubt you do, either. Besides, you are going to think I am crazy, anyway."

"Am I now?" Sullivan's brow drew down with a suspicious look.

"My sister can talk to ghosts," I told the

detective as I placed my hand on my hip. "We were having a charming evening at Griselda's—eating something, by the way, containing so much chocolate and sugar that it should, by all rights, be illegal—when some ghost came up to her and said Marianna Black was here on this property."

"You heard a ghost tell your sister—"

"I didn't hear anything," I interrupted. "I can't talk to ghosts."

Detective Sullivan stared at me with narrowed eyes. "So, your sister told you this ghost said Marianna Black was here."

"She did."

"And where is she?"

"Marianna Black?"

"Your sister."

"In my Jeep," I told her.

"And your Jeep is…?"

"Parked on Thompson Street in front of the property."

Detective Sullivan rubbed her fingertips back and forth across her brow. "My vehicle is parked on Thompson Street right in the front, and I didn't see any Jeep."

"Not surprised," I told her. She waited for me to say more. "Right now, it's invisible."

Detective Sullivan and I stared at each other again.

"Invisible?" she asked. "You said the Jeep is invisible."

"That's what I said."

I was actually quite impressed by Detective Emma Sullivan's reaction. Typically, people become pretty startled when they're informed of something existing they don't believe to be possible. Sullivan didn't even flinch an eyelash.

Before we go any further? I know what you're thinking.

Why did I even bother worrying about Detective Sullivan's reaction to a suddenly reappearing Jeep Rubicon if I was just gonna tell her the truth? Spill the beans, the tea, whatever one spills when they're divulging things that are supposed to be kept secret.

One thing you'll come to learn about me.

I hate lying.

Oh, I know sometimes we have to tell falsehoods to protect people, and lying isn't always evil or immoral. Sometimes people lie for perfectly valid reasons, and sometimes they say something false to save someone's feelings or protect someone from a truth that would hurt them. Heck, sometimes I have to lie to get information out of somebody.

But for the most part?

If you can tell the truth, it's always better to tell the truth. It's far easier to keep your story straight that way. And since my former employers decided that any supernatural being should be able to 'tell their truth' to anyone they wanted to, at any time, and for any reason? Well, why not just tell the woman?

Besides, she was a cop. As a soldier, I just didn't want to lie.

So I didn't.

"Look, Detective—"

That's all I got out before the gunshots.

* * *

SULLIVAN FLEW at me like a tigress taking down the slow gazelle in the back end of the herd, and we both slammed into the mud. "Stay down!" she hissed, covering my body with her own so thoroughly that I was only a few inches away from having a legitimate sexual harassment claim against the Forkbridge cop.

"Get the heck off me!" I growled as I pushed up, but she was an immovable pillar pinning me against the ground. "I need to get to my sister! I mean it, get the hell off!"

"I thought you said the Jeep was invisible," she whispered. Her gun was out, and its muzzle followed her eyes as she scanned the darkness for movement. "If they can't see it, they can't shoot at it, right? She's quite a bit safer than we are—if what you said was true."

"Yeah, Sullivan, it's true, and I said it was invisible. I didn't say it was bulletproof." I shot a glance behind us as Sullivan's attention was occupied in front but saw nothing. "I don't need you to protect me. Get off!"

I shoved her once—hard—and she finally slid off me and onto the muddy ground. Springing to my feet, I took off toward Ayla and the Jeep. "I swear if I find a single bullet that leads me to you," I mumbled to the invisible assailant as my arms and legs pumped, "I will turn you into a frog myself. You have no idea who you're messing with." Spotting an opening in the brush, I spun to the right and ran harder.

A bullet whizzed by me. Then another.

"You have got to be kidding me," I muttered as my feet slipped in the mud. I veered left and right in a zigzag pattern hoping anyone with a gun trained on me wouldn't have the aim to hit their target if that target was me. Out of the corner of my eye, I saw the flash of a gun coming from one of the broken-down buildings littering the old property.

Another whiz.

"Astra!" Sullivan shouted behind me.

I cursed to myself and almost stopped to punch Emma Bigmouth in the nose.

Sure, Detective, shout out my first name in this quiet field and tell the bad guys with a gun my name. I'm sure there are a hundred Astras in our tiny little town. There's no way the kidnapper bad guys would pinpoint me as the person poking around the old Thompson place. I mean, it's not like I found the woman's assistant drowning in a pond or anything.

I swerved to the right again and made it out onto the street. "Make the truck visible now, sis!" I shouted. "Right now!"

Seconds later, the Jeep shimmered into view.

I ran full speed toward the vehicle, yanked open the door, and dove over the front seat toward my duffel bag in the back. Rummaging around, I found the crystal cube I was looking for.

Ayla sat, stunned, watching me. Her jaw was dropped.

"Invicta!" I shouted brusquely. A white light flashed so brightly, it was almost like lightning. "Hold this," I told Ayla, handing the shielding cube to her. "You need to hold onto it at all times. Move over here into the driver seat, and when I come back with the detective? You need keep the door open, and when I get close? Grab my arm." I looked into Ayla's eyes. "Did you get all that? Are you absolutely sure you can do that? This is important, Ayla. Don't say yes if you're not sure."

Ayla nodded silently, her eyes wide.

"Do not let this go, Ayla. No matter what happens, you need to keep a hold of it and have it touching your skin the whole time." I peeled off my gloves and jumped back out of the car without closing the door. "Do not drop it, do not let it go. Even if something scares you, makes you jump? You have to keep ahold of it. Skin contact. Do you understand?"

My sister nodded again.

"Stay here." I ran back toward the field. I was just about to go back into the old Thompson place property when Emma Sullivan exploded out of a bush and ran toward me. "Come on!" I shouted as another bullet whizzed by us. Just as she reached me, I grabbed her arm, and we raced across the street toward the Jeep.

"So, I don't mean to be critical considering the situation," Emma shouted breathlessly as we ran, "but I can see that Jeep Rubicon plain as day. Nice lift, by the way."

We're running for our lives, and Detective Sullivan is checking out Aunt Gwennie's off-roading modifications. Which, honestly, were pretty cool—my aunt installed 35-inch mud tires, a 3-inch lift, and every piece of recovery gear you could think of on the thing. It was a monster.

But now wasn't exactly the time.

"It's visible now, you dolt! Hurry up!" As we crossed the last few feet to the Jeep, Ayla reached out with one arm while holding the shielding cube tightly in the other. I kept a hold of Emma Sullivan with one arm and Ayla with the other, then swept the detective forward. With a hard shove, I got Sullivan into the vehicle and then climbed in behind her.

* * *

"There's more than one door to this vehicle, you know," Emma responded as she settled into the backseat. "You didn't have to climb up my back like I was a bouldering wall."

"If you weren't touching me and I wasn't

touching Ayla, you wouldn't be in this Jeep," I told her from the driver's seat. "You're right, now you can see it, but now it's bulletproof. It's magic. You're welcome." A metal clanging sound reverberated as the first bullet pelted us and bounced off. "See? Bulletproof."

"Anything I can do?" Archie called from underneath the canvas.

"What was that sound?" Detective Sullivan asked, her voice nervous for the first time that night. "Is there an animal back there?"

"I have a useless bird in the back."

"No need to be rude," Archie grumbled.

"You have a pet bird? Here? In a Jeep?" She stared with a mystified look soon replaced by a suspicious one. Her eyes narrowed. "Are you an animal trafficker?"

"You're sitting in a bulletproof 4x4, and you want to question me about my bird? Yeah, that makes sense." I took a long drink of water from a bottle I kept in the car. Once finished, I glanced in the rearview mirror. "No, I'm not an animal trafficker. I'm a..." I paused, trying to come up with a simple one word occupation designation that adequately described my new identity. "Did you ever see that television show *Touched by an Angel*? No, not really like that..." I frowned.

"How about *Person of Interest*? You ever see that show?"

Detective Sullivan stared at me oddly. "Yes."

"I'm kind of like that guy in *Person of Interest*, only I'm not a guy, and I'm not crazy, this has nothing to do with the government, and the list of people that are in danger isn't coming from some payphone or computer algorithm, it's coming from a tarot card deck. Well, sort of." I stopped talking and looked out along the road, but as before, no one was there. At least no one visible. "Okay, maybe I'm not so much like the guy in that show. But I am ex-military." Another bullet clanged. "So, that part's similar."

Sullivan looked at me with an insincere smile. "Let me guess, they let you out on a Section 8?"

"Haha, aren't you charming," I told her. "No. The branch of the military I was in didn't have a Section 8. If they thought you were crazy, they just threw you in prison."

Little-known fact. The US military used to give Section 8s to crossdressers, gay, lesbian, bisexual, and transgender people. The military— any military—is not well-known for its celebration of individuality or differences.

"And what branch of the military was that, exactly?" the detective asked. She glanced around the Jeep calmly as if she hung out in a bulletproof vehicle with a vinyl roof, getting shot at, every day.

"No branch of the military you've ever heard of."

"Are we just gonna sit here all night while people shoot at us?" Ayla asked, looking back and forth between the detective and me. "You two are acting like nothing's happening, and I don't know who she is or why someone is shooting." Ayla swallowed nervously. "I feel like at some point they're going to see us here—"

"They've already seen us here, Ayla." I pointed toward the tree line. "That's why the bullets are bouncing off the shield around the truck. But yes, we're going to sit here until Detective Emma's backup gets here."

"I didn't call for backup," she told me calmly.

I turned and stared at her. "Well, aren't you the renegade."

"By the time anyone shows up, these guys will be gone." She hitched her chin toward the old Thompson place. "If they were going to chase us out of the darkness and show themselves, they would've done it by now."

"Astra, did you find Marianna? Was she

there?" Ayla asked me, her eyes eager to have helped crack the case.

"I didn't really get very far, hon. I barely got up to the house when Detective Quick Draw over here decided to corner me. Once she did that, she probably gave away our position and got us into this mess."

"I'm sure your trespassing had nothing to do with it. Ayla, is it?" Emma Sullivan leaned forward. "You're the one that talked to the ghost?"

Ayla turned back toward the detective and nodded.

"What did the ghost say, exactly? The ghost was male?"

Ayla nodded again.

"Did he say whether Marianna Black was alive?"

"Hey!" I snapped. "She's a thirteen-year-old kid."

"She's sitting in a magically bulletproofed car clutching some sort of magic box while being shot at, Ms. Arden—and you don't seem particularly concerned about comforting her or explaining things," Sullivan responded calmly as I bristled at the polite insult. "I assume she's probably not a typical thirteen-year-old girl if you're bringing her out on...whatever it is that you think you're doing."

"We're here to save Marianna," Ayla told the stranger sitting in our backseat. "He—the ghost— said that she was alive, and she was miserable. She was yelling at the guys that were keeping her tied up."

"Guys?" the detective asked, sounding surprised. "So there was more than one kidnapper?"

Ayla nodded.

Detective Sullivan pulled out a small notepad and took notes. "Did he tell you how many people were guarding her?"

"Just two, but there was another man that was coming and going. But he didn't stay there all the time."

I looked at Ayla. "You didn't tell me any of this when I asked."

"Well, you didn't ask any of that," she responded.

"Maybe you should leave the detecting to actual detectives, Ms. Arden," Sullivan said with that pompous, ego-puffed tone in her voice that all cops seem to be issued as soon as they got promoted to a level other cops envied. "All you've managed to do here tonight is to get shot at."

It dawned on me that Emma Sullivan thought she was better at tracking down a missing person than I was.

And that would just not do.

"I think they stopped shooting," I pointed out, noticing our conversation had not been punctuated by a clink or whizz for a while. I turned toward the back. "I'll drive you over to your car just to be completely safe."

Starting the Jeep, I inched forward toward the detective's downright boring Chevrolet Malibu as the car grew quiet. "I'm going to keep the bulletproof box running just a bit longer, though, so I'll need to help you out."

Detective Sullivan rolled her eyes.

After parking the Jeep inches off the Malibu's back bumper, I got out and pulled the seat forward. I placed both hands firmly on Emma, wrapping my arms around her so I could pull her out. All the way around her. Lots of contact. More than was necessary.

"Well, that was a little friendly," she said as I released her. She gave me a suspiciously raised eyebrow.

"Not as friendly as you might think," I told her, jumping back in the vehicle. "It was much less grabby than your tackle was over in that field."

"Stay out of police business, Ms. Arden," Detective Sullivan told me sternly. "The men that took Marianna Black are dangerous, and we don't have that many detectives on the force in Forkbridge, so the next case would probably go to me. I'd like to deal with just one at a time, and I don't want to deal with any paranormal shenanigans." I shifted in my seat, a little surprised at her nonchalant reference to the paranormal, but I didn't think this was the right time to ask about it. "Do we understand each other?"

"Probably not. I'm a very complicated woman," I told her with a wide smile. "But I do hear you. Loud and clear. You stay safe, now, Detective." She drew herself up and regarded me with an expression of self-important confidence. I closed the door, backed up, and pulled out.

"Astra, we're not really just gonna leave it to the police, are we?" Ayla asked. I glanced over and found she was still clutching the shield box with white-knuckled fists. "The goddess must think that we are the only ones that can save Marianna if she got the star card."

"No way," I told her. I reached down into my

tactical belt and pulled out the case notes notepad I surreptitiously filched from Detective Emma Sullivan. Tossing it to Ayla, I half-smiled. "Go ahead and put the shield box down. Take a look in Sullivan's notes and see if you can get any information we can use."

I said I don't like to lie. Didn't say I wouldn't.

I also said nothing about stealing.

CHAPTER ELEVEN

"*A*re we going to tell her the truth?" Ayla whispered as we crept in quietly through the side door. The house was quiet as a church on Sunday—which was making me very, very nervous.

"We're not going to volunteer anything," I whispered back. Scanning the dim kitchen for my mother, I pushed open the inside door and slowly closed the outside door behind us. Even Archie kept his beak shut while hitching a ride on my shoulder. "But no, we are not going to lie. For one, it's a terrible habit to get into. Trust me. Once you start, it's hard to stop. Two, if we do and she catches us? She'll never let you go out with me again." I sighed. "And remember, Mom always catches us in a lie eventually."

Well, me.

She always catches me.

It did occur to me that I was a thirty-three-year-old woman sneaking in the door I felt was most likely to be unobserved by my mother. My childhood was long gone, and yet here I was, still tiptoeing in like a teenager out past curfew while hoping not to get caught. I tried not to let it bother me as I removed my boots and padded across the floor in bare feet.

The voice—you know, THE voice—caught us halfway into the house like the crack of a thunderbolt. "Astra and Ayla Arden, just what do you think you're doing?"

Ayla froze as Mom's angry tone stopped her in her tracks. Seconds later, light flooded the room. My mother stood, arms crossed and cheeks pink, like a warrior queen in her royal purple sleeping muumuu. Her eyes scanned us both like she was looking for a head to chop off. My sister paled at the sight of her. "Mom, we just went for ice cream!"

Mom's eyes narrowed. "Ayla Arden, what have I told you about lying to me?" Her eyes jerked toward me. "Are you going to let your thirteen-year-old sister take the blame for this?"

I tried to maintain a firm (but polite) tone. "I didn't know there was any blame to be taken—"

"The ghost that spoke to her in the parking lot came to visit me," Mom thundered, her finger pointing across the room at Ayla while her eyes burned into me. "He told me that he informed you, young lady,"—she turned her gaze to Ayla—"about the missing woman at the old Thompson place, and that the two of you decided to go look for her yourselves—as opposed to doing what any normal two people would do, and calling the police."

Ayla stared back, her face pale and her expression stricken.

Mom's voice dropped an octave, and her eyes narrowed as she glanced back at me. "Is this the type of responsibility you learned in the military? Is this how you care for a child of—"

"I am not a child! You always treat me like a child, but I'm not! I'm not a child!" Ayla burst out. Then stomped her foot for good measure to prove that she wasn't, in fact, a child. "I'm a teenager!"

My mother stared at me for a long moment as if to say, "You see?"

"Everything you said is true. We were in the parking lot; a ghost came up to Ayla and said Marianna Black was at the old Thompson place. We went to check it out, but,"—I held up my hand as her mouth opened to speak—"Ayla was in the car the entire time with Archie, and the car was protected by an invisibility spell or a shielding spell the entire—"

"Neither of which you have a clue how to cast," my mother pointed out.

"Neither of which I need to cast when I have military-issued objects that are programmed to do it for me," I responded calmly. "Ayla was never in any danger, Mother." I leaned against a sewing table and slid my boots back on. "I would never let anything happen to any of my sisters. Or you, or Aunt Gwennie. I know you don't like me much, but surely you can't think I would put them in danger."

Mom looked at me with a stoic, contained face, and for the first time, I couldn't tell what she was thinking. "It doesn't help me to trust you, Astra, when you simply leave the house with your thirteen-year-old sister and act as if I'm in the wrong for being upset."

I could have bit back.

But I didn't.

STAR OF SAGE & SCREAM | 187

If I'd truly taken Ayla with me, I absolutely would have checked with my mother first. I never would have just disappeared with a thirteen-year-old—any thirteen-year-old—without talking to their parent. My mother had every right to be upset—if that was what I'd done.

The problem was that wasn't what I'd done.

But I couldn't say that without narcing on my sister.

"I understand, and I apologize for not asking you," I told her as Ayla bristled beside me. I reached out, grabbed her arm, and squeezed. "I'm not really used to asking permission to come and go, and it slipped my mind. I will definitely let you know in the future."

"I'm sure you misspoke. I'm sure you meant to say that you would ask me if you can leave the house with your thirteen-year-old sister," she said tersely. "Not that you would tell me what you plan to do with your sister without so much as a by-your-leave from her mother."

I could see Ayla out of the corner of my eye, fidgeting and shifting from foot to foot. I knew she was suffering from the discomfort of watching me getting in trouble for something she, in fact, did. The teenager wanted to admit that she hid in the Jeep, that I had nothing to do with it. She was practically bursting at the seams to shout the truth.

But again—my mother was right.

As much as I was loath to admit it.

Ayla was a child, and I was an adult. I should've turned around immediately and brought her back. At the very least, I should've called my mother and let her know that Ayla was with me. My sister had a form of qualified immunity because she was thirteen years old. Thirteen-year-olds do stupid things—a lot.

But I, the adult, gave tacit approval to her rule-breaking.

And I knew it.

"You're right, Mom, that's what I meant," I told her sincerely.

My mother blinked as if surprised by my answer. Her expression softened slightly as she looked back and forth between Ayla and me. "Ayla, I appreciate the fact that you want to use your gift to help with Astra's goddess-charged mission. Athena herself would be proud of you, showing such initiative. But you're still young yet, my little priestess witch," Mom told Ayla with a nervous affection. "Your sister is much more capable of assessing and eliminating threats because of her experience. You don't have that experience. Do you understand?"

Did my mother just say something positive about my military service? My heart raced, the blood pounded, and I shook my head back and forth in case I was hallucinating. I could've sworn that woman just said something nice about me. But that's not possible. Is it?

Before Ayla could answer, the doorbell rang.

"The police are here!" Ami shrieked so loudly that if the police were here, they no doubt heard her announce them. "Do I have to get my toothbrush? Are we getting hauled off to the clink?"

My mother's eyes narrowed. "What did you do, Astra?"

I ignored the reproachful look she cast in my direction and went to answer the door. "I'll get it!"

* * *

DETECTIVE EMMA SULLIVAN stood on our front porch and stared at me with a silent accusation. She said nothing, but as soon as I swung the door open, her hand was out, palm up. Her tactical boot tapped impatiently.

"Hey, those are great boots," I told her cheerfully. "Police issue, or can anyone buy them?"

"Yours, too," she said, glancing down toward my feet. "Hand it over, Arden, before I arrest you for theft, assault by contact, and anything else I can possibly think of that would elongate your stay in our fine establishment. And by fine, I mean filthy, dirty, dingy dungeon of a jail."

"Hand over what?" I asked innocently.

The detective looked me over, one eyebrow lifting. "You don't want to play this game with me."

I looked out past sullen Sullivan and wondered—not for the first time—what a detective was doing running around Forkbridge late at night by herself. I know she mentioned there weren't that many detectives on the force in this small town, which could be why she was alone. But my tracker sense was tingling.

"I'm not playing games, Detective Sullivan—"

"Look, let's put our cards on the table, shall we?" The detective let out a breath as if she was trying to be patient. "I know who and what you are. I know about Imperatorial City, I know about the Witches' Council being overthrown, and I know you were a tracker with the Ministry of Arcane Fugitives."

I blinked. "And how long have you known all that?"

"To be honest, about fifteen minutes. Well, the information about you, anyway. I called my brother and asked about you. He took a job for some shady characters in Las Vegas and wound up a vampire. Don't ask, long story, and I don't have the time to explain," Emma said with a shrug as if something like that happened every day. "They had some kind of weird overthrowing thing, too, so he left that job and all. But apparently, he's still a vampire."

I nodded. "Yeah, I don't think you can give that back like a company car. How did your brother know anything about my military service?" I asked suspiciously.

"You must be a bit more famous than you think in the paranormal world. You'd have to be if my brother knew who you were. Point is, I know who you are and what you can do. I also heard most of you folks walked out of the new and improved Paranormopolis with all sorts of gadgets and whooziwhatsis for crime-fighting. Not to mention training us mere mortals don't get."

The detective, still standing on the porch, was turning out to be surprisingly well-informed. It was a little bit unsettling. "Let's assume what you're saying is true. So what?"

"So let me borrow them, or help me out so we can save Marianna Black," the detective said point-blank.

I blinked again. "Pardon me, but weren't you the one that told me to stay out of police business just an hour ago? After shouting my name across a field, so the bad guys knew I was there?"

"You were a suspect at that point."

"And now you want me to be, what...a CI for you? Police psychic?" I waited to see if she had a response, but she didn't. "This is one hell of an about-face, Detective." I crossed my arms. "And to tell you the truth, I'm not buying it."

"Fair enough," Sullivan nodded. "Here's the thing. I'm dealing with four other detectives—all male, of course—who think I never should have been promoted, and also think I couldn't find a lost beagle howling 'I'm here' while sitting on the back bumper of the dogcatcher's truck." She delivered this comment as if it were simply a fact —without the seething resentment I would've expected her to have. "Not only do they think I can't solve a case, they actively sabotage me every time I turn around. None of the men will partner with me." She tilted her head. "That puts me at a disadvantage I'm tired of tolerating. You're obviously involved in trying to find her, too—why is that, by the way?"

"Just an interested citizen, Detective," I responded.

She stared at me for a moment, then raised an eyebrow. "You don't trust me, do you?"

I cocked my head to one side. "I think I said that already. I was a soldier for fifteen years, Detective. I don't trust anyone unless I have to. In my line of work, you survive longer that way."

Emma Sullivan nodded again, then tilted her head. "I can understand that. I'm ex-military, myself. I served two tours in Afghanistan, and being on alert all the time? It does a number on you."

A gust of wind blew over both of us, and I took a deep breath. The air was scented with the heady perfume of a humid Florida evening, and the moon shone over us both as if struggling to light our way forward. The whine of mosquitoes looking for their next meal buzzed—which, in the end, was probably the most significant factor in encouraging me to invite her in or send her away.

Quickly.

"How are you all doing this evening?" The detective called as her eyes glanced over my shoulder. I turned to find my mother, aunt, and three sisters staring at the doorway from the end of the foyer, listening to every word.

"I think you can trust her, Astra," Ami called down the hall. "She doesn't have a lot of black or brown at all. Not even a little dull gray." Black and brown colors in someone's aura usually denoted negative traits like greed or unjustified resentment. Gray could be a health problem. "And for a police officer, she's got, like, a lot of blue. If she was a witch, I would think she's clairvoyant." Blue denoted someone with great compassion and sensitivity, often the predominant auric color for a healer or seer.

"Black or brown is bad? Not to tell you all your business, but you realize how racist that sounds, right?" Detective Sullivan asked with a raised eyebrow.

"It's just color theory. You mix all the colors from light, you get white. Black is the absence of light, so not good. Interestingly, pigments work exactly the opposite way, so who knows what any of it means," I told her, stepping back and gesturing for her to come in. "Sorry about stealing your case notebook. Considering we were under fire, I didn't think asking you to share information was the way to go at that point."

"So instead, you opted for stealing police property?" she asked a little stiffly once in the foyer. However much blue Emma Sullivan had in her aura, it didn't seem like she was particularly amused I'd gotten the better of her.

"It was Plan B, and in my defense, it did work."

"If you mean it almost got you arrested, sure."

"Detective Sullivan, can I get you something to drink?" Althea, my fifteen-year-old sister, asked politely. "We have some wonderful chamomile tea flavored with watermelon. It's been cold brewing with some delightful clarity herbs."

"Althea is the herbalist in the family," I told Emma. I then pointed to Ami. "Ami's the seer, and Ayla—who you previously met—can, obviously, talk to ghosts. This is my Aunt Gwennie, the empath." Detective Sullivan respectfully shook hands with each person, murmuring a greeting. "And this is my mother, Minerva Arden. She's an all-around healer and can do a little bit of everything."

"Detective, welcome to our home." Mother bowed forward slightly and touched her hand to her heart in a regal fashion. "May your endeavors here be successful and blessed by the goddess Athena herself."

"Oh, right," Sullivan said as she bowed back slightly. "Rex mentioned you guys were actual Greek pagans."

"Rex?" my mother asked, confused.

"My brother, the vampire. He gave me a bit of a rundown on your family history."

"Of course. Well, your brother was somewhat correct," Mom said as we walked into the back of the house. "We're not Greek—we're witches. Being a witch is a cultural identity in and of itself. I am the high priestess of a Greek goddess, though. That doesn't make us Greek," she said somewhat defensively. "The goddess Athena chose me." Mom cleared her throat. "We wouldn't want to be accused of cultural appropriation."

"We're super woke," Ayla told the detective cheerfully.

"Of...course." Sullivan looked confused.

I smiled. "Don't worry about it. I don't get it half the time, either."

"That's because you left home at eighteen," my mother said under her breath. "Shall we all gather around the table and share what we know? Perhaps if all of us put our heads together, we can find poor Marianna Black before the sun comes up."

* * *

IT TOOK about an hour to go through everything that had happened. To my mother's credit, she did not throw things at me when Detective Sullivan and I discussed being shot at. I did notice the knuckles on her hands turned white, though, and Aunt Gwennie's clawlike grip never left her upper arm.

"If I had to bet, I would bet that Hayward Beals has something to do with it," I told Sullivan as she took more notes in her newly returned notepad. "Maybe Joel Clemens assisted him because he was there when we had that bizarre conversation. But the guy never said a word. One thing I can't understand, though, is when we met Marianna Black, she was—"

"She was horrible. Really horrible. Like a woman that couldn't see past her own wants to anyone else in her life," Ami interrupted breathlessly. "But it didn't make any sense. I kind of looked at her aura a little bit, and her colors just didn't make sense with the way she was talking."

I stared at Ami. "You didn't tell me that."

"Well, I mean, I kind of did. I told you that maybe she was just having a bad day." Sullivan looked back and forth between Ami and me. "You didn't ask me many questions about the reading, though."

I stared at Ami. "I was sitting ten feet away listening to the whole thing. I mean, I was there, so I didn't have to ask you much."

"Right, right, I know, but you never asked my impressions or anything." Ami shifted on the dining room chair and wrung her hands nervously. "I mean, I'm not saying you did anything wrong or anything. I'm just pointing out you didn't ask, right? What we found out on the internet about her? About the things she did to help the orphanage in Africa? That stuff made much more sense with her aura than the way she was talking to me today." Ami dropped her eyes. "That's all."

Detective Sullivan nodded. "What your sister said rings true with what I've found. I talked to some of the crew, and they had nothing but good things to say about Marianna Black—right up until two days ago." Emma put down her pen and closed the notepad. "Two days ago, the very kind and considerate Marianna Black turned into a selfish diva. Almost overnight. Nothing was right; she verbally abused the crew if they didn't do things the way she wanted. The craft workers reported that she turned over a table of sandwiches because they had mayonnaise on them."

"Craft workers?" Ayla asked. "Like arts and crafts?"

Sullivan turned. "Craft services. That's what they call movie set catering. For some reason, they can't just call it catering." The detective rolled her eyes. "Movie people."

"People—movie or otherwise—don't change that quickly," Aunt Gwennie said. "People's emotional natures, they are much more static than people want to believe. Sure, someone can have something happen, and they snap at people or get impatient. But the core moral nature of somebody and how they express that through their emotional interactions with other people? That doesn't change on a dime."

"No, it doesn't." The detective nodded. "At least not without an outside force causing that change."

"What could cause something like that?" Ayla asked.

"It could be any number of things," my mother

said. "Obviously, an enchantment or magic could do it, but we're not dealing with magical people here—"

"I wouldn't set that aside quite that fast, Mom. Marianna Black said she had a friend who had a reading." I looked up and thought back. "Rose? Rosa?"

"Rosie," Ami said as she got up and walked toward the store. "Let me go get my reading notebook and see if I can figure out who that was. If she was magical or a witch, I'd have a note of it. I can always tell if someone's paranormal. Even if just a little bit." My sister disappeared out of the side door.

"While she checks that, what else could it be?" Aunt Gwennie prodded Mom. "An illness, a brain tumor, maybe?"

"Drugs," Althea said with a shake of her head. "The most obvious answer is drugs. She's new to Florida, and there's this horrible new drug that people have been using here called gravel." She shuddered. "It's terrible."

"Gravel's been quite the problem." Sullivan raised her eyebrow. "It's not that widely known, though. How do you know about it?"

"I had to come up with a tincture that would help people come down off of it. It's an angry,

angry drug," Althea explained softly, her eyes downcast. "Every herb, every drug has a personality. Gravel is angry, and it wants people to be angry. Some people that take it just can't handle it, and they become violent, agitated, or paranoid. Anger is heat, and people can overheat so severely…" Her face paled. "Anyway, I came up with a tincture that cools the anger and counters it with calm and safety."

"What were you going to say after severely?" I asked her. "Is this stuff fatal?"

Althea nodded slowly. "It can be. It's terrible, terrible stuff. Just awful. Bodies aren't meant to hold that much heat. Too much of it or a bad reaction, they start to break down."

"Jeez. Why would somebody voluntarily take that?" I asked, frowning.

"I know, right?" Althea agreed.

"But maybe she didn't voluntarily take it?" Ayla said, her statement ending as if it were a question. "When you were walking through the Parrot Paradise, Ami told me there was this big place set up with all this great food anyone can eat. Someone else must make her food while she's acting, right?" she looked around at all of us. "What if someone slipped it in her food?"

"Let's hold on here. We're making an awful lot

of leaps," Detective Sullivan said, her tone cautious. Ayla's face fell. "I'm not saying it didn't happen. You might be onto something there, Ayla. I'm just saying there's a long way to go before we make that leap."

"Here it is!" Ami said, walking in waving a sheet of paper. She made a beeline for the detective and placed it in front of her. "Her name was Rosie Jackson. She was here last Tuesday. I was thinking about it after all this happened, and I didn't think it was her because she never said she knew Marianna Black or anything about movies. She told me she was a tourist from Orlando on vacation with her family." Ami shrugged. "Maybe they know each other some other way?"

"Why is that name ringing a bell?" Detective Sullivan murmured, picking up her notepad. She scanned the pages rapidly, and on the fourth page, she stopped. "Rosie Jackson. Craft services, *The Fabulous McCaws*." She raised her eyes. "Not a tourist from Orlando on vacation with her family." Sullivan glanced over at my sister. "Ayla, maybe you really are onto something. Nice work."

Ayla beamed proudly.

CHAPTER TWELVE

"We're going where?" I asked while climbing into Detective Sullivan's Malibu the following morning. Sullivan leaned forward and lowered the volume on a poppy tune blaring from the radio. "I must have misheard you. I could have sworn you said we were headed to a beach party." I pulled the seatbelt across my lap and struggled with the old buckle. "Criminy, how old is this car?"

"Thirty years. Isn't she awesome?" I didn't answer. "The movie shut down for a couple of days because of the kidnapping," Sullivan explained as she backed up, shifted, then pulled out into the road. "I called Hayward this morning and asked if we could stop by Parrot Paradise. He told me he was bringing the entire crew to the beach for the day so they could decompress from the trauma."

"What trauma?" I snorted. "It's not like anyone saw anything."

"Where's your magic owl?" The detective leaned forward and scanned the clear blue sky above the car as if she expected the owl to be pacing above. Which he was. Well, sort of. Just not above. Archie let me know he'd follow us out to the coast along the tree line and meet us at the beach. "Did he decide to stay home today? Afraid it might drizzle?"

"He's not a magic owl, and no, he's not home." We merged onto the highway on the outskirts of town, and I watched the scrub and trees roll by. "He let me know he'd be there, watching, if we needed him."

She nodded. "What can the owl do, then?"

"You want to know what owls can do?"

"Not owls," she responded. "Him. I figure he must be your familiar or something. Like in Harry Potter."

"Hedwig was Harry's pet and mail carrier. Mine's neither—and technically isn't really mine. But as to your question, besides be snarky and hide from water? No idea."

Once we were on the highway proper, Sullivan snaked into the fast lane and slammed on the gas. Without warning, the old car rocketed forward like the detective was a race car driver, and we'd just touched tires to the Autobahn.

I gasped. "Holy crap! How fast are you going?"

"Fast enough. It's a sleeper," the detective said offhandedly with a glance.

"What the heck's a sleeper?" I shouted over the roar of the engine. The wind noise was almost deafening, and the car's metal rattled like it would come apart.

"A high-performance car with a very unassuming exterior. This may look like an old 1980s clunker, but it's got a turbo Buick V6 under the hood with 600 horsepower and 28 pounds of boost."

I raised my eyebrow. "It sounds like English."

"People look at her and think she's old and ugly. Incapable." Sullivan chuckled. "They usually only do that once, though."

"Why not just buy a sports car?"

"I like being underestimated," she told me with another sidelong glance. "You can see those fancy foreign sports cars coming from a mile away screaming 'look at me, look at me.' I don't have that need for attention. You see a cop chasing you in an old, beat-up Chevy Malibu? You don't try so hard."

I glanced out the window again. "Fair enough."

Sullivan slowed down to only five miles over the speed limit instead of twenty and turned the radio back up. I glanced at her again out of the corner of my eye and spotted a satisfied look on her face. She may not have wanted a cherry red sports car so everyone would look at her, but her 90 miles an hour acceleration had clearly been done to get my attention.

I cleared my throat, and she turned the stereo down again. "Does it seem weird to you that a workplace would throw a beach party when a coworker gets kidnapped?"

"This whole thing seems weird to me." Another glance. "For example, isn't it a little warm to be wearing upper arm length gloves?"

I looked down at my military uniform and stretched my hands out. "Psychometry is a bit tough to control. Well, it's not as easily controllable as some of the other magical powers and much more dependent on the strength of impressions," I explained. "People with powerful gifts tend to wear gloves or some kind of blocking cream. I tried all the creams and lotions, but my skin's really sensitive, and they all made me break out in a rash. So, gloves."

"Did you get anything from Marianna Black the day she came to your family's shop? From your psychometry, I mean?"

"I never touched her. Hey, by the way, did you get one of the bullet casings from last night?" I asked her.

"Oh, right, yeah, I did." Detective Sullivan reached into her pocket and pulled out a Ziploc baggie. "I put all of them into evidence except for this one." She passed it over. "They shot a lot of bullets at us."

Unzipping the bag, I stripped off my glove and pulled out the spent casing. Immediately, the image of a box of bullets appeared in my mind. "A 40 caliber. That would have stung." Another image of a gun I recognized. "Glock 22. You know it?"

"Of course I know it. I carry it. So do half the cops in the country, I'd guess." She glanced at me. "Are you sure?"

"I can never be completely sure that what I'm seeing is exactly what I need or want to see," I told her with a shrug. "But that's the image I'm getting."

"Well, that's one of the most popular guns in

the country, so that's not a huge help," Sullivan said as she changed lanes. "Super popular with law enforcement, too, though I don't see why someone in law enforcement would be trying to shoot us at a rundown farmhouse in Forkbridge in the middle of the night." Sullivan frowned. "Say, can prop guns shoot bullets?"

"I don't think so. I think the whole point of the gun being a prop gun is that it doesn't shoot real bullets. But it's not exactly in my area of expertise."

"Let's ask the folks at the beach party about any replica guns that might be in the production. I'm not even sure what the movie is about. Can't get much from the title."

"Well, it clearly involves macaws," I pointed out.

Sullivan gave me a dark look. "So glad I brought you along. Never could've put that together without you."

* * *

WE PULLED up at about one in the afternoon. The hot Florida sun, brutal under normal circumstances, seared my pale white skin as soon as we were close enough to catch the reflected rays bouncing off the sand. "I really hope I don't get a sunburn," I mumbled sullenly.

Detective Sullivan reached into her bag and tossed me sunblock, SPF 80. "How could you grow up in Florida and not slather sunblock on half an hour before you hit the beach?" She looked my outfit up and down. "Never mind. Don't answer that."

"Did you tell me we were going to the beach? No, you did not tell me we were going to the beach. Over there." I pointed toward ten picnic tables surrounded by at least a hundred party-goers. The steady thrum of the surf competed with pounding rock music coming from giant speakers. "Well, gosh, they look positively broken up about Marianna's kidnapping."

"Don't they, though?" Detective Sullivan turned and looked at me.

"Let's go, then." I turned away, but her arm reached for me.

"Wait."

"For?"

The detective looked slightly uncomfortable— as if she just ate a bad clam. "I know we don't know each other very well, and I've just kind of glommed onto you in hopes that you can help me find this woman, but I want you to know I really appreciate your help." The wind whipped her long, dark hair into her face, and she tossed it back into place. "I can get kind of mono-focused, and I don't want to forget to thank you." She rolled her eyes. "The rest of the force doesn't even really think she was kidnapped."

I stared at her in surprise. "What do they think happened?"

"They think Marianna Black is upset about her pay, and she's disappeared in order to demand a higher salary from Hayward Beals."

"Where did they get that idea?"

"On that gossip website, *Z NUT*. You heard of it?"

"Yeah, I know who they are," I told her.

Z NUT, a national entertainment gossip juggernaut, was well-known for sharing just about any piece of information dropped in their direction that sounded remotely salacious—and if it wasn't naturally salacious, they shaded their words to imply it was. Unfortunately, it was also often right—the Ministry monitored their site for information on fugitives regularly.

Well.

They used to.

"I know. It's barely above the *National Enquirer*,

but from my perspective, leaking a fake story to *Z NUT* is a perfect way to get the police to look the other way or not try very hard to find her."

"Yeah, I could see that."

"Anyway, before we walk in there, I just want you to know I really do appreciate it," Sullivan said, circling back to her original point. "I'm not gonna give you one of those lectures about not stepping out of line, or being careful what you say, or following my lead, or whatever. You're a grown woman, and you chased fugitives for fifteen years." Detective Sullivan nodded. "From what my brother says, you know what you're doing."

I felt like I was living in the twilight zone.

Two months ago, I was chasing a fugitive elf across the Sahara Desert—while my mother texts passive-aggressively excoriating me for my choices. Then I came home with my tail between my legs to work the shop counter selling love potions to single women that couldn't land husbands.

Suddenly, goddesses were giving me owls and glowing cards were giving me missions. My mother gave me compliments on my skill set, and now a local detective gave me the "I owe you" speech like I was an expert consultant called in from the Feds.

Twilight Zone. I'm telling you.

"I appreciate the vote of confidence, Detective."

"Call me Emma. My friends and family call me Emma or Em."

"We're not friends," I said quickly—too quickly—without thinking. "I'm sorry, I know that sounded rude, but...but we're not...friends."

Way to stop digging, get a bigger shovel, and dig further, Astra.

"You're right; we're not friends," Sullivan said, her voice a little louder. "But I am a detective, and if I have to keep calling you Ms. Arden, I'm going to keep sounding like I'm about to arrest you. I can't help it. It's my cop voice." She smiled in an attempt to look agreeable. "I'd like to set aside cop voice."

I stared, unsure of what to say.

After about five seconds, Sullivan smiled even wider, but it looked...odd. When I didn't respond, she exhaled and dropped the smile. "Look, I want you to know I respect you, that's all. I've been told I'm unfriendly. I'm trying not to be. So, we're equals. Call me Emma."

I hesitated. Whatever equal footing she

wanted to put us on, Emma was the one with the handcuffs. On the other hand, Sullivan sounded sincere, and we were working together. It probably would be easier to be on a first-name basis. "Will do, Emma. Feel free to call me Astra. No nickname. Just Astra."

"Ready to start interviewing drunk people that look like they're ready to dance on Marianna Black's grave?" Emma asked.

"Why, Emma, you sound like you've already made up your mind about these people." We walked toward the raucous gathering. The attendees were talking loudly alongside young women in bikinis shrieking with drunken laughter. "This whole party's really rubbed you the wrong way, huh?"

"A woman is missing, her life is in danger, and they are at the beach getting drunk," Sullivan told me through gritted teeth. "You're damn right it's rubbed me the wrong way."

* * *

THE BEACHGOERS SEEM to sense our authority as we picked our way through them. I spotted multiple suspicious cigarettes suddenly disappearing behind people's sunblocked backs.

"Detective!" Hayward Beals shouted, his friendliness clearly feigned. Lumbering behind him, just as he had been in the grotto, was Joel Clemens. The quiet man eyed me with curiosity. "We didn't expect you for a couple more hours. Can I get you something to drink?"

"No, thank you—"

Turning toward me, he smiled just as widely and just as fake. "Astra Arden, was it? I wasn't aware you were friends with the detective." His expression turned lascivious as his eyes swept over my figure in the skintight bodysuit. "Or, are you more than friends, perhaps?"

I wanted to just kick this guy in the…shins.

Let's just say shins.

"Ms. Arden is consulting on the case," Detective Sullivan told Beals without elaborating. "Can you point out Rosie Jackson, Mr. Beals?" She turned and scanned the party-goers. "I'd like to speak to her first."

"Why would this woman"—he said woman in a scornful tone despite continuing to ogle my womanhood—"be consulting on the case? I assume you're aware that she was the one that found Christine Chandler nearly drowned." Hayward dropped the volume on his voice and leaned toward Emma as if he was confiding a secret. "I can't believe a suspect in Marianna's disappearance would be consulting on the very case in which she played a role."

Joel Clemens tensed, his eyes nervously bouncing between us. Emma's eyes cast over to me quickly and then moved back to Hayward.

"I didn't realize stumbling across a woman and saving her life was considered 'playing a role' or 'being a suspect' in the case, Beals," I told him tersely.

"Yes, well, if I were writing a movie, you would be pivotal as a suspect—even if you turned out to be nothing more than a red herring." Hayward leaned over and whispered conspiratorially to Clemens. "I'd like to red her herring, if you know what I mean."

"No woman would possibly know what you meant by that," I responded sourly. "And if you wrote the movie, it would no doubt bomb at the box office and destroy my career, so no thanks."

The pink on his cheeks from the sun became more pronounced as sudden rage blotched his face. This guy loved to dish it, but he sure couldn't take it. I'd known men like that.

Nothing good came from men like that.

"Astra?" I turned and found Richard Ford standing next to me. The parrot whisperer was tanned, and his skin shined slick with suntan oil. "What are you doing here?"

Detective Sullivan turned and raised an eyebrow at me.

"I came with Detective Sullivan. I'm consulting on the Marianna Black case." Rick nodded. "What are you doing here?"

Beals jumped in before Rick could respond. "Our hosts have been so generous, especially with the shutdown of the last couple of days, that I felt it only right to invite them to decompress and heal with the rest of us," Beals interjected. "I forgot that you and Richard knew one another."

"We went to school together," Rick said, his expression confused. "How do the two of you know one another?"

"Perhaps the detective and her friend should go over there to where Rosie is," Joel Clemens, his voice far deeper than I would've expected, broke in before either of us could answer. Clemens pointed to a small quiet group of women hanging about on the outskirts of the party. "I don't think we should keep them. They came here to do a job."

"Fine, the girl you want to talk to is over in that direction," Hayward Beals said, waving dismissively. "Richard, why don't you come with us? I'd like to talk to you about Blue and Jewel."

"Blue and Jewel?" I asked.

"Two of our birds. They—"

Hayward interrupted. "Come on now, Richard!"

Rick stood there for a moment as Hayward and Joel walked away. He gazed after us, a puzzled look on his face. The next time I glanced back, he had followed the producer and director to a table and was deep in conversation.

* * *

"You saw what I saw, right?" Emma whispered as we made our way toward Rosie Jackson. "On Clemens' face?"

"The fact that he tensed up when Hayward brought up Christine Chandler?"

She nodded and went on, "I saw it. He didn't hide it very well. What I can't figure out is why the mere mention of that sent his blood pressure up. All of us knew what happened. Well, you, Joel, and Hayward were there. He has to assume you told me about it."

"Have you talked to Christine Chandler?" I asked her. "Well, either of the Chandlers?"

Emma stopped walking and turned. "What do you mean, either of them?"

"Christine Chandler or her brother, Bart. Marianna's boyfriend?"

"The boyfriend isn't here," Emma told me. "He's back in LA."

"No, he's not; he's here. Marianna told my sister about all of the fights they'd been having the past couple of days, how she told him she wanted him to get rid of his dog, and how she didn't like his mother," I said, frowning. "If our theory is that she's normally a nice person and suddenly became this raging...well, you know."

"I know."

"Well, then the conversations and fights all had to take place here. Granted, it sounded at the time like it was this horrible two-year relationship with this horrible woman, but if someone's dosed her with something to make her nuts? Then she couldn't have been a horrible woman that wanted her boyfriend to get rid of his dog all that long. Right?"

Sullivan bit her lip, deep in thought. After a few moments, she looked at me with a wary expression. "She really wanted him to get rid of his dog?"

"Yeah. Anyway, some of the things she said

gave me the distinct impression that he was here in town with her. She never said as much, but Marianna specifically mentioned getting him to propose to her that night." I shrugged. "I don't know any woman, even if they're drugged, that would want to be proposed to over the phone."

"Fair point," Emma agreed.

"Why did you think he wasn't in town?"

"Because Hayward Beals told me he wasn't. Said she was alone in Forkbridge, only her assistant with her."

We both turned back and looked at the director with wariness.

* * *

"OH MY GOSH, YES, RIGHT." Rosie Jackson was a small woman, no more than five foot four, with brown eyes and long hair pulled into a ponytail. Her three friends stared and whispered as we stood a few feet from where they sat on an unfurled blanket. "That was me. I was the one that got the reading."

"Why did you tell my sister that you were on vacation with your family in Orlando?" I asked pointedly.

Rosie blinked. "Well, I was at the time. It was

right before the movie started filming, and my husband drove me here instead of me flying alone, so we could take the kids to Disney World." Her large, sincere eyes bounced back and forth between my face and Detective Sullivan's. "I came out here to Forkbridge to get my room set up while he took them to a water park. While I was here, I got a reading from the bruja Amethyst." Her voice wavered nervously. "Did I do something wrong?"

"No, Ms. Jackson, we're just trying to get all the facts. Marianna Black went into the shop the day of her kidnapping, and she said it was because you recommended she get a reading."

"I did." Rosie nodded vigorously. "She was acting so crazy that I thought maybe it would help her. I mean, the movie doctor certainly wasn't doing anything." Her pixie-like face scrunched up. "If anything, it seems like whatever he was giving her was making her worse."

"The doctor prescribed her something?" Emma asked. Rosie nodded. "Recently?"

She nodded again. "I tried to get her to go to a regular doctor, but she wouldn't. Marianna said it was just a few more weeks of filming, and she could see her own doctor in Los Angeles. But she seemed so...she was so bad, so different, and the reading I got from Ami was so accurate!" Her hand drifted to her midsection, and she rubbed her stomach affectionately. "I didn't even know I was pregnant, and she told me. It was a good thing, too, so I could be more careful."

I smiled. "Congratulations."

"Thanks. My family, we always go to the family bruja, you know? La Bruja Blanca always makes things better for me. She told me that I would get this job, and she was the one that told me to see the Forkbridge bruja when I was here," Rosie smiled shyly as if the two of us would make fun of her. "Amethyst gave me such good news, and Marianna was so sad; I thought that the Florida bruja would help her because she was obviously powerful with the gift." Her smile fell, and her eyes filled with tears. "But I guess she wasn't as powerful as I thought. Poor Marianna."

I felt a pang of guilt in her words. Maybe had I shaken Marianna Black's hand, I could have seen the darkness gathering around her. Had Ami looked past her words, she might have seen that something was wrong. The woman had come to us because she was in need—and if we had any doubt, that doubt was swept away when the star card fell for her. It felt like we'd failed her.

It felt like I'd failed her.

I tried to shake it off.

"You said something about the movie doctor giving Marianna something. What doctor?" Detective Sullivan asked.

Rosie's face turned stormy. "That doctor. *El mal de ojo*," she whispered and then shuddered. "I heard him and the director talking. They talk all the time in front of us because they don't see us, you know? We are just the people that make the food, the servers. You notice how they walk by us here and don't speak? But they eat our food." She frowned, glaring out over the revelers. "Anyway, Doctor Gerald was giving her pills with this white powder in them. The pills have no numbers on them, so I couldn't tell what they were, but they made her feel terrible. And then they made her angry."

"You mentioned you heard them talking?" I reminded her. "Do you remember what Doctor Gerald and Hayward said?"

"Yes, I heard them talking before Doctor Gerald gave her the pills," Rosie said, her eyes glancing around as her voice dropped to a whisper. "Mr. Beals told Doctor Gerald that Marianna was going to ruin his movie because she wasn't acting crazy enough for the part she was playing, and he wanted Doctor Gerald to give her something to make her crazier in her performance."

"Did Marianna know that's why they were giving her pills?"

"She's a good woman, Miss. She wants to do a good job, and so she would do anything they told her. Yes, she knew." Her eyes scanned from side to side, and she dropped her voice to a whisper. "But she didn't know they had a plan B."

"A plan B?" Detective Sullivan asked.

"I told her that they wanted someone else to play her part," the woman whispered sadly. "They said the insurance would pay to cover replacing her if she couldn't perform. She didn't believe it when I told her. Said they would never do that."

"When did you tell her that?" I asked.

"The day before she was kidnapped."

CHAPTER THIRTEEN

"*D*id you believe her?" I asked as Emma and I walked away from Rosie, her expression unsettled as she returned to her group of friends. "You seemed like you did."

Emma flicked her eyes to me, sighed, and then turned back to stare at Rosie. "She seemed sincere," Emma admitted finally.

"Yeah, I thought so, too."

We moved toward the main party's side and leaned against a short brick wall separating the picnic area from a beach volleyball court. "That doesn't necessarily mean she's telling the truth, though. I mean, psychopaths appear completely sincere even when they're lying to your face." She gazed back at Rosie once more. "I like to think I can spot a psychopath, though, and that young mother didn't strike me as one. Hayward Beals, on the other hand?"

I nodded. "Say, can I ask you something?"

"Shoot."

"Why are we here?" I asked seriously. Emma raised her eyebrow. "What I mean is all the information we have so far indicates we should be looking at the old Thompson place." Emma stared. "Well, I mean...doesn't it?"

"You're talking about the information from an anonymous ghost claiming Marianna was there? The one that spoke to your thirteen-year-old sister? That information? You think I should drop all normal investigative techniques and search an abandoned property based on the word of a ghost?"

"Well, when you say it like that, it sounds ridiculous," I admitted. "But to be honest, I don't really get what we're doing here. Something happened at the old Thompson place last night, and we know that for sure because we were shot at. Did you send investigators there, at least?"

"Investigators?" Detective Sullivan laughed. "Astra, what resources are you under the impression the Forkbridge Police Department has? We have one single forensic investigator. Jared Upton. He's part-time, sixty-two years old, and retired here from New York City. Every time we call him out for anything, he thinks it's a waste because everything in NYC was so much more dramatic."

"But you said there were four other detectives?"

She made a strangled noise. "I did," she answered bitterly. "And if you'd like to talk to them, I think their tee time is at three in DeLand —we could just about make it. You know how I know that?" I raised an eyebrow. "Because that's when it usually is."

I looked beyond Detective Sullivan, my eyes drifting over the crowd just over the first rise in sand dunes behind the volleyball court when a man in dark clothing caught my eye. He was tall and stocky—and on his hip, a large gun glinted in the sunlight.

A gun that looked suspiciously like a Glock 22.

"Hey, do you know who that guy is?" I waved my hand toward the man casually so as not to draw attention. Emma leaned back as if she were stretching and glanced toward him quickly. "Is he a cop? Florida isn't an open carry state, is it?"

Emma turned back, the hair falling into her face. "No, it's not. We have concealed carry laws for handguns, but you can't openly carry one." She hoisted up her purse and placed it on the brick wall, rummaging through as if looking for something. After a few moments, she zipped it back up and twirled around to face me. "If he is a cop, I don't know him. But we are in Daytona, and I don't know all the folks on that force."

I watched as the man scanned the movie set crowd, his eyes widening slightly when he spotted Hayward Beals. The director was still sitting at a picnic table with Joel Clemens and my high school friend, Rick Ford. Immediately, the mysterious armed man made his way toward the table.

"Let's get closer and see if we can hear what they're saying," Emma whispered, grabbing my arm. We picked our way through the crowd with some stealth and subtlety, settling behind several kegs just out of sight of the table.

"Yes?" Hayward asked in a faintly musical voice. "What seems to be the trouble? So much so that it couldn't wait until we got back?"

"I thought you'd want to know immediately—"

"That's generally why I keep a phone on me."

The man frowned and cocked his head. "Marianna Black's mother is landing in Orlando in less than four hours. Pictures from this little ill-advised excursion," he added curtly, waving toward the bathing-suited beachgoers, "are already up on the *Z NUT* site." He leaned forward, both hands on the table, and glared stonily at Beals. "You all realize you look like you're dancing on your female lead's grave?"

"Well, that's unfortunate," Hayward sighed. "Those people do pay top dollar for a whiff of a hint of controversy." Then he chuckled. "I couldn't buy publicity like that, and if I tried, it would cost me a fortune."

I could swear I heard the guy with the gun curse under his breath. "So you don't want me to find out who sent the pictures and take care of it, then?" Hayward shook his head no and laughed. "And the woman? What do you want me to do about her?"

"The mother?" Hayward took a long drink from his red Solo cup. "I'm sure she'll come here and get herself in front of the television cameras weeping and wailing about how worried she is." I cringed at Beals' arrogant dismissal of Marianna's situation and his snide comment about her mother. "It's just more publicity for my film I don't need to pay for. Let her do whatever she's going to do."

Oh, jeez. Really? How could anyone stand this guy?

I glanced back again and saw Rick was moving quietly from Hayward's side, his face troubled. I hoped he was troubled by the conversation he'd just heard, but...frankly, I couldn't know that for sure. Just because he had a pretty face and seemed like an okay guy fifteen years ago didn't mean he wasn't part of whatever this whole conspiracy was. And it was looking, sounding, and feeling like a conspiracy.

To what end, though?

The man with the gun told Hayward (in a reasonably menacing tone) he was playing with fire.

"Fire keeps you warm, Downing," he responded, his tone chipper and his posture relaxed.

"Rick's going over there to refill his drink," I whispered to Emma, pointing. "I went to high school with him. Let me go over there and see if I can find out any information."

"Before you go, I should warn you—Marianna was taken off the property through an exit no one on the film crew should have known about. The site manager gave us maps of where everyone would have any reason to be to track movements. That back area? It was technically off-limits."

"That doesn't necessarily mean that someone who worked in Parrot Paradise told them about it," I told her seriously, not wanting to believe Rick could be part of something so wrong.

"That doesn't necessarily mean someone who worked in Parrot Paradise didn't tell them about it or wasn't part of it. Or didn't get paid to look the other way and not ask questions." Emma looked at me pointedly, and I nodded as I stood up and walked toward Rick.

* * *

"THESE HOT DOGS FOR ANYONE, or do you have to be in the movies to snag one?" I asked, pointing toward a tower of barbecued hamburgers, hot dogs, and tofu.

Rick turned and smiled as if happy to see me, passing me an empty plate. "I think there's more than enough food to feed three times as many people." He smiled sheepishly. "Though, to be honest, most people seem more interested in the alcohol than the barbecue."

I grabbed the hot dog, some potato chips, and

a pickle. "You looked a little uncomfortable with your previous picnic company. Have a few minutes to sit down over there with me while I eat? We can catch up a bit."

"Sure." Rick looked out and found an empty picnic table, pointing. I nodded and followed him over. "I didn't know you were working with the Forkbridge Police Department. You didn't mention it when you and your sister came over the other day with the owl."

He could be making small talk—and he was right; I hadn't mentioned that (though I hadn't been working with the police at the time). On the other hand, he could be digging for information.

"It's just a temporary thing," I shrugged and took a bite of the hot dog. It was all beef, Nathan's or Hebrew National. My favorite. "Marianna Black came to get a reading from my sister just before she disappeared, so I was kind of interested in her disappearance."

"Your sister Ami?" I nodded. "Wow. That's crazy. So, interested how, exactly?" he asked earnestly, barely a pause between the two sentences.

I blinked.

Was he digging for information, or was this

just the most significant thing happening in our little town of Forkbridge right now?

I couldn't tell, and I regretted leaving Ami at home. She could have read him in seconds. "I don't know. Maybe interested isn't the right word. I was worried. I felt connected to her, I guess, since we'd met." I took another bite of my hot dog. "Besides," I added, my mouth half-full, "in my previous job, I used to find people for a living."

He nodded with interest. "Oh? What was your previous job?"

I stared at him. "I just told you. I used to find people for a living." I didn't mean to sound as snarky as I did, but I was feeling like I was getting the third degree for a reason.

Or I was utterly paranoid.

Which was possible.

My training at the Ministry was...heavy-handed? I guess that's a polite way of putting it. Subtlety wasn't something fugitive trackers were known for. We were like state-sanctioned bounty hunters, and we busted heads and threatened people and kicked doors in until we boxed our quarry into a corner.

Then we pounced.

This was requiring a deft touch I really didn't have.

Rick's eyes met mine, and he chuckled nervously. "Sorry, you're right, of course, you did." He reached into his pocket and pulled out sunglasses. Slipping them on, he tilted his head back toward me.

Mirrored sunglasses, so I couldn't see his eyes. Suspicious.

Or, um, Florida.

I sighed and hoped we'd get to the part where I'd need to punch someone in the face or something.

"How's the owl you're not supposed to have doing?"

"Who said I wasn't supposed to have the owl?" I asked him, my eyebrow raised. "And if you'll recall, I told you I don't have the owl. The owl, whose name is Archie, comes and goes as he pleases. Speaking of coming and going," I said as I leaned forward. "How do you think the kidnappers knew about the escape route through the waterfall?"

Rick's face remained smooth and friendly. "The escape route through the waterfall?"

Aha.

That trick, I did know.

You repeat a question back to someone to give yourself some time to gather your thoughts or prepare an answer. People could be trained to do it or just do it unconsciously to buy themselves time. It was usually done by people that needed to get their lie straight.

I nodded. "Emma and I were discussing the case, and she mentioned that area wasn't really a place anyone from the movie shoot would've been expected to be in." Rick didn't give much of a reaction to my observation. "Is that right?"

"Well, not really, but it wasn't exactly locked away or out of bounds or anything. It wasn't secured. I mean, they paid us a lot of money to use the place since we had to shut down—none of our staff would've told them to get out of an area unless it was bothering the birds." He paused and fiddled with his cup. Then took a drink. "I guess if you're planning something like a kidnapping, you find a way to escape without getting caught, right?"

Of all the questions Rick had, he'd had none about how close we might be to finding Marianna Black, whether we thought she was still alive. That could mean he wasn't digging for information.

Or it could mean he already knew the answers.

There were no offers to help. No expressions of worry for someone he'd seen daily for several weeks. His reaction just wasn't a "normal" one. Or so it seemed to me.

"You think it was planned?" I asked him.

"Well, yeah," he answered, surprised. "Don't you?"

"Don't really know yet. Hey, do you know who that guy is?" I asked quickly, jerking my chin in Hayward's direction. "Downing?"

Rick pulled down his glasses and stared at me, his eyebrow raised. "Were you eavesdropping on our conversation back there?"

"You guys didn't exactly run off and have it privately," I pointed out. "We were standing right there behind the kegs, so, yeah, we heard the whole thing. He was kind of hard not to notice—considering he had a gun strapped to his waist."

"He's one of the armed security guards Hayward just hired for the production."

"Security guards?"

Rick nodded. "I guess after Marianna was kidnapped, Hayward was worried he was being targeted, so he hired armed guards for the production. To tell you the truth, I felt a lot better after he did. It's really creepy knowing someone was kidnapped from our park. The birds have been agitated for days."

Wait a minute. "Why would Hayward worry he was being targeted if it was Marianna that was kidnapped? Has he said something about Marianna's kidnapping that leads you to believe he thinks it has to do with him and not her?"

"I, uh..." Rick looked around nervously, breaking eye contact and slipping his sunglasses back up his nose. He appeared to study me for a moment, then took a deep breath. "Look, I don't really know enough about his business to say one way or the other. I probably shouldn't have said anything."

"Dude, I don't work for *Z NUT*," I told him forcefully. "I'm trying to find a woman that's been kidnapped. You probably should tell me anything that you know that might help me to find her."

"Hey, my family signed one heck of a confidentiality agreement," he told me, his voice faltering. "I really do want to help. I don't want to see anyone get hurt. But I also don't want to lose my family's business because I don't know when to keep my mouth shut." He stood up from the picnic table and gathered the empty paper plates.

"It was terrific to see you again, Astra, but I really need to get back."

Rick hustled away without saying goodbye, and I watched him walk all the way back to Hayward Beal's table, a worried look on his face.

* * *

"WELL, sounds like your boy Rick knows something," Emma said after joining me at the table. "You're right; these hot dogs are delicious."

"How could you have never had an all-beef hot dog?" I asked, incredulous. "Kosher hot dogs. Only ever eat kosher hot dogs. They are the only ones worth eating."

"I'll remember that." She gave her red plastic cup a lazy swirl and then washed the rest of the hot dog down. Looking back up at me with a speculative look, she asked point-blank, "You knew the guy in high school. Do you think he had something to do with it?"

Richard Ford wasn't the sharpest tack in the box. The guy I knew in school struggled to keep his grades up, but never struggled to get a girlfriend or make a touchdown. He was, in many ways, the stereotypical dumb jock.

No one, though, is always the stereotypical anything.

His passion for the parrots at his family's park got him teased mercilessly by the other football players and the popular kids in his wealthy, judgmental little clique—but it didn't stop him from staying in Forkbridge and becoming the Parrot Paradise heir apparent.

"I think Rick could be used," I told her regretfully. "I don't think he would do anything deliberately malicious to someone. He's gentle, compassionate. Or at least he was, especially when it came to parrots."

"The ex-football player is gentle and compassionate?" Emma asked suspiciously. "I've watched a few football games, and gentle and compassionate are not the first words that come to me when thinking of football players."

"Stop thinking in stereotypes," I told her. Leaning back, I drummed my fingers on the table. "Here's how I see it. We have several suspects—Bartholomew Chandler, Hayward Beals. I'd add Clemens in there just because he completely creeps me out."

"Your friend Rick?"

"I don't think he would do it, but he might know something that points to who did. Add gun-toting Downing to the list, too. The doctor that drugged Marianna." I frowned. "We've got a basket full of suspicious people acting suspiciously, but what we don't know is what anyone would have to gain from Marianna Black being drugged or kidnapped."

Emma shook her head. "Rosie said Hayward Beals wanted to replace Marianna. Maybe she has a buyout in her contract that he didn't want to pay?"

"How big could that buyout be? Marianna is a B-list actress, and this is a movie about parrots. What about an insurance payout?" I asked. "Have you seen the paperwork on file with Forkbridge for the movie shoot?"

"No," she mused quietly, looking off toward the water. "But I think we should probably go pull those papers."

"And look into what armed security company is providing security for Hayward Beals now," I told her, pointing toward Downing. "He just hired the guy with the gun."

"That explains why he's open carrying. He's on the job."

"Open carrying with a Glock 22. Tell me that's a coincidence."

Emma shook her head. "I told you, that's a

smart gun for people in law enforcement. Maybe not quite as popular as others and a bit more gun than most people would carry. The 22 has a hell of a kick."

"Anyone else you want to talk to here, or can we get out of the sun?" I asked her. I could feel my nose beginning to burn.

Since we'd arrived at the party, the vast majority of movie employees were distinctly and deliberately avoiding us. The drunken revelry and dancing had slowly ground down, and I could see clusters of people whispering to one another, their eyes skittering about nervously.

"What are they all whispering about?" Emma asked.

"Probably the photos of them dancing and whooping it up when one of their coworkers is missing. Would you want to work with someone that fiddled while Rome burned?"

"I do work with people that fiddle while Rome burns, or more accurately, golf while crime rages. Does it look to you like any of these people think Rome is burning?" she asked with a touch of caustic judgment in her voice. "Hollywood people. I knew this case was going to give me indigestion."

"Want a Tums? Have one on my belt. Well, it's

an herbal tum-like tablet that Althea whipped up. She says it's much healthier, and it helps fight depression, too."

"If this case drags on another day, I might be able to use that," Emma admitted. "Come on, let's go back to Forkbridge and let these people party without feeling the eyes of condemnation staring them down." She stood up and waved toward the parking lot. "We can go back over to the old Thompson place, too, since you don't trust my department's forensic investigator."

"I didn't say that."

"Oh, right, that was probably me."

CHAPTER FOURTEEN

I could tell you about our return visit to the old Thompson place, but it was uneventful. We surveyed the property from top to bottom, trudging around in knee-high grasses, scanning for any clues. If there was anything there to find, it was well hidden or moved before we got there.

I was feeling like a non-detective since we— Detective Sullivan and I—had spent two days non-detecting Marianna Black's location, the conspiracy, who might've kidnapped her...it seemed I'd accomplished nothing more than getting a sunburn on my nose and getting an unpaid job with the Forkbridge Police

Department, where I was now waiting outside the station.

"She's been in there an awfully long time," Archie said after flying down onto the hood of the Malibu and facing me through the window. This being Florida, tourists walking by oohed and aahed at the unexpected sight and took pictures without asking. "What is she doing in there, anyway?"

"She went to pull the insurance papers for the movie shoot that should be on file with the city," I told him without getting out of the car. "They would've had to give the city a bunch of information to get the permit to film. We went to take a look at that info—hey!"

"Get off me!" Archie raised his wings and lurched toward a passerby who aggressively attempted to scratch his head. He punctuated the threatening movement with a bellicose screech that had the heavyset woman in Mickey Mouse ears scrambling back to a safe distance. "Don't you know I could snap your fingers off your hands like peppermint sticks? Are you daft?"

"Ma'am, that's a wild owl," I told her through the open window. "You may want to be careful."

"Oh, goodness, it's just so precious, though," she cooed, inching forward. "I'm sure he'll let me pet him. Why, look, he's just sitting there waiting to be snuggled!" Her hand slowly rose, fingers inching toward Archie's head.

The owl gave another ear-piercing screech, and she screamed while stumbling backward. "Somewhere out there, there's a tree working very hard to produce oxygen so that you can breathe," the annoyed owl snapped at the woman. "I think you should go and apologize to it."

The woman couldn't understand him, but she seemed to comprehend his general attitude and finally scurried away.

"Humans," Archie said with disgust.

"If you don't like them, why do you want to help them?"

"First, I didn't say I didn't like them." Archie swung his head swiftly in my direction, and his eyes opened wide. "I didn't like that one, but I don't think all of them are like that one. Secondly, I'm the goddess's own owl. What's the point of the gods if not to help the humans?"

"The gods don't exist for their own purposes? They just run around trying to be of service to humanity?" I asked curiously.

Eyebrows arched. "You want to have a philosophical discussion now?"

"I don't know, it came up—"

"It came up because you're running around behind the human detective doing absolutely nothing to find Marianna Black," Archie said with a matter-of-fact tone, swaying toward the front windshield. "Didn't it even occur to you that magic is necessary to find this woman? That maybe the star card flipped over because human policing and detecting wouldn't be enough to find her?"

I blinked. "I hadn't really thought about it one way or another."

"If ignorance is bliss, you must be the happiest person on the planet," the owl said caustically. "From where I sit—which is, I might point out, uncomfortably on the hood of an ancient car that's burning my tail feathers—you're using none of your powers to assist detective dimwit in there."

"Hey, there's no need to be insulting. Sullivan's not dumb, and neither am I." I rapped my knuckles on the windshield. "She invited me to participate, and we are in the human world. I've used magic when it was called for, but it's not always called for—"

"Again, though I hate to repeat myself? A magical glowing card showed up in Marianna

Black's reading." The owl walked forward with a dignified pace, and I winced as his talons scraped the metal hood. "A magical, glowing, goddess-provided card," he told me slowly and deliberately as if I was a small child. "You have only seventy-two hours from the time that card flips over to stop the death you've been charged to—"

"Hold up." I jumped up in the car seat and clambered out of the car. "What do you mean, I have only seventy-two hours from the time the card flips over? You never told me there was a time frame on this."

"Seventy-two hours, more or less, but about that, yes. And I absolutely did tell you, I'm sure of it," Archie responded emphatically, his shoulders rising and falling. His voice was a web of confidence and surety. "I would never forget to tell you something like that. The seventy-two hours—more or less—is very important."

"Well, is it more or is it less?" I asked with exasperation. My exasperation was only partially fed by a rising panic.

"I said more or less, and I meant more or less. It could be more. It could be less. Which is why I said more or less." Archie waved his wing in the air dismissively. "We already had this conversation. I told you this. Not my fault you didn't listen."

"But I did listen, and you absolutely did not tell me there was a clock ticking." I poked the bird's fluffy breast with my finger. "You said that a card would appear with the star, and it would be glowing, and I would have to stop a death that your 'goddess' decided shouldn't take place. You never, ever told me that was the beginning of a clock ticking."

Archie raised his head again, and his eyes searched my face. "I'm sure I did," he said finally, sounding a little less sure of himself.

"I'm sure you didn't."

We stared at one another.

"Okay, so, let's say I didn't." He waved the wing dismissively again. "Did you really need me to tell you that Marianna Black—the kidnapped Marianna Black—had a clock ticking on her life? The woman got the star card and was marked for a death that didn't need to happen, and then she was kidnapped by goons that dumped her assistant in a parrot pond on the way out." Archie blinked. "My point is, Astra, maybe it's time to take point on this investigation and break out some of your magical tracking tricks." He blinked again. "Or did we want to head back to the beach and get another hot dog?"

* * *

I WAS STILL SMARTING from Archie's lecture when Emma jumped back in the car. "I got everything. Do you want to head back to your house to go through it?" I nodded distractedly, and she started up the car.

I was sure Archie had not told me about the time frame involved with the star card flipping over—and to be honest, I didn't know that I believed the bird, anyway—but his point was valid.

I still believed none of the gobbledygook about the goddess Athena sending Archie. Didn't trust that story for a second. But if Archie was an enchanted owl my mother cooked up in her ritual room, and the star card was part of whatever spell she cast?

Everything Archie said might be true. More or less.

My mother had some power of prophecy, and I couldn't dismiss out of hand that she could have seen Marianna Black's death and enlisted me to stop it by using the owl and the enchanted card.

That vision might have entailed a clear time frame.

Even so, I frowned. It didn't necessarily mean I had to use magic to solve the thing. Detective Sullivan was used to operating in the human world. So far, all signs pointed to this being a human problem. Human problems required human solutions if human solutions were available.

And they were, I nodded to myself. The human world and the paranormal world were different—that, by the way, had been pounded into our heads in the Ministry.

Do whatever you have to, they told us, but make sure whatever you do is minimally magical so as to not upset the balance. That rule sounded suspiciously like the Prime Directive in *Star Trek*, and I often wondered which came first, but regardless...Humans evolved by doing. So, we should let them do. In general, it was a good rule with a noble purpose.

And, let's be honest—a self-protective one.

The last time the human world believed in magic, they came after us with pitchforks, stakes, and bonfires. Confirming our existence to humans? It was something we generally try to avoid on a larger scale.

"You're awful quiet," Emma said while we waited at a stoplight. "You haven't said anything since we left City Hall."

"That tiny storefront is actually City Hall?" I asked.

"Are you changing the subject on purpose?"

"Really, there's nothing to discuss." At least nothing that a detective in a tiny little town like Forkbridge could understand. "Archie stopped by while you were getting the papers, and he let me know there's a clock ticking on Marianna Black." I pulled out my phone and looked. "The card flipped over yesterday around two. That means we only have until tomorrow at two—no, wait, the day after at two—to stop whatever is destined to happen." I tapped on my screen and set a timer on my phone to countdown.

"Destined to happen, huh? That sounds ominous."

"Archie thinks we're using too many human investigative techniques. Well, he thinks I'm using too many human investigative techniques. That I should be taking the lead more and using magic—"

Emma suddenly steered the car hard right onto a gravel road. Without warning, she slammed on the brakes and brought the car to a skidding stop. Turning, she asked with exasperation, "Okay, who the heck is Archie? Is this another ghost?"

I stared at the agitated detective. "It's the owl's name. The magic owl?"

"And he can talk? Like a parrot, he says words, and you can understand him?" she asked.

"It's not like a parrot, no. Archie and I can speak to one another the same way you and I can speak to one another. He can do that with anyone in my family. To you, he would just sound like an owl." I stared at her with disbelief. Where was this coming from? "I thought we went through this already?" I said, echoing Archie from just moments before.

"You told me a whole lot about what you know with regards to Marianna Black, what happened when you found her assistant Christine, and if you use magic in front of me, you usually stop to explain it a little bit. Like with the magic box cube thing. But no, you never told me that you could talk to your owl or your owl could talk to you."

"Well, to be fair, Detective, we barely knew one another."

She raised an eyebrow. "I'm not Emma anymore?"

"What is your problem all of a sudden?" I asked her.

"I think we're using too many human investigative techniques, too—but I don't even know what to ask you to do. I'd hoped by asking you to work with me that you might have something better than what I have to find her, because I'm not finding her." Emma's shoulders were tense, and her hands balled into fists. "I'm a detective in a small town, and there are way too many suspects and too much information and history—much of which happened on the other side of the country, mind you—for me to get as far as I need to get to find her before something happens to her."

"I'll help any way I can—"

"But I don't know how you can help! You do, but I have no idea. You don't trust me, and you're not sharing any of the magical information with me, so I don't even know how I can use you!" She stared at me, her eyes fiery. "So, tell me how you can help me."

I was taken aback by her statements. Emma Sullivan had struck me as a tough cookie, and the pleading tone in her voice seemed out of character. "I was trying not to push into your investigation. You said your brother told you all about me, so I assumed if you wanted me to do something, you would ask."

"My brother's a vampire, Astra. He can give me a recipe for a really good blood martini, but as far as telling me specifics about what you as a witch or as an ex-ministry officer can do?" She held up her hands. "I know that in general, you have some kind of powers, but I don't know what to ask you to do. I mean, I just found out you have a sentient spy drone that can go and check things out and report back. That would've been really useful to know back at the beach. Archie could've followed Downing, and that might have led us to Marianna Black."

I frowned. "Come on. You don't know that."

"Right. Exactly. That's the point, Astra," she said, her cheeks reddening with a new flood of frustration. "I don't know that."

She must've seen something in my stunned expression, something that made her anger dwindle away. Emma took a deep breath, flexed her fingers, and looked at me. "Look, I don't mean to come down on you. I really don't. My parents don't know my brother, Rex, is a vampire. He doesn't tell many people. We've talked about it a lot, the paranormal thing. I get why you hide it."

"Do you?" I asked her sincerely. "Last night, to be honest, I said more than I should have to you. Showed you more than you probably should have seen. My world…" I turned my head, and our eyes locked. "Just a few months ago, I could have been executed for telling you who I was and what I could do," I confessed. "And then there was a revolution, and that rule was wiped away. But still, Emma, I have to tell you—there was a reason for it. For hundreds of years, we all hid in the shadows. To protect ourselves."

"Like I said, I understand why—"

"Don't tell me you understand," I said with a half-smile. "You may think you understand what it's like to have your people hunted, to have that in your history, but I guarantee you—you don't. People will do terrible, terrible things to others if they can't see their humanity."

"You're right. I probably can't understand what it's like to be what you are." Her voice was quieter. "But Astra, you're one of the few people on the planet that can do what you do. And you told me about this whole star card thing. There must be a reason you and I met. There must be a reason Marianna Black came into your shop. If you don't tell me what resources we have, I'm just gonna do what I normally do—"

"—and the whole reason you asked me to join you is that it's not working," I finished. She nodded.

Ami said I could trust Emma Sullivan. She wasn't specific, though, regarding what extent I could do so. But Archie and Emma both were right. I was useless if I wasn't candid. At least about what I could do, Emma seemed to want me to take point.

Which made sense since we were running out of time.

* * *

I SPENT the next ten minutes detailing the powers at my disposal, whether mine or object-granted thanks to purloined tools from the Ministry of Arcane Fugitives.

"Then we need to get you to Marianna Black's trailer," Emma said as she started the car and threw her arm over the seat to back up. "You can strip off those black gloves and grab everything that's not nailed down while I look through these papers." We veered back onto the road. "See if you get anything off the stuff."

"So, that's another weird idea I had." I buckled my seatbelt and pulled it tight as Emma's lead foot pushed the accelerator toward the floor. "I know you're having trouble finding any witnesses to anything, but you actually have tons of witnesses."

"I do?"

"The parrots in the park," I told her. "If she was grabbed near her dressing room the way you think? They would've had to pull her almost all the way through the park to get to the waterfall. The birds would have seen everything."

"Right, but...they're birds..."

"I can read objects, I can read people—and by people, I mean pretty much any sentient being. And don't forget we have access to a talking bird," I pointed out. "I know those macaws understood Archie. Maybe he can communicate with them in a way that we can't."

She thought about it briefly and then nodded. "I think this is a good plan. After that, I think you should try the thing with the necklace again? With the shirt direction?"

"Pendulum?"

"Right, the pendulum. See if we can get a direction." Emma fell quiet as the sunset highlighted her dark hair with shots of auburn. "Oh, and Astra?"

"Yep?"

"Thanks for trusting me." She glanced over at me in the passenger seat, and her expression was a mix of surprise and gratitude. "I'm not a psychic or anything, but it really feels like you're supposed to help me. Like we were supposed to find each other and save this woman." She looked back once more, a sheepish look on her face. "That sounds crazy, huh?"

"I have a talking owl supposedly gifted to me from an ancient Greek goddess. I'm not sure I'm in a position to tell anyone else they're crazy."

CHAPTER FIFTEEN

*P*arrot Paradise was quiet.

Detective Sullivan unlocked the front gate with a key, and we slipped inside. Just as I was about to close the gate, Archie swooped in behind us and then flew off swiftly into the park without a word. "Ford Senior gave me this to use during the investigation," Emma told me quietly. "I don't know if anybody's here. It looked like the whole crew was at the beach."

"The movie crew. There must be some employees from Parrot Paradise here to take care of the birds, right? And I didn't see Rick's father." If there were people in the park, though, I couldn't see any.

"Marianna's tent thing is this way." Emma

started down a dirt path in the opposite direction from the grotto where I'd found Christine. "We think she was grabbed just outside of it. Hey, speaking of that. Can you use your touchy-feely psychic vision stuff on a place? Like, touch the ground and know what happened there?"

"Sometimes. It depends on what happened there and how many people have walked across that spot. Public places can be tricky, though. They don't generally have an intense tie to the person I'm looking for. Or any single person, for that matter." I could see the sun setting through the tree canopy, and the parrots seemed uncharacteristically quiet.

"It's been cordoned off since she was kidnapped, but that part of the park is usually open to the public." Emma lifted her long hair from her neck and fanned herself as we walked. "I hope someone's around to turn the lights on," Emma murmured as we continued down the path. "Twilight's coming a bit faster than I expected."

"It's not, really. The trees are just really dense."

The dank pseudo-rain forest felt like it was closing in around me as we traveled deeper into the park. Light shot through the leaves only sporadically, and shadows grew denser the further we went along the path. The dim light that filtered down and the eerie quiet of the silent birds made me jumpy. I half expected something to leap out at me—even though I heard no voices.

"Here we are." Emma led me down a path to a makeshift campsite set up in a clearing. Small canvas tents had been erected in a semicircle around a large table at the center. Movie cameras, lights, and other equipment were dropped haphazardly. "Normally, this is the snack area." She pointed to the booths just beyond the outer ring of tents. "Now it's set up for the actors and crew to hang out in when they're not shooting. See that tent in the northwest corner? That's Marianna's. Christine stayed in there as well."

I pushed aside the canvas door and ducked under the crime scene tape to find a small "room." The floor was dirt, and I frowned—not conducive to reading the place, unfortunately. Soil has a long memory. One person being grabbed? Barely a blip on the timeline of a thing that's seen from eighteen thousand to two million years (or more) of history.

On one side of the tent, there was a small futon couch and sofa table. The sofa held a blue silk robe draped over it neatly. On the other side of the tent sat an elevated desk that looked like a makeup station with a large, brightly lit mirror. Next to the makeup station was a small refrigerator.

"That's exactly what I need," I told Emma, pointing at the mirror.

"A mirror? Really?"

"You know the story of Snow White? There's a reason that a mirror was pivotal to the story."

It might've been more beneficial to bring Ami —she could use the mirror for scrying. It wasn't a talent I had...though if you thought about it, I was kind of scrying. Just not the same way that Ami would, and I couldn't venture as widely in what I saw.

"Okay, school me," Emma said. "Why a mirror?"

"Mirrors reflect everything back at us, so they see everything. My sister could scry this mirror and flip through everything it ever saw—she, unlike me, can do proper captromancy. Unfortunately, my talent works a little bit differently."

I moved the chair to the side and stepped up to the mirror. Holding my hands in front of me, palms out and fingers splayed, I reached forward and touched the tips of my fingers to its cool surface and waited.

Hesitation.

I pushed forward.

It pushed back.

I stopped pushing.

The mirror relaxed and ever so hesitantly relaxed its guard. Slowly, carefully, I followed that relaxation until I was in.

Once I secured the connection and felt reasonably sure it wasn't dangerous, I took a deep breath, pressed my full palms against the glass, and opened myself up to whatever it wanted to tell me. "Get paper and a pen out. I'm going to tell you what I see as it comes."

"Got it," Emma said. Her voice already sounded somewhat faraway. "I'm ready whenever you are."

At first, it was just a haze, the fog you would see coming off a warm lake after a cold front blew in. It swirled and raced in my mind's eye. I waited.

There's no rushing this part. It's like the beginning of a date, the part when two people size one another up. As the object dials into what I wish to know, it seems to take some time to decide what it's willing to share.

Yes, I know I said items have no agenda, but when you're reading them? With some objects, they almost seem sentient. I've never understood it, but there's no point in fighting it. It's going to do what it will do. Eventually, the murkiness fades, and ghostly images take form.

"I can see Marianna," I told Emma. "She's wearing a black shirt with a checked pattern. Black, with white checks. She's sitting in the makeup chair, her chin in her hand. She looks sad and is staring at herself in the mirror, her back to the room."

"That's the shirt she was wearing the day she disappeared," Emma told me, her pen scratching quickly on her pad. "Is anyone with her?"

"Christine is sitting behind her on the futon." The assistant was pleading with her, but there was no sound yet. "She's agitated."

"Marianna?"

"Christine. She's talking rapidly, using her hands, but I can't hear what she's saying."

"Do you read lips?" Emma asked.

I opened my eyes and glared at the detective over my shoulder. "It's not enough that I can put my hands on a mirror and see what happened a day ago?" I asked with an eyebrow raise. "Now you want me to read lips, too?"

"Hey, you're the one that's been withholding information about your powers. How am I supposed to know what you can do and what you can't?" She waved toward the mirror. "Go ahead, finish before someone shows up. This would be hard to explain."

"Right." I turned back and watched the two women.

Christine stood up and paced while Marianna continued to stare into the mirror, looking dejected and miserable. "She stopped her rant at Marianna. Now Christine is walking over to that small refrigerator next to this makeup station. She's reaching in and pulling out a metal tumbler." I watched as she stood up and shoved it toward Marianna. Marianna shook her head no and pushed the tumbler away. "She's trying to get Marianna to drink whatever is in the tumbler, I think, but Marianna doesn't want to."

"You're still not getting sound?"

"No, but it's a mirror. Mirrors tend to really focus on what's seen, not what's heard. Joel Clemens just walked in," I told her quickly. "He's grabbing the tumbler and yelling at Christine. At least I think he's yelling. He certainly looks angry."

"Joel Clemens? The guy that hasn't spoken a word to either one of us since this whole thing started? The one that trails along behind

Hayward Beals all the time? That Joel Clemens?" Emma's voice traveled behind me, and then I heard a refrigerator door open. "Wherever this tumbler was, it's not here now."

"Christine's pushing him. Not hard, just hard enough to make an aggressive point. He looks frustrated. He's grabbing for the tumbler," I told her rapidly as the situation escalated behind my closed eyes. "Marianna is doing nothing, just sitting in her chair and looking helpless, like she doesn't know what to do. Ouch!"

"What?" Emma asked.

"Joel Clemens just knocked the tumbler out of Christine's hand," I told her, slowly peeling one hand off the mirror to point in the direction it rolled. "Check that way. They just kept arguing; it doesn't look like anyone went to get it."

I heard furniture being moved. "I found it! It rolled under the futon. How we missed this when we cataloged this room, I have no idea." I could hear plastic rustling. "We can get this to the crime lab, but honestly? I don't know that we'll get anything back in time."

"None of what I'm watching makes any sense," I told Emma. "When I met Christine, I would've sworn that someone had tried to kill her. But what I'm looking at?" Joel continued arguing with

Christine and looked like he was pleading with her. She looked angry, yelling back at him while repeatedly pointing at Marianna. "It looks to me like Joel was trying to protect Marianna Black." I opened my eyes and removed my hands. "From Christine."

* * *

BEFORE EMMA COULD RESPOND, Archie swooped in. "Hide!"

"We have to hide. Someone's coming!" I hissed, leaping to action. I grabbed Emma and dragged her behind the futon. With both of us crouched into the tiny space, I held up my finger to my lips, and she nodded in response.

Archie settled himself on the top of the futon, his talons wrapped around the back bar, and stared out over the room menacingly.

"This is where your daughter stayed, as far as I know," Richard Ford, Rick's father, said as he entered the tent. "Since there's crime scene tape, I don't know if I should be letting you in here. I wouldn't want to get into trouble."

"She's my daughter," a woman responded. I tried to move slightly to get a sense of what was happening (and a look at Marianna's mother), but

Emma reached out and grabbed my arm with more force than I would've thought her capable of. She shook her head no and pointed downward. I rolled my eyes. "It doesn't seem like anyone in your tiny little town is doing a damn thing to find her. The detective I spoke to didn't even think she'd been kidnapped. He thinks she's off partying in Miami."

Emma frowned.

"Well, the lady detective on the case has been looking for her. My son called me and told me she went to the…ah, gathering at the beach to ask questions about something or other," Richard informed her.

Suddenly, a second bird appeared on the futon next to Archie. The brightly colored tail feathers thwacked me in the face as it inched closer to the owl. "Rawk! I see you, I see you," it thundered.

"Shut up, birdbrain. They're hiding," Archie told the brilliant green Amazon Parrot. He puffed up to twice his size and glared ominously. "Get out of here."

"Rawk! Rude owl, rude owl," the parrot said and then let out what sounded like a giggle. "I know something you don't know. I know something you don't know. Rawk!"

"What on earth is an owl—"

"Focus on me, Mr. Ford! You're around these birds all day. And her fiancé?" the woman snapped. "Are they looking for him as well? He's been missing for four days."

"Her fiancé?" Richard asked, but his tone... there was something odd in his manner. He sounded like someone feigning surprise. Like he knew the information he was getting, but was trying to pretend he was learning it for the first time.

"Bart's gone, Bart's gone," the parrot said and then squawked. Its head snaked back and forth as the bird stared at the owl.

"Shut up!" Archie hissed.

"Rude bird, rude bird. Dingy feather brain," the parrot responded.

"Who are you again?" Mrs. Black asked.

"I own this park, ma'am."

The parrot made a sound like a siren and then said, "Dimwitted dunderhead, dimwitted dunderhead. Rawk!"

"You know, just because you can talk doesn't mean you should talk," Archie muttered. He glanced down at us with a worried look on his face. "We don't want the dunderhead to come over here. You get me, moron?"

"Rude bird, rude bird," the parrot responded. "Poseidon's a good bird. A very good bird. Rawk!"

Emma and I stared at each other, our eyes wide, as Archie and Poseidon argued with one another six inches from the tops of our heads. Luckily, Marianna's mother was not easily distracted by talking birds, and she relentlessly continued to question Mr. Ford.

"So, you're not associated with the movie shoot at all. Do you even know my daughter, sir?" Without waiting for him to answer, Mrs. Black continued. "Where is Hayward Beals? I want to speak with him right now."

"He took the entire crew to Daytona for the day. Since the movie is shut down for a couple of days, he thought it would be good for them to get away." There was a long pause. "You know, to decompress." Another long pause. "I guess they were pretty upset."

"Daytona."

"Yes, ma'am."

"Daytona is a beach?" Mrs. Black asked acidly.

"Yes, ma'am," Richard Ford responded nervously.

"Do you have any idea who I am, Mr. Ford?"

"You in trouble now, son," the parrot said quietly. "Trouble, trouble, trouble. Rawk!"

"You said you were Marianna Black's mother," Richard Ford responded. I wasn't sure, but there was something like fear in his voice.

"I am. Do you know who my husband is, Mr. Ford?"

"No, ma'am."

"My husband is Gerald Black. Perhaps you've heard of him."

Gerald Black was the CEO of Black Enterprises, a technology company headquartered in California that designs, develops, and sells consumer surveillance equipment so cheap, it was turning the entire United States into one gigantic *YouTube* video. I'd seen him on the cover of *Weeksnews*.

"I was unaware of that, ma'am." The surprise in his voice was no longer feigned. "Your daughter never mentioned her father. Or her family."

"Hello ma baby, hello ma honey, hello my ragtime gal," the parrot sang, bouncing up and down with enthusiasm. "Baby, my heart's on fi-i-i-i-ire—"

"Hey, Poseidon, read the room," Archie told him menacingly.

"My daughter is a liberal left-wing socialist and has rejected her moneyed capitalist upbringing—as well as put herself in opposition to her father's well-publicized lifelong ambition to ensure there is a camera in the doorbell of every home in this country," Mrs. Black told Richard Ford in a clipped voice. "Thanks to Gerald being a friend to nearly every paparazzi outfit in the world because of what he does, we were able to keep our connection to Marianna out of the papers. Something my daughter wanted but didn't seem to appreciate was due to her father's company and position of status," the woman added.

"Of course. I was lucky. My son appreciated what I did for a living and followed in my—"

"Mr. Ford?" Mrs. Black interrupted.

"Yes, ma'am?"

"I don't care."

"Yes, ma'am."

"Score!" Poseidon squawked, flapping his wings.

"You have an hour to get Hayward Beals here before I let loose every dog of war my money can buy," Mrs. Black told him. "And I guarantee you, Mr. Ford, the size of the pack I can afford is substantial."

"Oh, honey, baby, give me a kiss," the parrot said.

Archie looked down at me. "I give up."

Ford didn't respond.

"And I'm only giving you that hour out of respect for my daughter's choice not to be associated with her father. If two hours pass, that choice will no longer be consequential to my decisions, and your little bird zoo won't have enough parking spots for the number of press vans that will descend on this place. Do we understand each other?"

"Yes, ma'am."

There was a rustling sound of canvas, and then Ford's urgent voice.

"Beals, it's me. We got a problem. You need to get back here now."

* * *

"Plot twist," Emma said. We stood up and stretched as soon as we were sure Ford had left the tent. "The daughter of Gerald Black." She looked thoughtfully around the room. "If they are that rich, why did it take her so long to get here? Those people can afford private planes and teleportation machines. Well, if there are secret teleportation machines." Emma turned. "Are there? You would know, right?"

I ignored her question. "When did you talk to her? Mrs. Black, I mean."

"That's just it. The detective that gave her information? That wasn't me. Marianna's emergency contact was Christine. Not her mother," Emma told me. "I didn't call her family. Christine said she would do it."

Archie and Poseidon stood quietly, side by side, watching Emma and me as we spoke. Every once in a while, the owl would glare at the colorful bird.

"So, was it just me, or did it sound like Ford was involved with whatever's going on here?" I asked her. "You notice he said that 'we' have a problem, not 'you' have a problem. And we heard what Beals said about the mother to Downing."

"Yeah, he didn't seem very concerned about Marianna's mother coming at all. I didn't even see the woman, and just from what I overheard? I'd be concerned about that woman. I'd be even more concerned about her husband."

"Is it possible Beals doesn't know?"

Emma shrugged. "I suppose anything is possible. What caught my attention, though, is the claim that Marianna's fiancé is missing. Didn't you say that she was meeting with him two days ago?"

"I may be blue away from you, and then again, I may be gay—"

I whirled on the chatty parrot. "Poseidon, dude, you're adorable, and your repertoire of old songs is impressive, but you're also making this a lot harder. Be quiet."

The parrot whistled from high to low as if mimicking a bomb dropping, looking insulted. "I get no respect," he muttered. "No respect. Rawk!"

I turned back to Emma. "Anyway, I hear you. How could she have met with him two days ago and him be missing for four days?"

"Well, if I remember correctly, you didn't say she met with him; you said she thought she was meeting with him." Emma frowned. "Maybe."

I looked around the room once more. "Everything seems to be pointing to her fiancé and Christine being important pieces of the puzzle. We have no idea where her fiancé is, but Christine's still in the hospital."

"Time to go talk to Christine, then."

"After you get what you want you don't want it, if I gave you the moon, you'd grow tired of it soon," Poseidon crooned, his wings opening wide and his bright green chest thrust out as if he was Dean Martin appearing on...um, whatever Dean

Martin would have appeared on back in the day. "Rawk!"

"Hey, before we go—Archie, the parrots can understand you. Do you have some special way that you can communicate with the parrots? It would really help us to be able to ask them what they saw."

The owl's head turned swiftly on his neck, and his large, unblinking eyes bore into me. "I am the goddess Athena's own owl. I am a divine creature —a magical animal. There are myths about me. Bards have sung songs about me. There are statues in honor of me—"

"Well, of Athena, you mean—"

"I am a goddess's creature and that"—he flung out his wing toward Poseidon—"is a rain forest pigeon! And you think I can communicate with it? My intellect dwarfs that dimwitted twittering disco hussy!" he told me haughtily. "What do you think we would talk about? Birdseed? Pooping on cars? I think not."

"Rude bird, rude bird," Poseidon told Archie.

"I'll spare you the ego speech he just made, but Archie can't talk to the bird. Well, he can the same way we can, but he doesn't have any special communication ability."

"That's a shame," Emma said, frowning. "The

bird seems to be super nosey. I bet he saw something."

"Sounds of the rude world heard in the day, lull'd by the moonlight, have all pass'd away!" Poseidon sang, his head tilted so he looked positively coquettish. "Rawk!"

CHAPTER SIXTEEN

"*W*hat do you mean, she's not here?" Emma asked a petite nurse with a perpetual frown. "The woman almost drowned yesterday. Wouldn't that necessitate at least a few days in the hospital?"

"She was uninsured," the harsh nurse told the detective—as if this explained everything. "Besides, Ms. Chandler's lungs were completely clear, and she had no ill effects from her experience. No edema. There were no submersion injuries. Frankly, it was as if she hadn't drowned at all." The nurse looked at Emma. "Didn't the other detective tell you all this?"

"Isn't this some kind of HIPAA violation?" I

asked, my eyebrow raised. "You telling us her medical situation, I mean? Most of us think our medical and health information should be private. I think the federal government actually agrees with us now."

"Ms. Chandler is part of a criminal investigation. Victims have no such expectation of privacy when the police ask a question. Since you're a police officer," the nurse told me as she leaned forward and looked down her nose at my outfit, "I would think you'd be aware of that."

"I'm not a police officer."

"Scuba diver?" she asked snidely.

"When was she discharged?" Emma asked.

"Am I allowed to tell you, or is little Miss know-it-all over there going to complain about another HIPAA violation?"

"When was she discharged?" Emma asked slowly, her voice illustrating her exasperation.

"She was discharged from the emergency room." Nurse Ratchet scanned the computer screen in front of her rapidly. "Technically, she was never admitted to the hospital. Just treated in the emergency room and then sent on her way. Like I told you, there was nothing wrong with her."

Emma looked at me. "If she's not here, where would she be?"

My cell phone vibrated on my hip, and I unclipped it from its holster. The screen showed Ami's cheerful picture. I tapped to accept the call. "Hey, Ami, what's up?"

"Stephen Thompson's back and talking to Ayla," Ami told me as if I would know precisely who Stephen Thompson was. "Ayla is not sure what else to ask him, though, so she wanted me to call you and see if you are planning on heading home anytime soon."

"I wasn't planning on it, no."

"Oh."

"Anyway, who is Stephen Thompson?"

"Oh, oh, right. Stephen Thompson is old Mr. Thompson. You know, from the old Thompson place? The ghost that came to talk to Ayla in the parking lot?" She blurted the information out in a rush. "He was the one that told Ayla Marianna Black was at the old Thompson place."

"But Marianna Black was not at the old Thompson place," I pointed out. "There was a guy with a gun that wanted to shoot us at the old Thompson place, so not sure I need to rush home to listen to anything Stephen Thompson has to say. That ghost almost got me killed."

"Right, no, yeah, I can understand what you're saying, but he says that you guys were looking in the wrong place." She covered the phone and shouted back and forth with someone, but it was so muffled I couldn't make it out. "You were looking on top?"

"On top of what?"

Emma held up her hands as if to ask what was going on, and I shrugged in response.

"On top of what?" Ami shouted in my ear, forgetting to cover the mike. I winced. "Can you ask him?"

"That was my ear, Ami," I told her. "Who are you shouting at?"

"Ayla. Sorry," she said and then covered the phone with her hand again. The muffling returned but not as complete as before. "Should I just tell them to come back here? Or go to the old Thompson place?" A few seconds later, my sister uncovered the phone. "Ayla said you guys should just come back here. She can get you information so you can find exactly where they're holding Marianna Black, but she doesn't know if there's other stuff you might need to know. Or stuff you want to ask him. You know?"

I gestured for Emma to follow and walked toward the sliding glass door at the hospital's visitors' area entrance. "It's starting to get late, and we're trying to find Christine Chandler. Let me relay all this to Emma. Give me a sec." I turned to the detective and told her what Ami had told me—after making sure no one could overhear us.

"Christine's not here, and we have no idea where she is. Your house is just ten minutes away." Emma took off toward her Malibu. "Let's just go by there and see what this ghost has to say. While we're there, we can grab a sandwich or something." She looked up at the darkening sky. "Since we can't find Christine, we probably need to track down Marianna Black's mom. If there's even a tiny possibility I can do that while telling her I rescued her daughter? I'd rather do that."

We jumped in the car, switched on the ignition, and went hurtling toward Arden House at an utterly unnecessary speed.

* * *

"Your sister is in the great room talking to the ghost," Aunt Gwennie said as she came out of the kitchen to greet Emma and me. "If you'd like, I can prepare a couple of plates for the two of you. We had meatloaf for dinner."

"You, ma'am, are now my favorite person in the entire world," Emma told Aunt Gwennie, looking relieved. The detective haphazardly tossed her purse onto a side table like she lived here and turned. "Have I mentioned how much I like your family?"

"You haven't actually tried the meatloaf yet, so you might want to hold your opinion there."

"Astra Arden, how dare you insult my cooking. If I recall, you can barely boil water," Aunt Gwennie told me with affection. "My meatloaf would be world-renowned if I cooked it for anyone that didn't live in this house." I gave her a smile in return and moved toward the great room, but she reached her hand out and lightly touched my arm to stop me. "Just be aware that your mother is in there helping Ayla. Don't... Don't start anything, Astra."

"I never start anything, Aunt Gwennie," I told her with another smile. She looked at me with disapproval, sighed, and turned to head back into the kitchen. "I swear, sometimes I think she has no faith in me."

"I heard that!" Aunt Gwennie called over her shoulder.

"It's about time that you came back," my mother said as we walked into the great room.

The entire family (except Aunt Gwennie) sat along the side of the room on the huge couch, gathered together staring at Ayla—who looked frustrated.

"Mr. Thompson said that when you went to the old Thompson place, you weren't looking in the right spot," my thirteen-year-old sister told me with a sharp eye. "He said you were looking on the top, but Marianna Black wasn't on the top."

"Ami mentioned that when she called me," I noted. "But the top of what?"

"The top of the property. You know, on top. Like on top of the ground." Ayla waved her hands in front of her as she tried to explain, but her young face tightened into a frown of frustration. "She's not on top of the ground. She's underground. You didn't look underground at all, did you?"

"What underground?" Emma asked Ayla.

Ayla turned toward Mom with a pleading look. "I'm not explaining it right, am I?"

"You're doing fine, Ayla. Mr. Thompson let us know that you've been back to the property twice, and while he tried to show you where Marianna Black was being held, he said you ignored him," my mother told us. "You were on the wrong side of the property. She's being held closer to where the gunman shot at you."

"I wasn't ignoring the guy," I told her. "I can't see ghosts, remember?"

"Before we get much further, here. I don't want to forget to give you this." Althea stood up and handed me a glass bottle with thick blue liquid inside. "This is going to counteract that drug, gravel, you guys think she might have taken. From what Mr. Thompson said, I'm almost sure that's the drug that she's on." Althea frowned. "And from what he described, it doesn't sound like she's doing well. You really should get over there."

"The last time we were over there—well, the time before the last time we were over there—someone shot at us." I accepted the blue bottle and turned to hand it to Emma. "You asked us to come here, so give us the information we need to find her. Where is she?"

"Mr. Thompson says she's in the storm cellar," my mother answered. "Underneath one of the collapsed buildings is a hatch that leads to a storm shelter." Waving us over, Mom pointed to a piece of paper on the table. It looked like a hastily drawn map of the old Thompson property, an X marking a spot at the large building's northwest corner. "This is where Thompson claims she's being held."

"Is anyone with her?" Emma asked, scanning the map. "Any guards, anyone else being held down there?"

Ayla looked into empty air. "No, no one's been with her for about a day. It's just her down there. Mr. Thompson also wanted to tell you he doesn't think the people that were shooting at you were the bad people."

"Who does he think they were?" I asked.

"Mr. Thompson said they were scouring the place as well. It's possible they were doing the same thing as you," my mother said. "Looking for Marianna Black to rescue her."

It didn't occur to me previously, but it's possible. Especially now that we know Marianna's father is Gerald Black—those people could afford to loose a private army on Forkbridge to find their missing daughter. I stared at the map, thinking.

"I know you're probably going to deck me for suggesting this, but it would be way more useful to head back to the old Thompson property with old Thompson," Emma said under her breath.

"Mr. Thompson said he heard that," Ayla told Emma.

"I'm not bringing my mother, and I'm not bringing my thirteen-year-old sister," I told Emma. "That means we're out of options for that. So, let's figure out another plan."

"Not entirely out of options," Archie announced, swooping in through an open window. What looked to be an elegant landing quickly went sideways, and he skidded to an uncivilized stop on the floor. "This floor is incredibly slippery. Polished concrete on house floors. Who does that?" He leaped up on the coffee table and then once again to the back of a chair. My mother tilted her head in a slight regal bow even as she glared at the talons digging into her Victorian chair. "You can just use your star power."

"Star power?" I frowned. "What are you talking about?"

"Hold out your palms." I did. Archie looked frustrated. "Okay, maybe I should have been more specific. Take your gloves off, and hold out your hands, palms up."

I peeled off my long black gloves and passed them to Emma. Standing with my feet slightly apart, I raised my forearms and turned my uncovered palms up.

"Ayla, honey, go grab your sister's hands," the owl told her.

Ayla hopped up and placed her hands in mine. "Okay, now what do I do?" My younger sister looked excited, proud, and terrified in equal parts.

"Just relax," Archie said. The owl leaned forward and touched his forehead to our clasped hands. As soon as he backed away, our hands exploded a glow of bright white on the faces of everyone watching —as if our clasped hands held a star. "There, that should be done. You can let go now."

"I didn't feel anything at all. What did you do with your head?" Ayla asked Archie as she let go and turned around. "Wait, where did Mr. Thompson go?"

"I'm still here, of course," the ghost said politely.

I stared at the translucent man standing in my living room dressed in clothing that would've been super fashionable if it was the early nineteen hundreds. "Mr. Thompson?" I asked.

He broke into a smile. "You can see me?"

"I can see you."

"Wait. What? No. But...Well, I can't see him!" Ayla shouted, looking panicked. "Why can't I see him anymore?" Ayla whirled on Archie, her hands balled into fists. "Did you just give my powers to my sister? My sister, who has a magical cube that can protect her and probably a bunch of other—"

Archie looked unconcerned about Ayla's panicky outburst. "I did, but it's only—"

"I didn't say you could do that! You took my powers? How could you take my powers? You're a terrible bird!" Ayla shouted as she lurched toward Archie, her arms rising toward him with deliberate speed. My mother grabbed her just before she wrapped her hands around the owl's skinny neck.

Wrapping her arms around her furious daughter, my mother told my sister in the most gentle of voices, "Ayla, this is not the way we show respect to the goddess's owl—"

"Screw the goddess's owl, that butthead took my powers away!" she shouted, tears rolling down her face. She struggled against my mother's iron grip, but it was futile. "You give them back! I didn't say you could do that! Haven't you heard of consent, you idiot?"

Archie narrowed his eyes and raised himself up. "You, little girl, chose to priestess yourself to Athena. Do I need to remind you that was your consent?"

Sheesh. And I thought the military took that stuff seriously. Archie's expression wasn't that far from my drill instructor.

"I take it back!" she shouted, sobbing.

"No take-backsies," Archie told her with frosty triumph.

Emma stared at the unfolding drama with wide eyes. Considering she could only hear half of the conversation, I had no idea what she was thinking. Still, I could imagine we did not impress her.

"Is this permanent?" I asked Archie. "Did you really just give me her powers?"

"Temporarily, yes. Ayla's a thirteen-year-old girl, and it appears people are trying to kill multiple other people in this situation. You needed to be able to talk to Thompson, and we wouldn't want to put your mother or your sister at risk unnecessarily," Archie explained matter-of-factly. "This is what needed to be done, and so I did it. You can return her powers to her as soon as we recover Marianna Black."

I wished he'd shown Ayla more consideration. I was used to just following orders—although, granted, not orders given by an owl—and though I was a little annoyed about the lack of discussion beforehand? I couldn't argue with Archie's logic.

Ayla, on the other hand, looked utterly betrayed.

"Ayla," I said quietly as I moved toward my sister. "Thank you so much for lending me your powers. Without you, we might never have found Marianna Black. You were pivotal to rescuing her," I explained as if the rescue had already taken place. I held out my hand to shake hers. "When you're a little older? You'll get to do the exciting part."

She glared at my outstretched hand and rolled her eyes. "I can do it now," she muttered. "I could have come."

"I have no doubt. But you know what? It's really my fault. I would be completely distracted worrying about you. Even though you can totally take care of yourself? It's much easier for me if I just borrow your power. Just for a few hours."

She tried to avoid looking into my eyes, but my face was so close to hers it was tough. Finally, she looked into my eyes. "Well, I mean, if you're that easily distracted that you couldn't even do what you need to do." She reached out and shook my hand once. "Fine, but I want them back like, the moment you don't need them anymore."

"Deal."

"And you better be nice to Mr. Thompson. He

didn't have to help us," she warned me, shaking her finger at me. "He's a nice old man. Most of the ghosts are snippy, and he's not."

"Absolutely." I stood up and looked at Emma. "You ready for our third trip to the old Thompson place?"

"In the dark, too," she said with feigned excitement. "I mean, the last time we went, and it was dark, it was super exciting."

"This time, we take my Jeep," I told her. "On the way, we'll talk about all the cool stuff I stole from the military." My mother glared at me. "I mean the interesting things I picked up in Imp City that are in no way stolen and were absolutely legitimately bought and paid for." Mom continued staring. "That you could get at any paranormal outdoor shop." Her icy gaze continued. "And which never, ever explode."

* * *

"I REALLY LIKE YOUR FAMILY," Emma said again as she slid into the Jeep.

"I'd be happy to lend them to you. Just let me know what day you'll want to take them."

"Is the ghost, like, riding in the Jeep with us?"

The detective turned around and scanned the backseat.

"Yeah, he's here. He's sitting on your lap," I told Emma, pointing.

She pressed herself all the way into the seat and raised both her arms. Her face was equal parts curious and horrified. "You're kidding me, right?"

"Yes, I'm kidding. Mr. Thompson is sitting in the backseat." I glanced in the rearview mirror. "How are you doing, Mr. Thompson?"

"Quite fine, thank you, young lady," the older man answered. "I very much appreciate you coming to get the other young lady off of my property. Obviously, I'm not a heartless man, and I don't want to see anything happen to her, but I also don't want to see that woman die in my storm shelter for purely selfish reasons." The ghost sniffed. "There's only one ghost that will be haunting the Thompson property, and that ghost will forevermore be me."

"Don't you get lonely?" I asked him.

"Not really. You know the Cambridge property about an acre down?"

"I'm not familiar with it, no."

"Well, old Mrs. Cambridge and I often meet for bridge. She's been after me for fifty years to move into my property." Mr. Thompson shuddered. "If I was suddenly sharing a tract of land with a young, attractive ghost? Oh, dear me, no—I would never hear the end of it."

I quickly related the conversation to Emma.

"Everyone has their own motivation, I suppose." Emma looked back into the empty backseat. "I, for one, really appreciate your help, Mr. Thompson."

"Of course, young lady. I may be dead, but I'm still a citizen of Forkbridge. I don't want to see it go to crime and villainy."

I stepped down on the clutch, put the keys in the ignition, and started up the Jeep. "She's not as fast as your Malibu, but give me a big rock, and I can climb right the heck over it. My wheels are also way more fun than yours on a beach."

"I can get to the beach faster," Emma said as we pulled out. "Mr. Thompson, did you see who brought Marianna Black to your place and hid her?" I was impressed she had turned politely and asked the question toward the ghost instead of just shouting it into thin air.

"I did not, unfortunately," Mr. Thompson answered. "I did see a man, and then a woman, come to check on her. But I didn't see who brought her there initially."

"The man and woman you saw that came to check on Marianna," I said so Emma could get the gist of what Mr. Thompson was relating. "Did they come together or separately?"

"Separately, my dear."

"Emma, do we have a picture of Christine Chandler?" I asked.

Emma pulled out her phone and googled. "Here's one," she said as she made the small image bigger. "One of the benefits of this case involving a celebrity." She held the phone up between the seats toward the back. "Was this the woman?"

"Yes, yes, I believe that was her," Thompson said, sounding unsure. "She looked much different than that, but it certainly could be her."

"Everything points to Christine Chandler having something to do with this, but I have to be honest with you; I never ever would've thought it," I told Emma. "That girl seemed completely sincere and incredibly worried about her friend. And, I mean, I saw her drown. I did CPR, for goodness sake. I saw her cough up water. Could she have faked that?"

"It's a movie set, so maybe?" As we drove, Emma continued to flip through her phone. "Well, here's one reason she was totally convincing." Emma held up the phone toward me. "Christine Chandler is also an actress. In fact, it seems that Christine's career is the one on the downswing, while Marianna Black's is on the upswing."

"Ami can see through acting, though," I murmured. Even if I couldn't. "My sister didn't say anything about there being anything off about her."

"Your sister isn't used to being in a high adrenalin situation," Emma pointed out. "It's entirely possible she was too freaked out to sense anything. Holy crap!" Emma yelped. "Christine Chandler was in the running for this part. She lost it—to Marianna Black."

CHAPTER SEVENTEEN

"Be quiet," I told my growling stomach. "We have more important things to do than eat." My innards gave one more protesting groan and then fell quiet as I turned off the Jeep.

Emma slipped quietly out of the Jeep and scanned the overgrown brush at the front of the old Thompson place. "All seems quiet on the western front," she told me quietly. "Well, except for your stomach. And I should mention you're not the only one that's hungry. We really should have eaten that meatloaf. I also should mention that assessment—the 'quiet with no one around'—was my same assessment the other night, too." Emma paused. "You know, before we were shot at."

"Comforting," I responded in a low tone as I waited near the Jeep and scrutinized the dark street for threats. "Good to know I shouldn't trust your assessment."

"That's east," Mr. Thompson said as he floated out onto the street. "She said the western front, but that's east. My property is on the eastern side of the road." Mr. Thompson pursed his lips. "No wonder you people haven't found that woman. Don't even know east from west."

We parked half a block away from the property line, tucked in the shadows behind an extensive scrub of brush. Anyone lurking about the old Thompson place would have a tough time spotting us.

"What's the plan?" I asked Emma.

"Any possibility you can touch the corner of the old Thompson place and get a reading off the whole thing?" the detective asked hopefully.

"Not really, but we can send him in to report back," I told her, pointing toward the ghost she couldn't see. "Thompson can do a tour of the place and give us the lowdown."

"I'd be happy to, young lady." The old ghost bowed and floated swiftly off toward his home.

Suddenly he stopped, turned, and added, "Be back in a few minutes; it shouldn't take long." I nodded.

As I watched him drift off, my stomach growled again, and a sharp pang of hunger made me grit my teeth.

"Here," Emma said, and she held out a small plastic pouch of beef jerky. "I always carry some with me. Never know when an investigation is going to run long and not be conveniently located near a McDonald's."

"Thanks." I accepted the bag gratefully and chewed on the peppered beef jerky. I hoped my stomach would cease its demands for at least an hour. "You still haven't gotten a call from Marianna Black's mother?"

Emma reached into her pocket and pulled out her phone. "Nope. No call, no text, no nothing."

It seemed strange the detective assigned hadn't been contacted by the missing victim's mother. I know Emma said the other detectives didn't like to work with her, but there were many people I didn't want to work with back at the ministry.

I still had to work with them. Follow the rules. Follow operational regulations. A small police department was still a bureaucracy with, presumably, those same things. Wasn't it a given that you refer inquiries to the person formally handling the case? At the very least, wouldn't you have to report the contact?

"When you say the other detectives don't like to work with you," I asked quietly, "like, how far does this go? Would they really talk to Mrs. Black and not let you know they've done so?"

"A few days ago, I would've said no, but at the moment?" Emma shrugged. "I don't know. Maybe they realized who she was, and they're trying to get in with the rich people." Emma frowned and thought for a moment, her forehead wrinkled. Finally, she shrugged. "I just don't know."

"So, a theory. What if the detective that called her mother isn't actually a detective at all?" I suggested. Emma frowned again. "It just occurred to me that in the military and law enforcement, procedures are fundamental. Like, really stupidly important. Still true?"

"Yeah, of course."

"If you withheld information on a case, that case would be put in jeopardy. I mean, it would be a huge breach of duty. Right?" Emma nodded. "So, I'm just wondering if any of these other detectives really dislike you so much that they would risk getting suspended or fired just to trip you up."

Emma blinked. "I don't know that they would get fired for that."

"Well, I'm just saying. My feeling is if they're old school, they wouldn't. Regardless of whether they like you or not, they'd follow the rules, right? So, if we look at things objectively, we don't know that a detective from the police department called the victim's mother. We just overheard her claim that." My eyes widened. "And you mentioned the other detectives don't even think she was kidnapped. True?"

Emma nodded. "Last I heard."

"So if that's the case, why call the mother of someone you don't think is really kidnapped? And Mrs. Black isn't exactly easy to reach, right? Rich people, especially well-known rich people, are surrounded by gatekeepers. They're not listed in the phone book," I told her as I leaned against the car. "How did one of the detectives not working on this case even get the number? She didn't know her daughter was missing until someone told her. She wouldn't have known to call, herself."

Emma raised her eyebrows in surprise. "So the question is—"

"Who called her? And more importantly, why did they call her?"

* * *

A FEW TEXTS LATER, Emma confirmed none of the Forkbridge Police Force detectives contacted Mrs. Black. They were apparently a little saucy in their denials, and she looked even more annoyed.

"Okay, now I'm baffled," she admitted. "You think Hayward called? Or maybe that security guard dude?"

I went through the information again in my mind, trying to piece together what happened. We'd been operating on the presumption that the people we came across acting suspiciously were the people most likely to have kidnapped Marianna because, mostly, we still hadn't found much of a motive. "What if we're going about this all wrong?" I asked myself out loud.

Emma's eyes narrowed. "How do you figure?"

I paced. "I feel like I've missed something obvious. It seems completely clear and totally obvious—now—that Christine was drugging Marianna. The thing is, that's the only person we have any clear evidence against, right? Hayward Beals seems suspicious, but we have no direct evidence linking him to anything. Just a general icky factor in his attitude, and Rosie's report that Beals wasn't happy with Marianna's performance." I stopped pacing and looked at Emma. "What if that's all it is?"

"You think Christine is at the center of all this, not the movie or Beals."

"She's the sister of Marianna's long-term boyfriend. She's obviously known her long-term. The hospital said she didn't really drown. I saw her trying to give Marianna a drink; I saw them arguing. She didn't say anything about her brother being missing, and yet you talked to her —wait, you did talk to her at the hospital, didn't you?"

"Yeah, I did, and no, she didn't say anything." Emma crossed her arms.

"Most importantly, Christine is the only person that said anything about…No, wait," I said, stopping myself. "Someone ran in and said Marianna was kidnapped, while I was talking to Ford in the information building. Who reported that? You said there were no witnesses. If there were no witnesses, and I found Christine ten minutes later unconscious, then…" I held up my hands and raised my eyebrow. "Who told the guy Marianna was kidnapped? How did anyone know at that point?

No one could—at least if the unconscious Christine Chandler was the only witness."

Emma reached into her pocket and pulled out the small pad of notes she carried around with her. Flipping through the pages, she scanned quickly but intently and then let out a frustrated sigh. "I don't know how I missed this, but you're right. Joel Clemens told his assistant Marianna was kidnapped, and the assistant made the 911 call. But later, when I questioned him, he didn't mention it and claimed not to have seen a thing." Emma looked up. "Well, I do know how I missed it. I was focusing on you."

"I'm sorry I'm so astonishingly interesting," I told her, and she rolled her eyes. Remember how I told you I would regret not looking further into Joel Clemens? "What do we know about this guy, anyway?"

"Joel? He's a director—quiet mouse of a guy. A few of the crew said he's just mild-mannered, easy to work for. Kind of the complete opposite of Beals." Emma pulled out her phone and tapped on the screen. She swiped. She swiped again. Suddenly, Emma's face froze. Then she swallowed. "And, um, he knows Christine Chandler personally?"

My eyes narrowed. "How personally?"

"Personally enough to have a picture of the two of them on a beach in Fiji six months ago? A picture that indicates a close, personal relationship. That personally?" Her voice sounded shaky in the twilight silence as she turned the screen toward me. "How did I miss this?"

A smiling Joel Clemens draped one arm over the slick, tanned shoulder of a laughing Christine Chandler. The two leaned into one another with a limb-entwined intimacy as they squinted in the bright sun.

"You weren't focused on the victim as a suspect," I told her bluntly. "I don't think anyone would turn toward a young woman that almost drowned and go 'Gee, I wonder if you're part of a conspiracy to kidnap a movie star.' Up until a little while ago, Christine looked like just as much of a victim as Marianna, just with a slightly luckier outcome."

"I got played. That girl played me," Emma said with a cock of her head. "I don't like getting played."

"Boy, did you pick the wrong career," I pointed out. "Don't take it personally. People trying to cover up a crime are supposed to lie to you. That's the game."

Emma gave me a withering look. "Sure, you can be all nonchalant about it. It's not your career."

"It's not yours, either. Your coworkers don't think a crime even took place. You're still ahead of the game here, Emma."

The detective stared hard at me for a moment, a look of fury and disappointment thundering across her face. Then she took a long, deep breath and exhaled slowly. Then she nodded.

"Feel better?"

"I just don't like missing things." She pocketed her notepad and dusted off her hands like she was finished with this whole mess getting away from her. "Especially when I'm dragging a psychic all over town. We should have known all this yesterday."

"I'm not a psychic," I pointed out. "I do psychometry. There's a difference."

"Not to most people."

"You're not most people. If you were, I wouldn't bother with you."

Emma let out a quiet burst of laughter. "Astra, I think that's the nicest thing anyone's ever said to me."

* * *

FIVE MINUTES WENT BY. Then ten.

"Where is that guy?" Emma muttered.

"Hide!" Archie shouted from somewhere above. "Car coming from the main street! Get behind the truck! Quick! Hurry!"

"We have to hide," I told Emma as I scrambled to get behind the Jeep. "Archie said there's a car coming." The two of us sank into crouches near the bumper. The overgrown weeds and the Jeep provided ample cover, and what those didn't hide, the heavy darkness enveloped.

Seconds later, headlights crept slowly along the road and came to a stop in front of the old Thompson place. I heard a single car door open and then footsteps on the pavement. It sounded like a woman's heels.

Emma leaned slightly out and then back again. "That's Marianna Black's mother," Emma whispered. "I could swear it is. She's wearing the same outfit she was wearing at the parrot place." Emma looked once more and then crept back behind the 4x4. "It's her, and she's alone."

"What's she doing?"

"Just standing there looking at the property."

"Do we go talk to her, or do we wait?" I

whispered. Emma bit her lip, and I shifted, trying to get a better view, but the extra tire I carried in the back was blocking me. "You don't think she's part of it. Do you?"

Emma gave me a look like I was drunk or crazy or both. "Of course not," she whispered. "But what would she be doing here?"

"Go ask her?" I suggested, my tone more 'duh' than I'd intended, though the level of 'duh' was appropriate.

"She's not doing anything!" Archie shouted full-throated from somewhere above. The shriek the humans heard must've been impressive because Emma jumped. "She's just standing there! I'm watching her! No one else is coming from the street! Something is moving in the trees!"

"How does he catch anything when he's that loud?" Emma winced.

"I don't think he announces himself when he swoops down on dinner. He's just letting me know that he's watching Mrs. Black and that he doesn't see anyone else, but something is moving on the property."

"Where is that ghost?" Emma muttered, looking toward the tree line. As soon as the words left her lips, the brush parted, and a man's silhouette hurried toward Mrs. Black. "Who is that? Can you tell?"

"I can't see. It's too dark."

"Did you transfer the money?" the man asked politely in a quiet voice. "I just checked the account, and I see nothing."

"I want to see my daughter," Mrs. Black responded. Her voice was pained, almost hurt. She sounded overwhelmed at the situation she found herself in. "I'm not giving you the money you're asking for until I know that she's alive. I know this is your first kidnapping for ransom, but usually the people you're shaking down get proof of life, you know."

"You don't have to make this difficult," the man said.

Emma twisted and turned, trying to get a better angle. "Can you see him yet?"

"Sort of," I told Emma. "But I don't recognize him. It's not Joel Clemens, and it's not Hayward Beals. That much I can tell."

"How could you do this to my daughter?" Mrs. Black asked him. "She trusted you. She thought she was going to marry you. My husband and I thought of you as family, Bartholomew."

Bart Chandler?

"Whoa. Plot twist," I whispered.

"You didn't think of me as family. We met twice, and neither one of you admitted who you were. In fact, you dressed up like you shopped at Walmart just to fool me."

"Marianna wanted to be sure that anyone claiming to love her loved her for herself and not who her father is," Mrs. Black told him. "Considering what you've done, can you blame her?"

"Oh, I blame her. And you. And your husband. How could I do this to your daughter?" The mild-mannered voice seemed downright odd coming from the mouth of a man who was part of a plot to kidnap his girlfriend. "Your daughter knew that my sister wanted this part. She didn't care. It didn't matter to her. She knew that I lost my shirt on my startup, lost my car, was close to losing my house—"

Mrs. Black interrupted him. "What did you expect her to do, Bartholomew? The company wasn't hers, your income wasn't her responsibility—"

"I expected her to be honest about the fact that she was the daughter of one of the wealthiest men in the country," Chandler told the woman, the calm demeanor slipping away as the venom he'd kept tamped down bubbled up from somewhere inside him. "Be honest about the fact that she was the daughter of the man that destroyed my company. Maybe dig into her deep, deep pockets to make it right."

I moved to the side of the Jeep and looked. Marianna Black's mother and boyfriend/kidnapper stood six feet apart from one another. Between them, Bart Chandler held a gun.

"I explained that—"

"But not only didn't she tell me that her parents were uber-rich," he continued as if Mrs. Black hadn't spoken. "She gave away her salary to orphans in some country on the other side of the world instead of using it to help me get back what's mine. Tell me—is that a partner?"

"He's got a gun," I whispered to Emma.

"I can see that," she whispered back. "I have to intercede, but I'm afraid I'm gonna make the situation worse." The detective was slowly pulling out her weapon. "Do you have any—"

"I've got it!" Archie shouted. "Don't you worry, I got this!"

I looked up, but I saw only stars and darkness.

When most birds fly, their wings flapping creates turbulence in the air. That air turbulence? That's what produces sound. Mostly, the larger and faster a bird is, the louder the sound of their flapping. You can hear them coming a mile away.

Okay, maybe not a mile. But they are loud.

Owls?

Virtually silent.

Owls have enormous wings relative to their body mass, compared to other birds. That allows them to fly unbelievably slowly—unusually slowly for a bird their size. On top of that, they have comb-like separations on the leading edges of their wing feathers to break up the air, acting as a built-in silencer. That sound absorption is a huge part of why owls are such deadly predators.

Their victims never hear them coming.

Since Archie was yelling at the top of his lungs, obviously, Bart heard him coming. But since Archie stopped screaming before he dove at boyfriend-of-the-year, Bart never knew what hit him. The owl had the gun in his talons and was back into the trees before anyone realized what happened.

"I'm bleeding, bleeding!" Bart shouted, cradling his arm.

Oh, yeah.

That the owl raked Bart's forearm with his talons probably had a little bit to do with his distraction.

Archie shouted, "I got the gun! I got it! I—"

Suddenly, a gunshot pierced the quiet night.

"Oops," the owl said quietly. "Dropped it."

Emma jumped out, her weapon trained on the doubled-over Bart Chandler. I raced toward Mrs. Black and threw my body in front of hers to protect her from whatever confrontation might ensue. As Emma moved on Chandler, though, it became increasingly clear he was in no condition to fight back.

"Police! Get down on the ground! Now!"

Bart collapsed to the street with what looked like relief. "I'm unarmed. Something...ow, damn...Something swooped out of the sky and ripped my gun out of my hand!"

Not a bright guy, this one.

"Yeah, um, I did do that," Archie called from somewhere in the trees. "Don't quite have it at the moment. I'm gonna look for it, though. I'll find it." I heard a rustling in the bushes. "It's here somewhere."

CHAPTER EIGHTEEN

*E*mma snapped the cold metal of the handcuffs around Bart's wrists. The ratcheting sound of the cuffs as they locked made him wince. "Okay, buddy, get up," she told him sternly, dragging him up by his arm.

"Who are you people?" Mrs. Black asked, looking back and forth between the two of us. She pointed excitedly, her face twisted with agitation and worry. "That man has my daughter! You need to let him go! If not, his partner will kill her!"

"Yeah, uncuff me!"

Emma and I stared at Bart.

"Though not because of what she said or

anything," Bart added quickly. "Because I'm innocent." He paused. "And injured."

"Mrs. Black, I'm Detective Emma Sullivan," Emma told Marianna's mother, ignoring Bart. "I'm the primary Detective on your daughter's case."

Mrs. Black blinked in surprise. "You're not. Detective Clemens called me this morning—"

Now I was the one blinking in surprise. Joel Clemens used his own last name while posing as a detective? It was a little embarrassing that we hadn't caught these people until now—considering how stupid they were.

"Joel Clemens is the director of your daughter's film, Mrs. Black," I told her while Emma wrestled with an indignant Bart Chandler. "He's not a detective. He appears to be the boyfriend of this man's sister."

"My arm. Something shredded my arm," Bart announced angrily once he was on his feet. "I'm a computer programmer! I need my arm! Someone get me an ambulance! The handcuffs are digging into my wrist! I swear, I will sue you for everything your department has!"

"This is Forkbridge, Florida—we don't have much. Stop tugging and jerking against the cuffs, and you won't have that problem," Emma told him. Turning to Mrs. Black, she said, "I can assure you that no detective from our department called you. We didn't have your number to call. No one from the movie's staff gave us your information, ma'am."

Mrs. Black swallowed. "Marianna didn't list me as a contact?" Without waiting for an answer, the elegant woman nodded and said softly, "Of course she didn't."

"We'd realized Christine Chandler and Joel Clemens were likely the kidnappers—or at least participants in the plot to kidnap your daughter. We didn't know why." Emma looked Bart up and down. "We weren't aware that Mr. Chandler was also involved."

"Speaking of Marianna, where is she?" I asked Bart.

He glared at me, looking me up and down. "What are you, some vigilante superhero?" Bart snorted with derision—which was impressively egotistical considering he was the one in handcuffs.

"Let's just say yes. It'll save time. Answer the question." With one hand firmly around Bart's forearm, Emma fished out her phone with the other while I questioned him. "Where can we find her?"

"Yeah, dispatch, I need officer backup and forensics to the old Thompson place. Will need to cordon off the property as a crime scene," Emma told the person on the other end of the phone.

"I don't know what you're talking about," Bart said haughtily.

"You said you knew where she was!" Mrs. Black cried.

"I said no such thing," Bart sniffed. Then he looked away.

"I have a suspect in custody, and more suspects may be on the premises. Also, need a bus," Emma continued relaying into her phone. She spun Bart around and lifted up his arms by the handcuffs. "Better make that two buses, just in case." She went silent and then frowned. "Good thing there's no emergency, then, Smith." Another silence. "That was sarcasm, Smith. This *is* an emergency."

"No one on duty?" I asked.

"Nothing and no one moves quickly in this town," she answered, a warning note in her voice. "ETA is five minutes. Should be enough time for lover boy here to lead us to Marianna." Emma stuffed her phone back in her pocket.

"I'm not taking you anywhere! I don't know anything," Bart spat. "I want a lawyer!"

"I haven't even read you your rights yet. You're jumping ahead."

"Well, then, you can't use anything I've said!"

"You didn't know we were over there, and we hadn't talked to you yet," Emma told him. "Come on, Chandler—cut the crap. The jig is up. Where did you stash Marianna?"

"Screw you, lady," Bart sneered.

Mrs. Black bit her lip, her face twisted with worry.

Emma looked at me and raised an eyebrow. "Can you?" she jerked her head toward Bart. "I've had enough of Mouthy McGenius over here."

Bart's head snapped toward me, and he looked wary. "What does that mean? What is she talking about?"

"Oh, I could do a lot of things," I muttered with a surly return glare at Chandler. "But yeah, I got this." I stepped over to Bart and placed my hand on the back of his neck. "Just relax. This won't hurt a bit."

"What are you doing?" he demanded, trying to pull away. He turned his head toward his shoulder, trying to look at me. When that failed, he tried to jerk forward out of my grasp. In the end, he was just too restrained to put up much of a struggle. "What are you doing to me?"

Mrs. Black looked confused. "I'm a bit confused myself. What is she doing, Detective?"

"Police psychic, ma'am," Emma told her. As if that explained why I had the suspect's neck in an iron grip.

Mrs. Black gasped, and her eyes filled with tears. "My daughter's going to die, isn't she? If this is the best way forward that you have...Oh, dear lord, I feel sick." The wealthy woman rocked unsteadily on her feet.

"Astra?" Emma prodded. "Do what you do. Let's just find her."

I nodded and closed my eyes.

Bart Chandler was so adrenalized and had so little control of his mental or emotional state that a flood of images slammed into my mind within seconds. Unlike the mirror, I saw through his eyes (and heard) the most critical moments he was carrying with him. I felt his anger, his greed, his deep resentment.

"They have her back there," I said, opening my eyes. "I know where. There's an old pool toward the back of the property. It was built in the late eighteen hundreds, I think. Fed by a sulfur spring." I walked toward the property. "It's been out of commission for years and years, but they—Beals and Clemens—checked it out as a possible filming location. Someone sealed it up to use as a storm shelter."

"She's there?" Emma asked.

"She's there," I said, my steps growing more anxious.

I'd seen a clear image of Marianna Black lying on the floor.

She didn't look good.

* * *

THE TWO GHOSTS argued near a collapsed building I realized had fallen onto the swimming pool/storm shelter area. Mr. Thompson was looking henpecked, and a round, older woman I didn't recognize shouted at him. At the top of her lungs.

Well, if she had lungs.

Ignoring them, I scanned the ground for the hatch but didn't see it. It was clearly in this area, but I couldn't find the exact location thanks to the darkness and the debris.

"And if you think I'm gonna stay in a relationship with you even though you just wander off with a bunch of women and don't tell me where you're going, you have another think coming!" The old woman placed her hands on her hips and jutted her chin out. "I didn't stick around here in my afterlife just to be thrown over for a younger ghost! If I wanted to be mistreated and cheated on, I could have moved on with my husband! That young woman? Seconds from death! Seconds!"

"Clara, I—"

"Don't you sass me, Stephen!" Mrs. Cambridge snapped at him. "You've been haunting this place for darn near—"

"Clara, there are the—"

"Did you just interrupt me?" Clara Cambridge asked menacingly. "I know you didn't interrupt me."

"Hello!" I called out. The two ghosts stopped, turned, and stared at me. "I don't mean to interrupt. Mr. Thompson," I nodded. "We were waiting for you back at the road."

"I got a little sidetracked." The ghost glanced at Mrs. Cambridge, who stood with her mouth open. "You know how it is. The women folk can get a little—"

"You don't want to finish that statement," Clara snapped. "Who the hell are you? You're not one of those spiritualists from over in—"

"Look, I get that you're in the middle of your afterlife, and I surely don't mean to interrupt anything, but we're concerned with the living, and we need to find the woman in the storm cellar," I told Clara before she could make the requisite comment on my outfit. "My name is Astra, and I need you to help me save a woman's life. Can you do that?"

"Who is she talking to?" Mrs. Black asked as the rest of the group joined me. I was impressed that the woman kept up with us in the muddy field. Her expensive Italian heels would never be the same. "Is there someone there?"

"I told you. Police psychic," Emma answered without answering.

"My arm feels like it's on fire," Bart complained. "If I can't type on a keyboard, I'm going to sue you for damages and lost—"

"Do you ever shut up?" Emma asked Bart. "That right to remain silent? Why don't you utilize that one for a few minutes? Try something new for a change."

"I must've got him good!" Archie called from above.

"Is someone up in that tree?" Clara asked, craning her head and scanning the treetops. "I heard someone talking from that tree, right there."

"It's a bird, dearest," Thompson told her. "They can talk now."

"Thompson, where is she?" I asked firmly. "That's all we want to know. I know that the hatch to get in the storm shelter is supposed to be right here. Where is it? How do I get in? Just show me that, and you can get back to your discussion."

"Goodness gracious, dear, you don't have to shout," Clara said, looking irritated. "The hatch you're looking for is right over there behind the tree stump. You just turn the lever on the top."

"Stay here," I told Emma and raced toward the tree stump. Leaning over it, I scanned the ground and immediately spotted a dark reddish metal hatch. With a turn and a yank, I had it open and scurried down the cold metal ladder. "Marianna?" I called into the dim expanse when I reached the bottom. My voice echoed back. "Marianna!" I called again, louder this time.

I heard a groan, but the lack of light made it impossible to see where it came from. "Marianna, I'm here to get you out. Can you make another noise? Anything will work." I stood still and listened. Nothing. "Marianna!"

It smelled of dust and dampness, and it was difficult to breathe. The walls were lined with cement blocks—no doubt added when it was converted to a storm shelter. More cement blocks stacked up in the middle at different points to make pillars that, I assumed, supported the old roof. This was the very definition of a dungeon you would lock someone in to forget about them. Marianna could've screamed for hours in here, and no one would ever hear her calls for help.

"I am here," a voice whispered weakly. "Please help me." The sound of soft crying broke my heart—but it also gave me a noise to follow.

When I found her, which I did pretty quickly, I wanted to punch Bart in the face until his perfect patrician nose was the size of a watermelon.

She was filthy, her face covered in dirt and tear-stained from crying. She clutched a tiny flashlight tightly. Her clothing was torn as if she'd been attacked by a werewolf. It was pulled demurely across her in an attempt at modest dignity. Her eyes had a haunted, sunken look.

"Marianna? Are you hurt? Is anything broken?"

Her eyes, and only her eyes, moved to my face. "Just me," she whispered. If she was still suffering from the drugs' effects, she had passed the stage where it gave her any energy.

Marianna Black looked spent and broken.

I kneeled down beside her and gathered her gently in my arms. "I need you to drink this," I said quietly, handing her the blue liquid Althea said would reverse the effects of the drug. Her hands tried to clasp the bottle and slid off. Her eyebrows scrunched up, and she lifted her left hand once more, but she just didn't have the strength. She looked devastated.

"I can't. I can't." More quiet weeping.

"Yes, you can. I'll help you." Her skin was hot, so hot it was almost uncomfortable to touch her. Drenched in sweat, her skin glistened a bright pink as if she'd been severely sunburned. "You have to drink this. I promise you, it will make you feel better. I can help you, but you have to try with me. Can you try, Marianna?"

"I'll try...I'm so thirsty," she whispered hoarsely. "But my throat is so sore. It's so hot. It's so very hot." I held the bottle and tilted it against her lips carefully. It took almost five whole minutes for her to drink the full measure of the medicine. Marianna attempted tiny sip by tiny sip, with breaks between for her to regain her strength. It was like watching someone climb a mountain by their fingernails.

"I can feel your body cooling," I told her. "You

should feel a pretty immediate effect." Because magic, but we'll leave that explanation out for now. "How do you feel?"

"Like I could sleep for a year," she told me, her voice already slightly stronger. "What happened? How did I get here?"

"You don't remember?"

She grabbed on to me and pulled herself up to a sitting position. Marianna swayed ever so slightly but then seemed to regain her equilibrium. I had to admit—Althea's concoction was impressive. The pink had almost faded from Marianna's skin, and the scorching heat coming off of her was gone. "I don't." She looked at her wrists and rubbed red welts. "I think I was tied up? I don't know why I'm here." She looked up at me. "I don't know you."

"You were kidnapped. Your boyfriend Bart, his sister Christine, and Joel Clemens kidnapped you from the set. The drugs that were in the tumbler Christine was giving you? They affected your demeanor and possibly your memory," I explained. Her eyes widened, and she looked confused. "You don't remember any of this?"

"That's not possible." Marianna trembled, her hands clutching onto me. "That's not possible. Why would Bart kidnap me? That doesn't make any sense. And Christine...I don't even know Joel...He's just the director."

I bit my lip.

If Marianna Black remembered nothing, all we had was what we overheard Bart say. Mrs. Black could testify that Bart shook her down for money, but unless he turned on Christine and Joel? We had little hard evidence of anything they'd done.

"Are you sure you don't remember Christine or Joel doing anything? Coming to visit you here? Saying anything?"

"Athena can help her remember," Archie's voice called from the darkness. "It's justice, after all."

"How?"

"How what?" Marianna asked, her voice even more robust.

"You're not gonna like it," Archie warned me.

"I don't have to like it. It just has to work."

Marianna looked into my eyes. "What don't you like? Who are you talking to?"

"Just ask her. You know, beseech the goddess for a favor?" Archie explained. "People have been doing it for thousands of years. You just gotta ask and have faith the goddess will grant you what you ask for. It's straightforward. Just do it."

* * *

I CARRIED Marianna out of the storm shelter and into the waiting arms of a paramedic without further engaging with the talking bird on the subject of faith. By the time I got her back to ground level, she looked almost normal, if weak.

"I got her, thanks," the paramedic said with a smile. "We'll take good care of her."

"Marianna!" Mrs. Black screamed, racing over to her daughter. I breathed a sigh of relief and turned to find Emma Sullivan staring at me.

"Makes you feel good, doesn't it?" Emma called.

"It was a nominally successful day," I agreed cautiously.

Emma turned back and talked with the paramedics, giving details and orders and taking charge. At least her lazy coworkers at the Forkbridge PD couldn't claim Marianna Black hadn't been kidnapped anymore.

"Marianna!" Bart shouted, spotting the girlfriend he'd nearly killed strapped into a stretcher. A fierce-looking patrol officer held him as he struggled to get to her. "Marianna, tell them I didn't do anything! Baby, tell them that we're in love! I would never hurt you!" He glared at Emma and then at me. "Don't believe these two! They are liars! Your mother, too!"

"Jeez, what an absolute pig that guy is," I observed. "Yep, everybody's lying except for you, Casanova."

"Casanova?" Emma rolled her eyes. "You're giving him way too much credit. Casanova was a jerk, but he wasn't a sociopath. That guy? That guy is a sociopath, and if he isn't one now and I'm wrong? I think he aspires to be."

"Are you going to ask the goddess for justice?" Archie called down from the trees. Yet again, his screech was so loud to human ears that two police officers and a paramedic jumped. "All you have to do is ask!"

I sighed and turned my back to the direction of his voice, my eyes scanning the scene.

Emma was right; it did feel good to save Marianna Black's life. Despite my first impressions of the woman when she came in to get a reading, everything I'd learned about her since then seemed to indicate she was a gentle soul just trying to make her way in the world on her own terms—someone who'd accomplished things without using her family's prominence to grease the wheels.

I—obviously—admired that.

Unfortunately, she also found the people around her didn't appreciate her accomplishments so much as they wanted to profit from them.

"So, problem. Marianna doesn't remember anything."

Emma's smile faded.

"Yeah, I felt the same way," I told her.

"We need to find Christine and Joel Clemens and place them under arrest. The thing is, though, unless Bart over there flips?" she shrugged. "I don't know that the arrest is going to stick. Did she remember anything? Anything at all?"

"Not a thing. Doesn't know how she got down in the storm cellar and doesn't think Bart would ever do anything to hurt her." Emma's surprised eyes met mine. "I know. This case has been weird from the start, and even though we found her? It doesn't look like it's getting any less weird. Look," I told the detective, my tone sympathetic, "at least we found her. We saved her life."

"But if we don't get all of them, for how long?" Emma muttered. "Is she out of danger, or will they just try again?"

"Just ask the goddess!" Archie shouted.

I shot a dirty look at the treetops and hoped he saw it.

CHAPTER NINETEEN

*U*ntangling the threads of this conspiracy would take some work, but that part wasn't my job. With a handshake and assurance that Emma could take it from there, I walked back to the street. Opening the door to my Jeep, I got a mouthful of feathers as Archie swooped in through the driver-side door.

"You think you're all done, huh?" he asked while clambering into the backseat. I winced as I heard the distinct tearing of leather. "The card flipped over, it glowed, you saved the girl. All done, are you?"

"You're a real pain in the butt, you know that?" I slid into the car, shut the door, and started the ignition. "I'm not a cop. I was supposed to prevent a murder, and I did. Time to go home and eat dinner."

"Did you, though?" The question hung in the air.

"I did."

"Confidence. I like that. So, let me ask you something." Archie leaned forward and stuck his head between the seats. "When you worked in the military, you just went and got your fugitive, and that was it? Bada bing, bada boom, get the bad guy and head back to Impy?"

"Essentially." I paused at the stop sign, made a right, and accelerated. "What else is there?"

"You tell me."

"There's nothing."

"Well, I guess we'll find out soon enough." Archie leaned back. "Not where I would have called it, what with two murderous people on the loose and a woman still in a relationship with her kidnapper. But, you know, I'm sure you're right."

I glanced in the rearview mirror. "Emma's handling it. It will be fine."

"Sure, sure. If you did everything you're supposed to do, then the card won't be glowing anymore. If the card's not glowing anymore? You're right, and my discomfort is likely just a bad rabbit." Archie sniffed. "Of course, this is

STAR OF SAGE & SCREAM | 337

your first job, and I'm the goddess's own owl sent to guide you. Sent to explain what Athena expects, what she would want to see. All the things you need to do." He sniffed again. "But, you know, maybe you're right." There was a long pause and another sniff. "What do I know? I'm just an owl. I'm sure you're probably right."

I love how Athena could never be dominated by other goddesses in mythology. Still, I'm somehow supposed to let myself be run right over by a smart-ass owl.

If there are gods—and I'm not saying I'm questioning my ultimate belief there are not, in fact, gods—they're likely just another race of paranormals with more advanced powers than the rest of us. I mean, I met some pretty sharp and powerful cookies in Imperatorial City. There were rumors of near-omnipotent beings controlling the witches of the Witches' Council. The circus people, too—

"What are you thinking about?" Archie asked.

"Eating dinner," I told him. "I'm starving."

So, say there is some being like "Athena."

Not a god.

Again, I don't believe in gods.

But some superpowerful paranormal being

that resembles the Athena of mythology? If you ask something like that for help?

It seems to me you're just buying a world of problems.

"Did you know that Athena was born in full armor?" Archie asked quietly. "She's the smartest god on Mount Olympus. She can argue circles around Zeus. I've never met another being as intelligent as she is." He grew quiet for a moment, then chuckled. "I've never met one as stubborn, either. You remind me of her."

"You're not going to convince me she exists. For one, she's not even a particular myth. She's Athena in Greece, and then she was Minerva in Rome. The humans created the gods they needed, Archie."

"Her children all have the flaw of hubris. She knows it, but it doesn't seem to bother her very much," Archie continued as if I hadn't spoken. "I think she gravitates toward witches with the same flaw." He grew quiet and then added, "You may want to reread the myths. Hubris rarely helps in a situation. Even if you're a god."

I looked in the rearview and briefly thought of asking Archie to fly home so I could get some peace and quiet, but his serious demeanor gave me pause. "What are you trying to say?"

Archie assessed me with a severe look, but I broke the intense stare to watch the road. "Astraea was a minor goddess, but she was a goddess—and you've been entrusted with her divinity. She was best known as a goddess of justice. In fact, many believe that Astraea is the goddess portrayed on the Justice card of your sister's tarot deck. Since I met her many years ago, I can tell you the likeness is striking."

My eyes widened. "You met Astraea?"

He clambered clumsily into the front seat and settled in. "I did. When humanity realized she left Earth for the heavens, they prayed day and night for her to return." Archie gazed out as we passed the center of Forkbridge. "They prayed to her, apologized to her, and wailed at the stars begging her to change her mind. Her leaving ended the Golden Age of Man, and the humans wanted it back."

"How did Athena become the guardian of her energy?" I asked the question before I thought about it. Archie's story and intensity were sucking me in. "Not that I believe any of this, mind you," I added. "But it's interesting."

Archie sighed. "Some people believed Astraea was actually the daughter of Zeus. Those people? They were right. Zeus was—and is—prolific."

Archie glanced at me. "Athena knows well her own faults, aspects of her own personality that are not well suited to...care. She is a warrior, possibly the most intelligent being in this or any other realm—but she is not a mother figure. Astraea, her sister? Now that goddess loved humanity in a way that Athena did not. Does not. Probably will not ever."

"Then why go through all this?" I asked as we pulled in the driveway at Arden House. "Sending you, sending Astraea's energy out into the world. What's the point if she doesn't care?"

"Because she's smart enough to know that someone needs to," Archie said with more than a touch of admiration. "Because she can see the way the world is moving, things that are happening, and she knows that someone has to care about justice. Too few do."

I turned and looked at the owl. "So, then my job is—"

"Your job is to seek justice," Archie interrupted. "The card, the murder to stop? That's important. But the energy you carry with you? That energy wants justice. It wants to make things right, Astra. You understand? It wants the evildoers punished and the righteous free of fear. Suppose Athena has chosen to get you involved.

In that case, the smartest person in the entire universe realized justice can't happen without you, without your magic." The owl tilted his head. "So, you know—if you've done that?" Archie shrugged. "Then, sure, I suppose you are done."

* * *

AUNT GWENNIE ENTERED the kitchen as I sat at the kitchen table eating a microwaved slice of meatloaf. It sounded as though my sisters were already asleep—young women with no social lives apparently have no reason to stay up late. "Everything get resolved?" she asked, sitting down at the table, her nightgown and robe fluttering around her.

"Don't know," I told her with my mouth full. "I'm kind of afraid to wake Ami up and ask her where the card is. She'd make me recount everything that happened, and now that I'm done, I'd like to get a shower and some sleep."

"The card? Of course, the star card," she said, answering her own question instantly. "Yes, I think she has that with her. She's been guarding it like it's the key that unlocks the gates to Atlantis."

"If it's still glowing, I'm not done. If it's not glowing, I did my job." I sat up straighter, lowered my fork, and turned toward Aunt Gwennie. "Can I ask you something?"

"You can always ask me anything, dear, you know that." She pulled her robe tighter around her and leaned forward.

"Is this all some con job that Mom cooked up?"

Aunt Gwennie blinked in surprise. "Is what a con job?"

"This whole goddess's owl delivery on my birthday thing." Aunt Gwennie brought her lips together in an expression of prim disapproval. "Look, I know you guys believe in this stuff—"

"Let me stop you right there." Aunt Gwennie placed her hand on my arm and squeezed. "I know that you've been away for many years, and I know that part of the reason you left is the difficulty you and your mother seem to have communicating. But as much as you have difficulty with communication, your mother has never been dishonest with you. She's never deceived you." Her eyes narrowed. "And you, my dear, cannot say the same. You started your new life initially with a lie and a betrayal."

Ouch. That stung. A lot. "Look, Aunt Gwennie—"

My aunt held her hand up to stop me. "Yes.

Minerva is a difficult woman, and no one recognizes that better than me," she said. "But your suspicion that she's manipulating you by lying about her religion? That she manufactured or enchanted an owl to spin a great—but false—tale?" Aunt Gwennie's eyebrows arched. "That type of accusation, Astra, is beneath you. And your mother doesn't deserve that."

My eyes dropped, and I felt like a chastised child.

My mother was much like Archie described Athena—intelligent, arrogant, full of hubris. But if I set aside my own suspicions and looked at facts, my Aunt Gwennie was right. Mom had never deliberately hurt me that I could remember. She'd never intentionally lied that I could recall. We just...clashed—a lot. "You're right, Aunt Gwennie. I'm sorry."

"I accept your apology, though you really should be apologizing to your mother." Aunt Gwennie paused. "Considering your previous paranoia, though, I think perhaps I will accept the apology on her behalf, and we'll just let it lie, shall we?" Aunt Gwennie pinched the bridge of her nose and leaned back in her chair. "It would be a kindness not to tell her what you suspected. Just for Pax Templi, you understand."

"Pax Templi" translates roughly to "peace of the temple." It essentially means that we will drop this dispute and leave it outside for the harmony of everyone in the house.

I chuckled. "Sounds good."

"You found Marianna Black, I take it?"

I nodded. "We did. She was in the storm cellar at the old Thompson place. She was in bad shape, too. I'm not sure that she would've lived through the night. When I found her, she could barely move."

"Did Althea's tonic help?"

"Absolutely."

"Wonderful. She's becoming an incredibly talented master herbalist. When you add in the magic that Minerva's been teaching her? Wonderful, just wonderful. I expect great things from the girl." Aunt Gwennie smiled happily. I suspected my aunt had been Althea's principal teacher, and she was justifiably filled with pride. "Did you and Emma managed to find out who did such a dreadful thing?"

I frowned. "It was her boyfriend, her assistant, and her assistant's boyfriend who also happened to be her director. Oh, and the assistant? Her boyfriend's sister. Weird spaghetti mess of relationships." I took another bite of the meatloaf, chewed, and swallowed. "Emma arrested the boyfriend—and Archie took a chunk out of the guy's wrist disarming him—but I don't know about Christine and Joel, though. Emma's not sure she has enough evidence to arrest them and make it stick."

Aunt Gwennie frowned and scratched her head. "If there's not enough evidence to hold them, how do you to know for sure that they were a part of it?"

"Psychic stuff, unfortunately. I saw Christine trying to force Marianna to drink that garbage in a vision. Joel Clemens called Marianna's mother and claimed to be a detective—that one might be easier to prove. I'm sure they can trace the phone call." I reached down to grab my phone and check for any text messages from Emma and cursed.

"Language," Aunt Gwennie said absently.

"Thirty-three years old," I responded. "I think I'm old enough to curse now."

"I think I can cast a spell to make sure that no one in this house could curse if you're going to insist on it," Aunt Gwennie responded sternly. Her face softened. "What's wrong?"

"My phone. I must've dropped it at the crime scene." As soon as the words left my lips, the house phone rang. I launched out of my chair and grabbed it before it could wake anybody up. "Hello?"

"Hey, Astra, it's Emma. I found your phone by the hatch."

"That's funny. My aunt and I were just talking about that. I just noticed I lost it."

"I'm actually on my way to your neck of the woods. Want me to bring it by?"

"If it's not too much trouble, that would be great. Let me just check with my aunt." I turned toward Aunt Gwennie and explained the situation. She nodded. "Yeah, come on by. I'll wait up."

"Well, that was very nice of her," Aunt Gwennie said as I sat back down at the table. My meatloaf looked cold now. It just didn't have that steamy, warm 'eat me, I'm yummy' vibe anymore. "Do you think you'll be seeing Emma again?"

I gave her an odd look. "We're not dating, Aunt Gwennie."

"There would be nothing wrong with that if you were, dear."

I rolled my eyes. "Thank you for your acceptance and approval of the alternative sexual lifestyle I don't have."

"Before you go to wait for Emma," Aunt Gwennie said, reaching toward my arm again. "I just want to reassure you that what's happening to you? Archie showing up, Athena entrusting you with Astraea's energy?"

"Yes?"

"These things are genuine and very serious." Aunt Gwennie studied my expression before continuing as if to assure herself I was taking what she said as seriously as she meant it. "You have been chosen for a great task, Astra. Some people hear the stories of old and think heroes are the ones that do big things—like those Marvel people. Those Marvel superhero people are always running off to save the entire world all at once in a week. That? That is fiction. That's not how the world is saved, niece."

I frowned. "I don't understand."

"It is only in the heavens that there are gods who can save an entire world. Here, on this mortal plane? We only have heroes. And heroes can only save the world one moment, one action, one person at a time." Her calm gaze held me as if I was under a spell. "Heroes are the best we have, and you have been made one. To one person, you are a champion. To one—or several—villains, you are justice's wrath."

I shifted uncomfortably in my chair. "I didn't ask for this, Aunt Gwennie. I didn't choose this."

She started to speak and then hesitated. After a few moments, she smiled. "You can always choose to send Archie back and refuse. No doubt the goddess would take your newfound power—and possibly your psychometry as well."

I blinked. "Wait, what?"

Aunt Gwennie smiled. "Athena is a stubborn goddess, Astra. She is always sure that she knows better than everyone else—and most of the time, she does." My mother's face flashed before my eyes. "I suspect she would not be pleased with your refusal. But until you talk to her—"

"How am I supposed to talk to her?" I asked with exasperation. "Let's say for a second I set aside my incredulity. I tamped down my skepticism, I boxed up my doubt, and I stopped all the questions. Just took a gigantic leap and said, okay, sure, a goddess sent me an owl." I searched Aunt Gwennie's gentle face. "Does she have a phone number? An email address? Do I have to fly all the way to Greece and hike up a mountain?"

My aunt let out a full laugh. "Oh, Astra, I have missed your sense of humor!" She reached out and hugged me tightly, still laughing.

I wasn't making a joke, but okay.

"Your mother is the high priestess of Athena!

We just need to cast a circle and ask for her to stop by."

So, no email address, then.

* * *

I saw the flash of headlights strike the window and ran out to meet Emma at the police cruiser she was driving. She got out of the vehicle and handed me the phone.

"Thanks for this," I said. I tapped the screen to make sure it still worked, and it turned on… despite a suspicious-looking talon mark across the back case. "Didn't notice I dropped it."

"No problem." Emma was subdued, her face troubled.

"What's wrong? You're making the face."

"You've known me for two days. If I do have a face, I'm sure you don't know what it is yet."

"Psychic, remember?" I said, pointing at myself.

"No, you're not psychic; you're a psychotrist."

"Psychometrist," I corrected.

"I think I like mine better," she told me with a half-smile. Then she shrugged. "The prosecutor told me that if I pick up Christine and Joel, there's not gonna be enough evidence to take to the grand jury. Well, what he said was he could outline all the evidence I had against them within three minutes, and that despite common belief? He could not, in fact, indict a ham sandwich." She leaned against the car and crossed her arms. "Though the jerk did mention indicting a ham sandwich might be easier."

"It's been, like, an hour. He went through all that evidence in an hour?"

"As Mr. Fancy Pants lawyer mentioned, ain't much to flip through."

"You can ask the goddess for some he-lp," Archie from somewhere above. "It wouldn't take more than a minute. Maybe two if she was busy!"

"What the heck is he screeching about now?" Emma asked.

I bit my lip.

"Now you're making a face. And I don't know your faces, but I know that face is a face."

"Archie thinks we should petition the goddess Athena for assistance in uncovering hard evidence to get justice for Marianna Black."

"We can do that?" Emma asked.

"My aunt and the bird seem to think so."

"Cool." She stared at me, not moving. "So, uh, why aren't we doing that?"

"I'm not sure I believe in gods," I told her. "I

don't want to pray to a god I don't know I believe in. Who knows what this being Athena really is, you know?"

She looked at me like I was crazy. "I'm not sure I believe in God either, but my butt's in the pew every important holiday just in case. I light the candles, say the prayers, the whole nine yards. Do I think it does anything?" she shrugged. "I have no idea. Maybe someday I will know, maybe someday I won't, maybe I'll never know for sure. It makes my grandmother happy, though, and that's enough for me." Emma gave me a once-over glance. "So, again—what's the problem?"

"I have no idea whether it would really work or not, though." This reasoning sounded much more logical and obviously brilliant in my head.

Emma rolled her eyes. "If all you have to do is mutter a prayer and genuflect to a myth to find out, why wouldn't you do it?" Emma asked seriously. "I mean, sure, okay, if they want you to strip down naked, slather yourself in honey, and sleep on a fire ant bed overnight? Maybe we should have a conversation. But if you just have to ask a godlike being for help?" She held up her hands and tilted her head. "I'm not getting the issue. I'm also not getting how it's any different than you having a conversation with the talking owl or sending the ghost in to scout a crime scene."

"We can help!" Ami hollered through the window. I looked up to find all my sisters leaning out over the second-floor window listening. "We've got everything ready to go! We thought you might need to!"

"Yep! We are all up. We can just do it now!" Althea called.

"If it gets my powers back? I'll do whatever I have to," Ayla shouted angrily. "So let's go, people! I interrupted a good book for this."

CHAPTER TWENTY

My mother was already waiting in the ritual room. She sat toward the front of the room where the altar was, in a long flowing purple robe, her hair decorated with flowers.

For a moment, I was agitated—maybe this was her plan all along. No one could get ready for a ritual in just two minutes, right? She looked like she was expecting this.

A harsh glare from Archie (who was also waiting in the ritual room and who almost seemed to know what I was thinking) stopped me from saying anything.

"Are we actually going to have a human in the

ritual?" Althea asked, spotting Emma behind me. "That's so exciting! It's been ages since we've had one!"

"I'll get the candle for the human protocol," Ayla said. She spun on her heel and took off toward the storage room.

"The human protocol," Emma said.

Althea nodded eagerly.

"When you say a human in the ritual, can you describe what that means? Exactly?" Emma asked Althea nervously.

My sister's eyes widened. "Well, it means—"

"Exactly. I mean exactly." Emma's voice cracked, betraying her nervousness. "Step by step. Go on."

"Emma, take a deep breath," I told her. Despite sounding confident outside on the driveway, her expression made her appear more than a little startled at this sudden turn of events. "It's going to be okay."

She gave me a pointed look. "Look, I'm all for religious tolerance, but I do have some lines I absolutely have to draw. I won't sacrifice anything, and I don't want to see anything sacrificed, and I don't want to be a sacrifice." Emma tilted her head. "If I arrest your sisters for something and the ACLU comes after me? It's just gonna be a lot of paperwork. Know what I mean?"

Now it was Althea's turn to look startled. My sister glanced toward me. "She's kidding, right? What does she think we are, vampires?"

I smiled. "Emma's mostly kidding, Althea. Right?"

"Yes, I'm mostly kidding," Emma agreed. "Mostly." The hesitation in her eyes, though, subtly communicated her apprehension. Althea stepped forward and placed a comforting hand on the detective's shoulder. She explained briefly in low, gentle tones what would take place.

"We're simply going to stand in a circle, light some candles, do the gods' blessings on everyone, and then Mom will call Athena here."

Emma searched my sister's face suspiciously. "What happens after that? What will she do? Say? Should I have my gun drawn in case some demon comes through the portal and tries to eat us?"

Althea seemed at a loss for words.

"There's no portal or demons, and what happens from there will depend on Athena, really," Ami said, coming to Althea's rescue. "We really can't speak for her. Athena may have something she wants to say, and then she'll go. The goddess might ask Astra what she wants from her or make her oath to something." My sister glanced back toward my mother. "It's all pretty loose, really. We'll just have to see." Ami straightened and glanced at me. "You never really know what mood Athena's going to be in."

"I know, right?" Ayla muttered as she sped by with a large candle. "Remember that one time we called her for the solstice, and she was so angry that she—"

"Maybe now isn't the time to go over that," Althea interrupted quickly, her eyes cutting nervously toward Emma. "We wouldn't want to tell tales out of ritual, would we?"

"Girls, it's time," Aunt Gwennie called from near the altar. "Minerva seems quite ready. If you'll all take your places? Alexa, set the lighting to ritual, please?"

Emma looked around. "Who's Alexa?"

I pointed to the Amazon Echo in the corner.

"Okay," the computer's well-known voice answered. A second later, the lights in the room dimmed. My sisters immediately took their spots next to the candles Ayla had placed and waited quietly.

"What do we do?" Emma whispered.

"I guess we stand here," I whispered back. "I don't know. I stopped coming to these when I was ten." Emma looked confused. "Atheist, remember? I got a wish from my mother for my tenth birthday. I wished to never have to come to one of these again."

"Ouch. Harsh."

I felt Emma at my elbow as my mother took her place at the head of the circle. I know what you're thinking. It's a circle, right? How could a circle have a head? Well, all I can tell you is a ritual circle has a head, and it's impossible for you to miss the head.

"Blessed are you, the daughters of Olympus," my mother intoned. The flames of the candles seem to flicker higher. "Blessed are you who are the chosen of the goddess Athena, the heirs to the temple."

"Blessed are we, chosen of the goddess," my aunt and sisters answered. Simultaneously, as if part of a rehearsed dance, they all bowed their heads. "Honored are we among the witches."

"As Athena is the daughter of the great Zeus, so are we her daughters. We are the daughters of strength, daughters of clarity, daughters of conviction," my mother said, her voice getting more robust.

"We are the daughters of skill," the coven called back.

"As Athena is the provider of gifts to humankind, so will we provide our gifts to humankind," my mother said as she stepped forward again toward the center of the circle. "Gifts Athena has given to us we must give to the world."

"We thank you for our gifts, oh, goddess," the coven called back.

Emma seemed enraptured by the ritual—and I had to admit it was almost always a little bit breathtaking. I didn't believe it, but every woman in the circle (other than Emma and I) did. Their devotion was quite beautiful in the flickering candlelight.

"The blessings of the gods of Mount Olympus are upon us, and in that blessing and favor, we call for Athena herself to come upon us," my mother said, her voice rising as if the goddess might be a little hard of hearing. "Keeper of cities, we vowed to be your shield in this sheltered city of Forkbridge. We protect those who dwell here, shelter those that need us and serve as their strength. But we need your help!"

"We are the daughters of strength," my sisters called out.

"I am the olive branch," my aunt followed.

"I am the shield," my mother called, her voice rising. "But justice has been left undone. We call upon you to help the daughter of stars finish what you charged her with undoing!"

Daughter of stars, huh?

I swallowed, glancing around the room as my mother's wide, unfocused eyes assessed me. The silence grew heavier and denser, like an invisible fog, and I shifted casually to a steadier defensive stance.

Look, I may not believe in any of this, but I was sure something would show up.

I just didn't know what it would be.

The coven women in the room stood silent, eyes closed—except for my mother. In the center of the circle, her arms upraised and hands wide, she stood like a majestic queen. She threw her head back and froze as if waiting for something to happen.

Thirty seconds went by. Then sixty.

It was so quiet you could hear a pin drop.

Finally, after about two minutes of silence, my mother dropped her arms, slowly pulled her head back up, and drew back her shoulders. Her expression was stern. My mother opened her mouth as if she wanted to say something but then shook her head and pursed her pink-stained lips together.

Great.

The goddess that didn't exist didn't show up, and now it would be one more thing my mother could blame me for somehow.

I looked toward Archie for help, but he sat perched on a chair calmly staring at my mother like he didn't have a care in the world.

I rolled my eyes. Thanks, owl.

"Look, Mom, it's fine," I told her, shrugging. "I'm sure Emma and I can figure this all out on our own. We don't need a goddess. I don't know what a Greek goddess would know about the rules of evidence in Forkbridge, Florida, anyway," I joked, trying to lighten the mood.

Ayla stared at me, making weird motions with her fingers. I raised my eyebrow. She continued pantomiming frantically, but I had no idea what she was trying to get across.

"You would be surprised at what I would know, Astra of Forkbridge," my mother told me in a voice that sounded...distinctly un-Minerva-like. She moved stiffly toward me, her eyes steady and unwavering. "Have you been treating my owl well, champion?"

* * *

"You know what drawing down the goddess is," Althea whispered fiercely from her position in the circle. "What did you think we were going to do, teleport to Mount Olympus?"

I did remember the whole drawing down the goddess ritual garbage from my childhood. The high priestess danced around, said a few words (probably after smoking something before the ritual to make them a little woozy and trance-y) and then pretended to embody the energy of some ancient goddess.

A symbolic ritual.

Key word being symbolic.

I mean, they are supposed to be invoking gods. You would think if you're inviting a god to hang out, if they would really show up, they'd have the power to do so with at least as much substantiation as, say, a ghost would?

But nope.

Yet again, you had to take some things on faith.

Which was, you may have figured out, not one of my strong suits.

"But who is that?" Emma asked, her hands shaking.

"It's my mother." I pointed. "What's gotten into you?"

"That's not your mother, Astra. Can't you see it?" Emma pointed at Minerva's face. "It's dark, like a shadow. But it's there. Can't you see it?"

"She sees what she wants, shieldmaiden," my mother told Emma. "When she is ready, she will see more. Or she won't. It is, truly, up to her." She nodded once as if that settled the question. "For now, what is it you want from me?"

"You're not going to make me bow down, swear an oath of loyalty, become a priestess?" I asked the "goddess." The others were crowding around my mother, their faces slightly awestruck. "I just have to tell you what it is we need, and you'll do it? That's it? That's the whole deal?"

"There was nothing unduly sinister in the question, Astra," Minerva responded with a slight smirk. "I gave you a job. It seems to be unfinished." She lifted her hand and held her palm out. In a single eye blink, the glowing star card appeared. "The woman I asked you to save is still in danger. I ask again—what is it you want from me?"

I blinked.

That took me aback, just a little bit.

The star card appearing in her palm was

unexpected. We all have our talents and strengths, but my mother didn't know translocation. As far as I was aware, only Ayla knew how to translocate objects. I turned and raised my eyebrow at my youngest sister.

As if she knew what I was asking, she shook her head no.

"I will allow you to come to wisdom in your own time, but I will not shield you from the way things are." My mother held out the glowing card. "I will also not ask you again after this third and final time, star champion—what is it you want from me?"

"Don't you know?" I shot back without thinking.

Minerva smiled. "Of course I know. But your aunt was right."

"I have to ask."

"You have to ask."

"Why did you send Archie to me? Why did you send me this goddess energy?" I asked, also without thinking. I really needed to work on some of my impulsiveness. Especially regarding my mouth and my mother. "Why would a goddess supposedly living on the other side of the world on a great big mountain bother for a hot minute with Forkbridge, Florida?"

"Every city needs a champion," Minerva shrugged. "Some champions need a city. This seemed a good fit."

"That's it?"

Minerva looked at me with amusement. "Does there have to be more than that?"

"And what if I fail?" I asked her. "What if one of these cards flips over and they're glowing, and I can't stop someone from dying?"

"Then you get justice for their death if justice is called for."

I paused, examining my mother's face. I had one more question but wasn't sure I wanted to ask it. In the end, I convinced myself it was all meaningless, anyway. "And what if I refuse?"

With a wave of her hand, Minerva somehow removed my left glove without touching me. She grabbed my exposed wrist. Instantly, images flooded my mind of ancient battles and cities and people in dusty, far-off places. The face of a gentle goddess smiling flashed, her eyes glowing with starlight. Just as I focused clearly on her face, she disintegrated into dozens of stars and flew up into the heavens.

Minerva released me.

We stared at one another.

I didn't believe in gods.

But whatever the energy was that was sharing space with my mother? It was old, and it had seen things that hadn't been seen for thousands of years.

"I thought you said what I see is up to me?" I asked. Mostly because I couldn't think of anything else to say.

Minerva frowned. "Astra Arden, if you couldn't block out the visions that just came to you, I picked the wrong champion for this place."

I bowed my head and closed my eyes.

I hated to admit it, but that vision...it changed things.

In, like, an instant.

I was suspicious of a lot of things. People, for one. Myths, for another. One thing you learn quickly as a fugitive tracker—and a soldier—is that nothing is exactly as it seems. The victors write the narrative that becomes accepted as truth—even if it's not.

But I trusted my gift. I trusted what I saw with my own eyes, whether those eyes were on my face or in my mind.

And what I'd just seen I couldn't explain away.

Even if this was a goddess...it didn't mean I had to worship her. It didn't mean I had to bow down to my mother and do everything she wanted me to and everything she said.

Right?

I was feeling like a petulant child rejecting my mother's religion just because of all it kept me from.

Knowing my father, growing up in an average family, and deciding pretty much anything about my own path without having my mother feel it was a betrayal. Being who I was and not who they wanted me to be. I resented those things. And if this energy was to be believed, she was the reason.

I looked up and stared my mother in the eyes.

Emma was right.

I saw the goddess shadow.

"I will work for you, but let's get one thing straight—I'm not one of your followers," I told her. Her expression didn't waver. "I'm not a worshiper. I'm not going to bow and scrape at your feet just because of what you claim you are. And I won't follow you blindly." I pulled my glove from her hand and put it back on. "That's just not me."

"I didn't choose you because you are a talented supplicant," Minerva said with a sharp nod. "I chose you because you are smart and clever, and you wish to do good."

"Why did you want me to save Marianna?" I asked. "I mean, why her?"

"Within the year, Marianna will return to Nigeria. Sometime after that, she will adopt the orphan girl Daraja she's grown so attached to," Athena explained. "They will return here to the United States, and eventually, Daraja will grow into a fine young maiden and go to medical school. Her talent at medical research will be such that the top hospitals in the world will be desperate to have her."

"She's going to cure something someday?" I guessed.

"If all goes well, that potential is there," Athena nodded.

"But that should happen now, right? I mean, we saved Marianna. Why is the star card glowing, just because we haven't caught Christine and Joel?"

Minerva's face hardened. "Because they betrayed a friendship, and they do not deserve to have the chance to betray another. Justice must be done."

"Justice must be done," my sisters murmured.

I swallowed. "We've hit a wall with that. Will you help us?"

"Done," Athena said quietly. Two seconds later, the shadow left my mother's face, and she crumpled to the ground.

* * *

"WHAT DOES THAT MEAN, DONE?" Emma asked as we sat on the back porch.

My sisters were attending to my mother—I'd tried to assist, but my aunt gently informed me that since I was not a priestess, I was not, strictly speaking, welcome. "I don't know," I answered.

"Do we wait? Do we have to go do something?" Emma tapped her fingers on the armrest. "I mean, far be it from me to criticize a goddess or anything, but we really could have used something other than 'done,' you know?"

"Again, I don't know. I'm new to all this," I told her. Gazing out in the backyard, I heard a rustle in the trees. I hoped against hope it wasn't Archie taking another one of Ami's rabbits from the garden. Goddess's own owl or not, Ami might very well cage that bird. "I really don't know what happens here."

Emma dropped her eyes. Without looking at me, she asked, "So, you believe now?"

"Believe what?"

I knew what she was asking. I just wasn't sure I was ready to talk about it yet.

"I'm telling you, Arden. Butt in the pew no matter what you think. I make sure my keister is there, and I promise you—I have never seen anything that proved my grandmother's beliefs to me the way that your mother's beliefs were just proven to you."

"Let's just say I'm slightly less skeptical."

"Man, you're tough," Emma said with the hint of a smile.

"Look, when I was in Imperatorial City, I met brownies, elves, fairies, vampires. I know there are powerful beings. This wasn't that earth-shattering." And it really wasn't. I was willing to believe when I walked in there that something would show up. Maybe there was an old, powerful energy walking around with the name Athena. It was like meeting a celebrity—yeah, okay, you're a famous entity. Good for you. "Just because Athena exists in some form doesn't mean everything my mother believes is true."

"Boy, you're tough." Ami walked out onto the back porch in sweatpants and a t-shirt. "The goddess gives you a magic talking bird, you get a glowing card, you find a woman just minutes from death, and you just can't believe that anything Mom believes is true." My sister sat down in the papasan chair and pulled her legs up. "Have you ever thought, Astra, that maybe your issue is less with the goddess and more with Mom?"

"Not really, because when I lived in Imperatorial City, I didn't have to think about any of this stuff at all," I pointed out. "So no, I haven't thought about it. I had no need to. I had other things to do."

"In other words, you haven't dealt with anything that happened between you and Mom before you left," said Ami, squinting. "Got it. Good to know."

"She's got a point," Emma agreed.

"Not everybody feels the need to take a deep dive into their psyche and pull out what's under rocks."

"It does seem, though, that you might want to call on Athena again at some point. If Athena talks to you through your mom…" Emma held up her hands and raised one eyebrow. "I'm just saying. The whole chip on your shoulder thing? Might be a problem."

"Yeah, and I may never have to call in Athena again because we may wake up tomorrow, and nothing's happened. So, let's not worry about deep diving my psyche until we know Athena is actually useful. I do just fine the way I am."

Ami glanced toward me and then shook her head.

CHAPTER TWENTY-ONE

"*A*re you ever going to get up?"

Not if I can help it.

I often went to bed with my mind racing backward. Lying in the darkness, I'd go over everything that happened that day or that week in my mind like I was replaying a game repeatedly. Where did I go wrong? What should I have done? What could I have done better?

It helped me fall asleep.

It wouldn't go on very long, this nightly mental replay. Usually, I was satisfied with my actions—even if I wasn't always comfortable with the outcomes.

Last night was different.

I went to bed, and my mind was blank. There probably was a lot I could've thought about, a lot I could've replayed, a lot I needed to consider. But I didn't even know where to start, so I just closed my eyes and tried to sleep.

I slept eventually, fitfully. The ritual replayed over and over in my dreams.

"I'm awake," I mumbled to Archie without lifting my head from the pillow. "You ever considered it's a little creepy to have an owl staring at you while you're trying to sleep? For me, I mean." No answer. I yawned. "I left the window open for you. Why don't you go, I don't know, catch a rabbit or something?" I pulled the cover up over my head. "Let me go back to sleep."

"You just said you're awake. So, I'm not watching you while you sleep. I'm watching you refuse to get up."

Through my eyelids, I could see the bright light of the late morning. Maybe even early afternoon. "What time is it?"

"I'm an owl, Astra," Archie responded with a huff. "I'm not a timekeeper. I'm not a clock. You want to know what time it is? Open your eyes and look at your phone."

I opened my eyes and stared up at the owl. He

was gazing down at me judgmentally from his wall perch, eyes wide. Though, to be fair, his eyes were rarely anything other than wide. "You're nocturnal. Shouldn't you be asleep, too?"

Suddenly there was a thunderous pounding on the stairs. "Astra!" Ami shouted. "Astra, are you awake?" Before I could answer, she burst into the room and peeked her head around the dividing wall. "Oh, good, you're finally awake. Look!" Ami waived the star card in front of her.

It was no longer glowing.

"Still want to go back to sleep?" Archie quipped.

"Of course she doesn't want to go back to sleep," Ami said, racing across the room. Throwing herself on the foot of the bed, we both bounced from the force. "Come on, sleepyhead, don't you want to know?"

"Know what?" I mumbled and pulled the covers over my face.

Another set of feet clomped up the stairway. "It's on the news!" Ayla shouted. "Is she awake? Ami? I have the news report on the tablet!"

"She's still in bed!" Ami shouted back. "Come on in!"

"Oh, don't come in," I mumbled. Ami jerked

the covers off my head. "You guys are ruthless, you know that?"

More footsteps.

More excited discussion.

More sisters gathered in my bedroom until we had the entire contingent before I even sat up. "This attic isn't big enough for everybody in the entire house!"

"This is it," Althea said.

"Mom and Aunt Gwennie are in the shop," Ayla added.

Blearily, I sat up in bed indignantly and reached for a lamp on the night stand. With a saucy huff, I glared at all of them. "Can you at least let me brush my teeth? Maybe go to the bathroom?"

"You know, if you had gotten up at a normal time, you would have been able to do all that," Archie pointed out.

Ami crawled up next to me in bed while Ayla and Althea hopped in.

"Did anyone bother to bring me coffee, maybe?" I asked.

No answer.

Ami grabbed the remote control to my newly installed television. "It's a smart TV," she informed me. Turning to Ayla, she waved her hand toward the tablet. "You know how to cast, right?"

My thirteen-year-old sister shot Ami a look back that said, "You're asking me that? Really?" With a few taps on the screen, the news report played on the mounted flat screen.

"Joel Clemens and Christine Chandler were arrested at Orlando airport early this morning in connection with the kidnapping of Marianna Black," reporter Sally Blane announced. Images of the two being led away in handcuffs played over her shoulder. "The couple was stopped by the TSA when the drug gravel was spotted in their carry-on luggage by an eagle-eyed agent running the x-ray machine. Brad Parsons has more."

"Well, Sally, it was an uneventful arrest, and according to the airport? One that they are still having trouble believing took place at all. We spoke to Joel Taggert, head of security, just a little bit ago."

"Our agent did a proper search of the couple's luggage after he saw the stuff on the x-ray, and when he did? He found evidence that seemed to show the couple, along with Bartholomew Chandler, had orchestrated the kidnapping of Marianna Black," Joel Taggert, dressed in an airport police uniform, told Brad Parsons. "There were some papers, copies of ransom notes, and several thumb drives containing digital video of the kidnapping."

"I'm sorry, did you say video of the actual kidnapping?" the reporter asked, incredulous. "The couple had evidence of their participation in the crime?"

"I did say that, and it appears they did," the man answered with a chuckle. "Now, they are Hollywood types, and so the prosecutor's going to have to do some work substantiating what it was we saw, but between you and me? I imagine these two won't be winning any awards for brightest criminals any time soon."

"What a stroke of luck for local law enforcement," Brad pronounced with a smile. "Back to you, Sally."

"As our viewers may know, Marianna Black was kidnapped several days ago. There was some confusion about whether she had gone on vacation or left due to a contract dispute. That confusion, which delayed the police search for the missing starlet, was thanks to an unsubstantiated report on the Hollywood gossip site *Z NUT*," Sally Blane explained. "In the coming days, as we learn more of what transpired, I imagine the site will have some explaining to do."

"I imagine so," the surprised weatherman chimed in. "How awful."

"Yes." Sally's face flashed from faux-concern to overly cheerful. "We hope you'll stay with us. Bo is next up with the weather." Sally smiled widely and gathered the papers in front of her to tap them neatly back in a stack.

"They didn't mention you or Emma at all!" Ayla complained.

"We didn't do it for credit, Ayla," I told her. "The important thing is that everyone who needed to be arrested got arrested. And, as a bonus, they didn't mention who Marianna Black's father was."

"Wait, who's Marianna Black's father?" Althea asked me, her eyes narrowing. "Is he famous?"

"Okay, that's it, everybody out." I pointed toward the stairway. "Just because there's not an official door on my attic doesn't mean you guys can just bounce in here whenever you want, you know. I need to get changed."

"But who's Marianna Black's father?" Ami asked, getting up and turning to look down at me. "Come on. You have to tell us."

"I do not. Now go."

"I'm not going anywhere until I get my powers back," Ayla said, glaring up at Archie. "You do whatever it is you have to do with your head." She lurched across the bed and grabbed my arm. "Come on. Let's go, owl."

* * *

THAT AFTERNOON, I drove over to Parrot Paradise. Emma was stuck there wrapping up the last of the investigation. From what she told me on the phone, the whole movie was packing up and going back to California.

I strolled past the few police cars, several large tractor-trailers, and clusters of unhappy below-the-line workers toward the Parrot Paradise gates.

"Astra?"

I looked around and spotted Rick standing on the information building's porch. He was dressed in his uniform but, thankfully, didn't have a parrot on his shoulder.

I walked over. "I see you're not in handcuffs, so that's a good sign."

He looked surprised at my observation. "That's what that was about at the beach the other day, wasn't it? You thought I might be involved in

Marianna's kidnapping." He sighed. "Wow. Well, I guess I can't blame you, considering."

Rick seemed more relaxed than he had been at the beach. I still suspected he knew more than he'd let on. Not enough, clearly, to keep the star card glowing, though. "Yep, I did. Or, at least, I thought you knew more than you were saying."

Rick looked at me for a moment and nodded. "I guess I understand that. But why didn't you just ask?"

I laughed. "Because that's not really how an investigation works, Rick. Bad guys don't generally answer direct questions." I wiped my hand over my face. It was a typical Florida afternoon with relentless heat and humidity I could feel even in the shade. "You guys going to be okay now that the movie is pulling out? Financially, I mean."

"My dad's a little bit upset, but we'll be fine." Rick leaned against the wall. "Dad thought the park being in the movie would bring in a lot of visitors, but we do get to keep the location fee. So that's taking the sting off."

I nodded. "Glad you guys aren't out anything. Anyway, I'm going to go in and find Emma. Glad everything turned out okay for you and your dad, Rick."

"Yeah, thanks." He squinted at me. "I guess I'll see you around."

The park was much quieter than it had been, and the parrots seemed more peaceful. Almost relieved. I couldn't double-check that, though. Archie hadn't come with me—the owl really had a thing about parrots. I turned a corner in the path and spotted Emma almost immediately. "Hey."

"Well, apparently a prayer and two stupid criminals can accomplish a whole lot really fast, huh?" Emma said brightly. "I didn't expect the whole thing to tumble down so quickly." Suddenly, she frowned. "It makes me feel a little useless. Like, why don't we just do that for every case?"

I tensed. "I'm sorry, did you say we?"

Emma flashed me a look. "Really? You're just going to go back to selling love potions until the next person's life is in danger? Maybe this was a one-shot deal. I mean, how many people get murdered in Forkbridge? Like one every five years?"

I looked at her. "Are you proposing something different?"

"I need a partner—"

I held up my hands. "I'm not a cop—"

"No, I'm the cop. You'd be a consulting psychic." She grabbed my arm and pulled me behind a bushy palm tree. "Look, you know what my situation is with the other detectives. And this is Forkbridge—again, it's not like kidnappings and murders happen all the time. I mostly sit around and wait for the phone to ring. You're going to sit around and wait for the card to glow. Yours won't happen often, and when my phone rings, it's usually a tourist that got pickpocketed. Boring stuff that rarely gets solved."

"In that case, maybe selling love potions would be more fun," I joked. "You're not making this very appealing."

"I'm not done. When I'm sitting around?" Emma tilted her head. "I'm sitting near the evidence room. Do you have any idea how many cold cases we have? How many items we have sitting in that evidence room that could tell a story?" She saw the flash of interest in my face. "Now you're getting it. See? More fun than love potions."

"Okay, first, you have to stop mentioning love potions because we don't sell love potions," I told her. "Second, I can't just disappear and not work at the shop—I can't put all that back on my sisters, and I really don't want to have that

384 | LEANNE LEEDS

conversation with my mother. But third, yes, that actually does sound interesting—as long as it's not full-time."

"Whatever time you can give me. It'll break up the monotony of sitting at my desk and staring at the phone, waiting for it to ring." Emma shrugged. "I might have picked another career if I knew that being a detective was going to be substantially similar to high school."

* * *

I ARRIVED back home after dinner. The family has gathered in the living room to watch "Natural Magic" for the three-hundredth time. Ayla looked up as I entered and waved. "How's Emma?" she whispered.

"Happy the case is over," I whispered back, then headed toward the kitchen to get a drink. Within a few moments, I turned with my glass of apple juice to find my mother staring directly at me. Her eyes were fierce, and for a moment, I wondered what I had done now.

"I'm glad you're finally home. I wanted to talk to you about the way you spoke to Athena yesterday," my mother began. Without thinking, I put the apple juice down on the counter just a little too loudly and grabbed the corner as if bracing myself for a dress-down. Her eyes lowered and scanned my gloved hands, and her expression turned from disappointed to offended. "I'm sorry," she said with an edge to her voice. "Do I, as the high priestess of the goddess Athena, not have the right to—"

"You know what? Stop," I told her suddenly and then winced. I didn't mean it to be aggressive but considering my automatic reaction to her, I could hear that it sounded that way.

Her jaw dropped. "I beg your pardon?"

"You heard me," I told her, cursing myself again for the additional aggressive retort. We—my mother and I—seemed perpetually caught in an automatic loop we just couldn't seem to get out of. "Look, I'm not trying to make you mad. I just...I don't want to keep doing this."

She blinked in surprise. "Keep doing what?"

"You're about to tell me that you don't like the way I spoke to your goddess. And I get that. I didn't talk to her like a supplicant, like a priestess. I didn't bow. I probably didn't address her properly. I understand all that. You telling me that when I already know?" I took a deep breath. "It's just going to piss me off."

386 | LEANNE LEEDS

She looked insulted. "Well, I'm sorry that the proprieties you have to follow—"

"Mom, that's just it. I don't have to follow them," I said, forcefully relaxing my hands, so they didn't hold the counter in a death grip. "If that goddess trusted me with this whole star card thing and the protection of Forkbridge? If that's really what's going on here? She knew who I was when she did that. I'm not gonna do anything just because you tell me I have to. I'm thirty-three—if that was going to happen, it would have happened a long time ago. And I think you know that by now."

My mother looked like I'd kicked her puppy.

Well, if she'd ever let us have a puppy.

Which she didn't.

"Astra, I—"

"Look, Mom? I'm sorry," I said gently. "I'm sorry that I left the way I did. I'm sorry that I didn't call, that I didn't come back for holidays. I'm sorry if that hurt you. Maybe I should have tried harder. Maybe I should've realized that just because I couldn't see your pain, it still had to be there. Maybe there wouldn't be a chasm between us so wide it seems impossible to cross."

My mother stared at me without moving.

"Last night? Those two people that got

arrested? I could not have done that without you. Whatever Athena is—goddess, powerful spirit, priestess-manifested entity stemming from your intense desire to make me believe? It doesn't matter. She did help, and I couldn't have gotten that help without you."

Mom blinked in surprise. "Thank you, Astra."

"You're welcome."

"And I...I am very proud of you. Proud the goddess chose you for such an important task." Mom smiled, took a deep breath, and added, "I just want to help you do it bett—"

"Mom?" I interrupted before she could turn the compliment into a criticism. "We did well just now. Let's call this a step and stop here. Okay? One step. Let's not risk hitting a wall."

For a moment, she didn't respond to that. But then she forced a smile and nodded. "A step. A step is good." Her face softened. "I love you, Astra. I hope you know that."

"I love you, too, Mom."

"I just want to make sure that you—"

"Mom?

"Yes?"

"One step."

* * *

THANK YOU FOR READING!

I hope you enjoyed Star of Sage & Scream! Please think about leaving a review! Astra, Archie and the whole Arden family continue their adventures in Book 2, Owl's Fair!

KEEP UP WITH LEANNE LEEDS

Thanks so much for reading! I hope you liked it! Want to keep up with me?

Visit leanneleeds.com to:

Find all my books…

Sign up for my newsletter…

Like me on Facebook…

Follow me on Twitter…

Follow me on Instagram…

Thanks again for reading!

Leanne Leeds

FIND A TYPO? LET US KNOW!

Typos happen. It's sad, but true.

Though we go over the manuscript multiple times, have editors, have beta readers, and advance readers it's inevitable that determined typos and mistakes sometimes find their way into a published book.

Did you find one? If you did, think about reporting it on leanneleeds.com so we can get it corrected.

ARTIFICIAL INTELLIGENCE STATEMENT

Portions of this book were created with the assistance of AI tools used for editing, proofreading, and refining the text. However, the ideas, storyline, characters, and overall creative vision remain my own original work.

While some aspects of the cover image were generated using AI tools, it was done so under my creative direction and curation.

I want to acknowledge the use of these technologies as part of my creative process, while affirming that the essence of this work comes from my own imagination and effort.

Leanne Leeds

www.ingramcontent.com/pod-product-compliance
Lightning Source LLC
Chambersburg PA
CBHW021427240626
47153CB00001B/54